A Kingdom to Remember

K. Malady

To my family.
Except...I hope most of you won't read this because I'd rather not discuss my inspiration for the sex scenes at Thanksgiving. Kthx!

(The answer is almost always fanfic.)

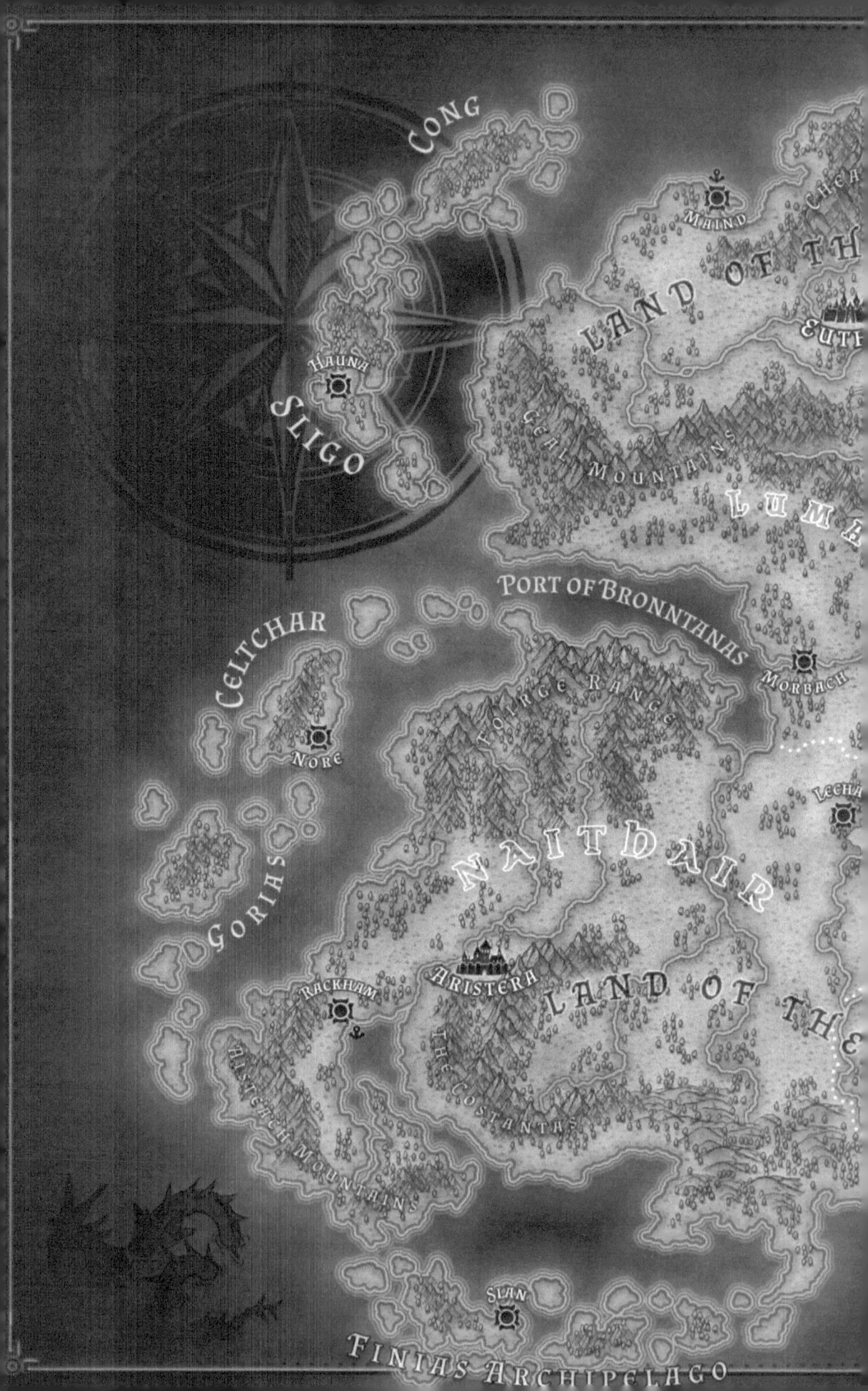

CONG
SLIGO
HAUNA
LAND OF TH
MHIND
CHEA
EUT
GEAL MOUNTAINS
LUMA
PORT OF BRONNTANAS
CELTCHAR
MORBACH
FOIRGE RANGE
NORE
LECHA
GORIAS
NAITDAIR
RACKHAM
ARISTERA
LAND OF THE
THE COSTANTAS
MOUNTAINS
SLAN
FINIAS ARCHIPELAGO

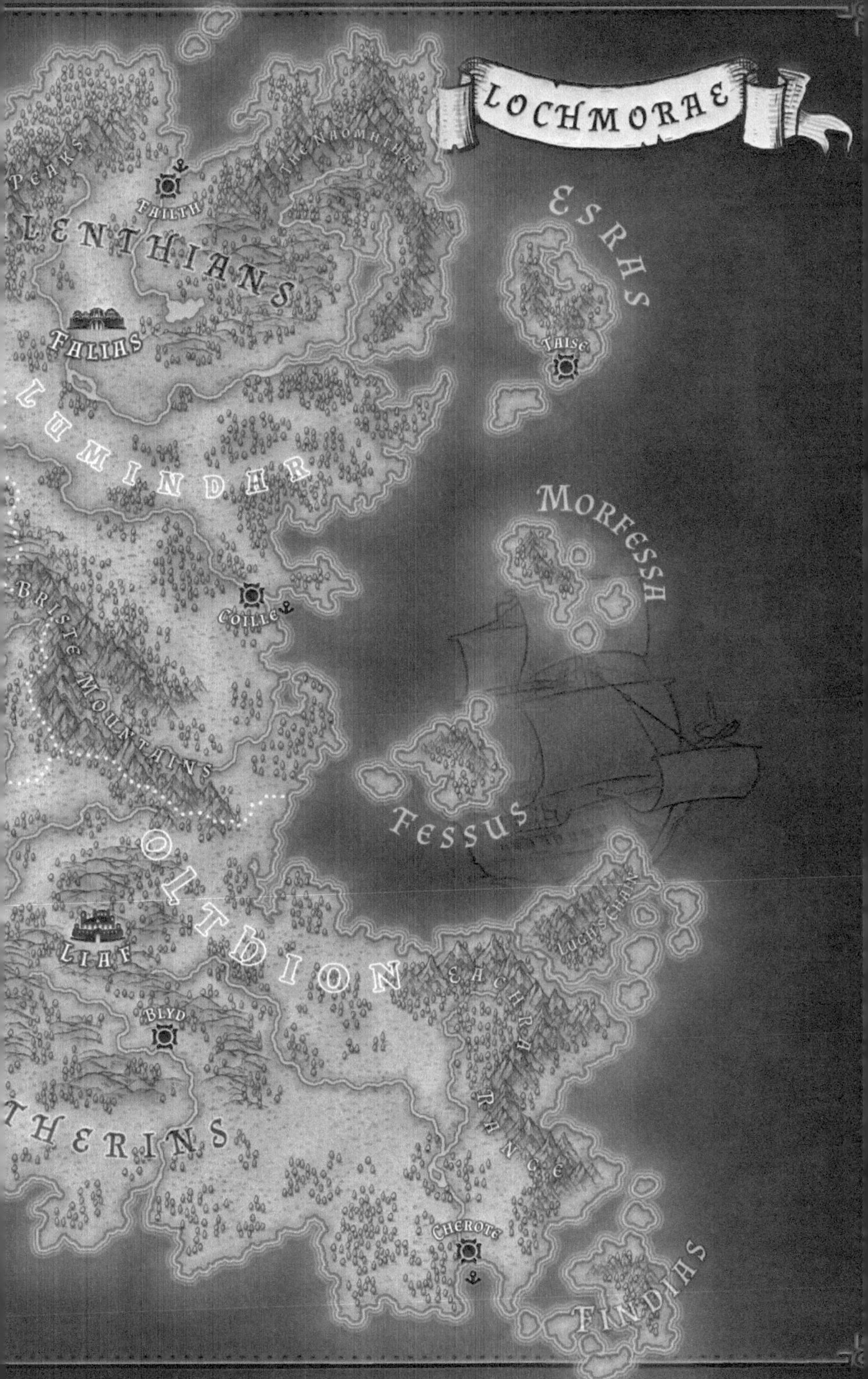

LOCHMORAE
ESRAS
PEAKS
THE NAOMH THAS
FAILTH
LENTHIANS
FALIAS
TAISC
LUMINDAR
MORFESSA
BRISTE MOUNTAINS
COILLE
OLTDION
FESSUS
LUCH'S CHAN
LIAF
EACHRA
BLYD
RANCE
THERINS
CHEROTS
FINDIAS

Also By

Chapter 1

Enna

"Why are you keeping the meeting a secret?" Tierney, my younger sister, says as she hugs her stomach. Her petite frame hunches over the oaken meeting table, her long brown hair cascading down past her knees like a waterfall. Worry etches over her features as she stares down at the map spread out before us. Although her features may *appear* sharp, she is anything but.

I don't normally hide things from her. Whenever I need advice, she is always there, ready to share her wisdom as my most trusted advisor in Lumadh. But in moments like these, when the burden rests solely on my shoulders, I must keep some things to myself.

"It isn't that it's a secret," I say, walking towards the wardrobes that line one wall of the war council room. Within them, rows upon rows of armor hang, normally worn by my personal battalion, but now untouched. Along another wall, mounted racks display an array of lethal weaponry: piercing swords, razor-sharp daggers, and finely crafted bows, all untouched and in need of polishing. Although the centuries-long war rages on, I've halted the conflict in order to test out a new strategy.

I pull on my leather armor. The fabric stretches over my slim shoulders with a soft creak. When I return, it will need a good buffing to ensure it has a shine, as my ceasefire will be lifted. I rub a scuff from a spot over my stomach; it barely looks like the traditional blue Lumadh armor in this state.

I turn back to Tierney, who is staring up at the tall banners bearing the sigil of House Lumadh hanging from the rafters. "It's that I'm not risking anyone else," I say, pulling back my dark brown hair into a tight bun. "Not after what he did last time."

"Which is why we should be involved *this* time," Cat says, her arms crossed over her slender chest.

Ever since I took command at nineteen, following my brother Liam's untimely death at the hands of the Netherins, Catriona has faithfully served as my second-in-command. She served Liam too and has always favored a more collaborative method of working. It was Liam's reliance on others that let the Netherins overtake him, something Cat hasn't understood.

Cat continues, frowning. "There's reducing risk and there's stubborn naivety, En."

I heave a breath as I tighten the laces on my pants. It isn't naïve to believe things are best done by my hand. Had I not brought others with me the last time I'd met with Mouric, they'd still be alive. I shouldn't have given him the benefit of the doubt. I should have known better than to expect *rational* behavior from him at negotiations. Uncle Conroy's sudden and shocking death forced Mouric into a position of power at a young age, dealing with advisors who treated him as a misguided orphan instead of a new king. Mouric rightly dismissed them all, but then thought he was above needing advisors. He made himself, at fifteen, commander of the Lumindaran army, and acted as no better than a despot over a dying land ever since. It was as though becoming king made him grow up... wrong.

I'd attempted to negotiate merging our governments, assuming he could behave logically, and he'd killed two of my soldiers instead. Despite retaliating by destroying half of his battalion and taking the rest hostage, it didn't bring my people back to life. He needs to be removed as 'King,' appointed as only a regent, with Father and *good* advisors staying his hand. And I can overpower him one-on-one. Even with his mind reading skills, he's a shoddy soldier. Plus, I've spent the last several years surviving in the wilderness through war training and battles. He hasn't. I'll have the upper hand when we meet in the Briste Mountains, the range that separates our two countries.

"I need to meet with him. Alone," I finally say. "I won't make the same mistake, by bringing others again. But if this plan fails, we'll go to the next one. And then we can do it your way, Cat. I promise."

Cat twists her lips in disagreement. "It would be best to reengage Olthion instead. Lumindar's army remains aligned with us. Before Mouric acts again, at least let us *reduce* our enemies before adding another."

Our world, Lochmorae, has been split into two (and then four) for as long as history remembers. Mouric's and my people, the Valenthians, have been in an ancient battle with the Netherins, who are also split into two: those living in Olthion, under the tyrannical rule of King Elric, and those living in Naithair, under the *similarly* tyrannical rule of Lord Rian. Of the two, Elric is the worst. But I had a plan for

Elric and Olthion. Maybe. It's something to consider after dealing with Mouric.

"Not until we look into that rumor about Elric," I tell her, kneeling to tie up my boots. "And Mouric made *himself* an enemy, remember?"

Cat exchanges a worried glance with Tierney but remains silent.

When I've finished dressing, I put a hand on Cat's shoulder and try to reassure her. "We can't be like the Netherins: battle, battle, battle. And I can't treat Mouric how I'd expect an enemy to behave. I'm going to make an appeal to Mouric's desire for power. He and Father can act as regents over our combined people. If he won't agree, I'll take him down. Either way, the fully united Valenthian people can then turn our sights back to stopping those fucking Netherins. It's a solid plan. Right, Tier?"

Tierney jumps, chewing on her thumbnail. "Err. Right."

Cat turns from me to retrieve my favorite daggers from their spots on the racks and begins polishing them. "You could at least tell us where you're meeting Mouric," she mutters, her fingers vigorously rubbing the blades as her black braid whips back and forth.

My superior hearing easily catches all the murmurs and whispers around me. But I ignore it now, allowing her disgruntled mumbling to continue uninterrupted.

Interruption finds us anyway as the heavy oak door opens behind us. Loughlin slips in wearing an emerald green tunic that contrasts beautifully with his white blond hair. He's braided it and it trails over his broad shoulders, stopping above his generous chest muscles. A smile accompanies his bright blue eyes, which fades when he takes in the room and my leather armors. "I've been looking for you, Enna... or is it General today?"

I wince. "It's still Enna. But not for long." When I'm not acting as general of the Lumadhan army, I am simply "Enna," firstborn of King Colum and Queen Kennis, rulers of our land. Enna relishes in her conquests and indulges in fleeting romances. Yesterday it was Balor; if not for my current mission, tomorrow it could have been Eaman. I study Loughlin's form and the look of disappointment in his eyes.

"We had plans tonight, didn't we?" I ask, already expecting the answer.

He nods. "I reserved a boat for us to head to the waterfall."

Disappointment pulls at my stomach. Behind the waterfall is one of the most sought after places to fuck in the kingdom. I've had many a fun evening there. I'd taken Loughlin once before, but we'd been interrupted by a messenger needing me for a war council. All I'd managed to do was undress him and lick a stripe up his pale stomach. "I'm sorry, Loughlin," I say, meaning more than I can express, given how delectable he looks today. "Luck is against us."

Cat scoffs and mutters something about my choices being what's against us today, before stalking forward and shoving my daggers in their holsters.

The impact is strong enough to knock me off balance, but Loughlin is quick to catch me. I lean against his sturdy frame, shooting Cat a piercing glare, but she responds with a smug smirk, showing no remorse. As Loughlin's hands trail down my arms and he steadies me, an idea takes shape. I flash a teasing smile in Cat's direction.

"Loughlin, don't waste the reservation," I suggest. "Why don't you take Cat?"

I'd propose Tierney, but she'd likely faint from shock. When it comes to sex, she is the most reserved out of everyone in the kingdom. I suppose it makes sense. As an advisor, she is shielded from danger, but the rest of us confront the uncertainty of our fate every day and seize every opportunity for pleasure in case it will be our last.

Tierney's cheeks turn a faint pink, as though she can hear my thoughts, but she isn't a mind reader. Only Mouric possesses that irritating skill. She ducks her head back towards the map, the light revealing a whip-thin scar on her cheek.

I frown, I'd almost forgotten when she earned that, just before Liam's last battle. Apparently none of us have escaped unscathed from the ravages of war. But it only strengthens my resolve to bring an end to it all.

While I'm inspecting Tierney, Loughlin drags a heavy gaze over Cat, starting at her heavy boots, up to her strong thighs, over her trim chest and ending at her face. A slow smile spreads across his handsome face. "I'm game if Catriona is."

Without missing a beat, she grabs ahold of his shirt and yanks him down until their faces are inches apart. "I prefer Major in bed."

Loughlin swallows audibly.

I suppress a laugh. "And we can celebrate my success when I return," I tell them. "Assuming Cat hasn't worn you out. That work, Loughlin?"

He looks star struck, too distracted by the filth Cat is whispering into his ear, to answer.

I resist the urge to roll my eyes. "Cat, before you kill Loughlin with your cunt, make sure the advisors are ready. And Father if necessary."

She salutes me and goes back to fondling Loughlin.

Tierney's delicate features are etched with concern as she hands me my travel pack, her fingers trembling slightly. "You'll be safe, won't you?"

"Aren't I always?" I reply with a reassuring smile, but she's still uneasy. Pulling her into a hug, I whisper into her ear, "You know I'm always careful."

"Can't you at least take Niall with you?" she mutters into my shoulder. Her best friend, Niall, was not only a committed soldier but also a talented spy and my resident spellcaster. But I can manage without Niall's help.

"I sent him out a week prior to check into the rumors of Elric's unbeatable sword, remember?" I remind her, cupping her face in my hands so she can see the sincerity in my words. "I have everything under control. If you don't hear from me in a week, then you can worry. Until then, find something fun to do."

Her eyes flick to Loughlin and Cat and the color drains from her face. "Not that," she mutters under her breath before forcing a smile.

"I hear knitting is quite therapeutic," I tease, trying to lighten the mood.

Tierney lets out a laugh that doesn't quite reach her eyes. "You'll have to wear whatever monstrosity I make for you."

"Not only will I *wear* it," I say with a grin, "I'll flaunt it at the next war council."

⸻ ◆ ⸻

Callum

The atmosphere in the throne room is thick and oppressive, heavy with the weight of responsibility and authority. None of it my own, of course. My father, King Elric, sits upon his grand throne at the front of the hall, surrounded by his loyal lieutenants and esteemed generals. As a child, I always found the room to be imposing, with its towering arches and intricate tapestries decorating the stone walls. But I knew one day I'd be in that room as its leader, guiding the Olthion army under my father's command.

Pity things don't work out.

Instead, *Darroch* stands beside Father in the post I'd wanted, before I realized my skills lie in strategy rather than battle. He acts as second-in-command, the favored son and general, and he and the others attempt to appease Father's current rage. I remain hidden in the shadows, unnoticed and unacknowledged—a mere afterthought in the eyes of my father and his court.

Father loves war. He told me once—before I'd disappointed him the first time—that battle is in our blood. How fortunate for him that we exist in a world *drenched* in violence.

A dispute over land boundaries ignited centuries ago, sparking a relentless war between the Valenthians and Netherins that still lingers today. The Valenthians were the sole gatekeepers to the northern sea, controlling the most advantageous trade routes. Our people sought access and the greedy Valenthians refused. Since then, we've been locked in an ongoing, brutal conflict. The Valenthians are under the divided rule of Colum and Kennis of Lumadh and Mouric of Lumindar. But everyone knows the actual power of the Valenthians comes from Princess Enna, the Pompous Princess, their General. She and Mouric are committed to destroying my people, the Netherins.

As if taking our sea routes wasn't enough.

The Valenthians most recently defeated us this summer and promptly ceased their aggression. They shifted their focus, no longer interested in engaging us, and instead the Pesky Princess set her sights on consolidating power. The Valenthians had a conjoined army, but separate kingdoms. But that wasn't enough for Lumadh, who wanted a single monarch to unite *all* the Valenthians under one banner. Lumindar resisted the change, meaning they fought each other instead of us, something Father couldn't abide. Lucky for him, and our violent soldiers, he still has his war.

With the Petulant Princess and Lord Mouric focused inward, Rian, my cousin and leader of the Netherins from Naithair, took advantage. The Peevish Princess declared an unofficial ceasefire, but Naithair saw its chance to gain control over Olthion. Seizing the opportunity, Rian used the temporary lull in hostilities to demand battles on Olthion soil, aiming to merge his rule over the Netherins.

"Has no one any ideas?" Father roars. From my seat in the back of the room, I can't see him but can conjure up the image of his mouth foaming and the vein on his left temple pounding like a drum, his hands clenched tight around his sword.

"We could send another battle invitation to Lumindar," one lieutenant says. The sheer number of them made it impossible for me to identify the speaker.

Olthion's main battle strategy involves pitched battles—where both sides agree on a date and location. Our previous pitched battles have generally proven successful, gaining us ground against the Valenthians before we were beaten back. Now we remain at a standstill, where our invitations go unanswered, and Father and his soldiers cannot sate their desires for war. Much longer and they'll start attacking each other again, just to experience the adrenaline of fighting.

While fighting may not be inherent to our blood, it is undeniably part of our nature. We demand physical conflict from the children in our training school, the Oige. But for those who graduated and enlisted in the army, there's been no need to sate their bloodlust outside war since we've always been entrenched in one.

"We could... sneak over the border into Valenthian territory," another says hesitantly. "Not a planned attack but a surprise."

The room is quiet, except for the occasional gasp, until the unmistakable sound of skin meeting skin shatters the stillness. I wince in sympathy. Though I dislike all the men present, I know the pain that accompanies the impact of Father's hand.

Father's voice is no more than a growl. "I will forgive your idiocy this time, Alistair. Do not let it happen again. I do not seek counsel regarding the Valenthians. Not with that *bitch* refusing to answer my invitations." Unsaid is that she hadn't answered his *last* invitation either, but he'd tricked her into appearing. It was a bloodbath against us. "But that whelp Rian and his foolhardy threats... Have we sent *him* a battle demand?"

"Not yet," Darroch says. His tone carries a hint of unease. "Although we planned to attack on Naithair soil as you requested, we, too, thought to sneak over the border and launch a surprise attack. Instead of awaiting a response from Rian."

There's a rustling sound as Father shifts in his throne. We're all waiting for the next strike of Father's hand, on

Darroch's face this time. But the punishment doesn't come this time.

"Darroch, you've been repeatedly told that we are a civilized society. We do not 'surprise attack,' not like the barbarians. Honestly, you're acting as idiotic as Callum."

The room titters, and I try not to wince, feeling the all-too-familiar pang of inadequacy gnawing at my insides. Despite my best efforts to contribute, my father had always dismissed my ideas, deeming them unworthy of consideration. But Darroch's silly ideas are always acceptable. He's barely five minutes older, but he—and Father—act as though it has meaning. That and his graduation from the Oige, Olthion's mandatory training school, which I withdrew from.

"We should join with Rian," I mutter when the laughs die down.

"What was that?" Father snaps. "Who dares hide from their king?"

Something stirs within me—a glimmer of hope that perhaps, just perhaps, my voice would finally be heard. Or it's fear that Father is planning on hitting me again.

I emerge from behind the huddled group of men, their gazes filled with contempt and resentment- nothing I'm unused to. I try to stand tall, my posture straight and my chin held high. I'm taller than Father, but you'd never know it from how he behaves. "We should propose a brief alliance with Rian," I suggest, swallowing any trembling in my frame.

"Join with Rian?" someone jeers. "Idiot," says another. "That's who we're attempting to slaughter," comes another.

"Not permanently," I explain, my voice slowly growing in confidence. Father hasn't struck me down yet. "But a brief alliance to attack Lumindar. With Lumadh's dissension against them, Lumindar cannot succeed against attacks on two fronts."

Father cradles the sword at his hip. Its silver-etched blade gleams even in the dim light, a mesmerizing shimmer that seems to pulse with an inner life. His own eyes beam down at it, staring at it like a lover might, although I've never seen him with a lover... nor do I have any personal experience with one myself.

"Won't Lumadh help their kin?" Father asks sharply, though we all know a larger battle wouldn't deter him.

The Parasitic Princess? Not likely.

Darroch responds in my stead, "A weaker Lumindar helps Lumadh too. And if they do counterattack, we'll get the battle Lumadh has been denying us since the summer."

Father finally stops admiring his sword to rub his bearded chin. "Prepare a plan and bring it to me within the week."

Grumbles of discontent fill the air, and I resist the urge to duck. Any sign of weakness is an invitation to attack me in the streets. But, of course, Father will listen to Darroch instead of me, even though it was my idea.

"Callum," Father roars. "Do not ignore your king."

Startled, I jolt in place, causing another wave of laughter to erupt from the advisors. "I'm sorry, Father," I say as meekly as I can. "I assumed you were speaking with Darroch."

He glares at me. "Perhaps I should have. But no, I'm offering you a chance. Do not disappoint me again."

I leave immediately after, not wanting to be caught by the others, my steps filled with a renewed energy as I head back to my cabin outside the city. Today was... good, for once. I might not even need the hybrid lily tea to sleep tonight.

Chapter 2

Unknown

The air is heavy with the scent of damp earth and a distant whisper of unseen creatures. I'm no stranger to waking on the ground outside, listening to the pixies cackle in the trees and the faewisps skittering under the brush. But this time, something feels off, and I can't pinpoint what it is. I open my eyes, struggling against the weight of exhaustion and confusion. It's nearly dark, the sun's rays barely visible through the thick foliage. My hands instinctively search for the daggers that should be in holsters on my hips, but they're not there. Instead, the holsters are empty and slick with something wet. I'm alone in these woods, unarmed and vulnerable, two things I know are unusual. The last thing I remember was—I frown. I can't remember what I last remembered.

Where am I? And... who am I?

The voice in my head is feminine, and must be mine, but I don't recognize it. My body protests as I force myself to sit up and inspect my head. I wince, fingers grazing over matted strands of hair tangled with leaves and twigs. I can feel the tackiness of dried blood on my fingertips. As I lower my hand to my eyeline to confirm, I notice that the skin looks unfamiliar, covered in a dark blue dye I instinctively know is the dye from an Oros, giant lumbering apex predators. *Fuck.*

I try to remember what happened before I woke up, but nothing comes. Irritation, rather than panic, claws at the edges of my mind and I struggle to stand, limbs protesting with every movement. The blue dye obscures any further damages to my skin, but the pain tells me something sinister has happened. That dye is only used in hunting spells when someone seeks to capture enormous beasts like those the Oros eat. The scent and magical song of the dye acts as bait that attracts predators that, once lured to the location of the dye, can be snatched by the Oros. Blearily, I glance around, but there's no Oros in sight. But predators could still be on their way, drawn to the dye's scent. If I stay in this small glen too long, I'll become prey to whatever might be found in this forest. Like the kelpie whinnying softly in the loch to the east.

I could attempt to wash the dye off, but I can't fight off a kelpie in this state. A fragment of memory teases out of the fog in my mind, and I realize that perhaps I've dealt with kelpies before. Under the dye and my left pant leg, I'll find a rope burn from a successful encounter with the creature, one that left me permanently scarred. The image vanishes just as I try to follow it towards something else familiar. *Like my name, the location, what I did this morning, or why I'm annoyed rather than afraid.*

I stagger towards the south. The ground beneath my uneven footsteps feels uneven, the terrain and mix of soft moss and gnarled roots. My vision blurs as I lurch through the dense foliage. I'm going to pass out soon and I must hurry for shelter. It's winter, and I can't survive without supplies.

Otherwise, whatever befell me before I woke up will be the *second* worst thing to happen to me today.

The sun sets while I stumble through the towering trees. But then, something in the air shifts. There's a distant creaking of timbers, the unmistakable sound of wind colliding with a log cabin. I follow the sound towards a clearing where the moonlight casts a pathway on the forest floor. The clearing reveals an old house illuminated in the dark. Massive rough-hewn logs form the sturdy walls of the cabin, rising to meet a steeply pitched roof. Wooden shutters hang open from the narrow windows, offering a glimpse of a glowing hearth.

I approach cautiously, the crunch of fallen leaves beneath my boots echoing through the stillness. Protective symbols cover the doorframe, ones I intuitively know are used for warding off evil spells. *How can I know* that *but not my name?*

The door is slightly ajar, and a warm glow spills from within. Feeling almost compelled, I enter a dimly lit hall that takes me to what must be the main room. In the sudden warmth, I slowly recognize the numbing cold creeping through my body. I slip to the rug laying before the fire and warm my hands. The light exposes what the forest's shadows couldn't: split fingernails and streaks of rust-colored blood making a sickening pattern in the dye on my skin.

Once I've warmed through, I leave the fire in search of something to clean my skin and patch up whatever wounds may be hidden beneath it. The staircase by the door leads to an upper floor cloaked in shadows, one where I might find cleaning supplies or (*dare I dream it*) a bed. I shuffle towards it, the warmth (and probable concussion) making me lethargic. A mirror hangs on the wall by the landing, and, curious, I stop before it. The reflection reveals a stranger with tangled brown hair streaked in blue and rust, and troubled brown eyes. My figure is trim, muscles prominent even through the dye, which, combined with my survival skills, makes me wonder if I'm a soldier.

The mystery must remain unsolved, for now. I crawl my way upstairs, the only sound the cracking fire behind me and my own labored breath. The second level reveals more rooms. In the first room, I discover a bed draped in faded linens. The head injury tells me I shouldn't lie down and sleep, no matter that it's all my body wants to do. Wincing, I touch the coarse fabric, leaving blue dye in my wake. I *could* nap for just a second.

Don't fall asleep in strange locations, a voice says, the one that must be mine. *But I want to*, I answer back.

Perhaps when I'm healed, I'll discover whether talking to myself is a panic response or a normal facet of my personality. I trudge back toward the hallway, searching for a washbasin and water.

Before I can exit the room, my gaze catches on a portrait hanging on the wall behind the bed. The subject is a man, handsome and compelling. His ebony hair looks silky soft as it falls neatly over his forehead and down to his shoulders. His well-groomed beard frames a chiseled jawline with sharp cheekbones and supple lips. Strong shoulders and a noble posture hint at both strength and grace. His eyes are a bright green, like spring grass, ones I wouldn't mind getting lost in once I've handled the head injury. A sense of familiarity tugs at my chest. *Do I know this man? Did I live here?*

I stumble into the hallway and make it two steps before I trip and slam my knees on the wooden floor. The fall irritates my head, my teeth rattling in my skull. Black spots swirl in my vision and I reach my arms out to steady myself. I catch on something, a black blur that feels solid and warm. I squint up towards the blur and see the man from the painting. He's beardless now and instead of a sharp gaze in those gorgeous green eyes, they're filled with confusion and concern. One final thought coils through my mind before I pass out: he is *much* more attractive in person.

Callum

With only one more day until I'm to present my plan to Father, I feel as though I'm walking on air. No one has jeered at me in the streets, no one has tried to mar the student-issued armor I must still wear since I withdrew from the Oige. No one had even bothered me when I stopped into town for some pre-celebratory wine before returning to my cabin to go over the plan once more.

The fire is still lit (thank you, Allanagh, for buying magical kindling from a spellcaster) and I was dying to remove my unused armor and fall into a bath with a vat of something alcoholic.

The door being open when I arrive doesn't immediately set off my alarms because Allanagh always drops by when I'm avoiding everyone. She told me her skills at mind reading don't work from afar, but she always seems to know when I'm planning on hiding out for days at a time. Plus, the wards on the doors keep out anyone who would harm me.

(Although the wards never keep *Allanagh* from stealing all my wine, which should count.)

As I toss my overcoat towards a chair, a faint whimpering reaches my ears. I tense, gripping the hilt of my virgin sword I haven't yet released from its holster. Even the wards can't protect me from my own paranoia. Silently, I ascend the staircase that leads to the upper chambers.

The whimpering grows more desperate as I approach the shadowy hallway. I scan the corridor, revealing the dim outline of a figure huddled against the doorframe of my bedroom. I cautiously approach. My jaw clenches as I take in the dye of the Oros beast on her skin, smeared with what can only be dried blood, and her garments stained with evidence of a brutal encounter. The holster drops to the floor with a clang as I slide towards her, my arms outstretched before I can think better of it. I catch her shoulders just as she grasps the clasps on my tunic. Her eyes meet mine and they're familiar, brown like the earth with flecks of the gold as bright as the sun. But her features are too obscured by the matted coil of her hair clumped over her face and the blue dye disguising her skin, and I don't recognize her. The heat of her fingers seeps through to my skin. One shaking hand releases my tunic and reaches upward towards my face. I flinch. Battered stranger in need of medical care or not, those fingernails look sharp. But before she can touch me, she passes out.

Although Allanagh is the healer between the two of us, born with the bite of healing magic in her blood, I've picked up enough field training through books to assess the stranger's injuries. Dark splotches of dried blood mar her armor, but it isn't sliced or torn. Her stained and sun-faded leathers confirm she spends time outdoors. With the dye obscuring it, it could be the dark red color of my father's soldiers. Some of his higher ranked officers know of this safe house, but it was their idiotic pranks that made me need the wards. No soldier that knows the owner of this cabin would ever come here. But maybe the emergency meant they had no options but to find the closest safe space.

My fingers twitch before I finally muster the courage to examine her skin. Streaks of rust cover her forearms, but I can't find the source of the injury that created them. Faint cuts and scratches mark her fingers and hands. Inspecting her head exposes a tender lump by her temple. She whines as I run my trembling fingers over it. At least it isn't bleeding.

I stare down at the woman in my arms. Allanagh might come by later if she doesn't find company at the nearby public house. But there could be wounds that need tending that can't wait until Allanagh sates her libido.

With no better idea and unable to let her accidentally bleed out, I gather her up and carry her down the hall to my bathing chamber. Darroch has the brawn in our family, my strength more wiry, but she's light in my arms, delicate in a way that belies her clothing. The pull of a lever starts water pooling into my copper bath basin, one large enough for two and overwhelming the small room. I gently rest her on the floor beside it, unwilling to undress an unconscious woman. An aroma of herbs fills the air. I'd forgotten I scattered some in the tub yesterday in anticipation of needing to de-stress after dealing with Darroch all day. But the scent is mild and none of the herbs will harm the strange woman lying on my plush rug.

I dampen a soft cloth and cleanse her skin, searching for any open wounds that need immediate tending. Since I'm still not undressing her, it's a somewhat fruitless endeav-

or. Pulling off her boots reveals that who—or what—dyed her was thorough in marking her. The delicate arches are smeared with dye and dirt but otherwise unharmed. I can only lift her pant leg enough to just reach her calves, which are first taut with tension but slowly relax with every pass of the cloth.

I move upward, hesitating over her stomach. The leather is intact but stained and there could be blood hiding beneath it. I can feel my cheeks heat as I bare her skin. Her stomach is smooth and blue. And uninjured, except for the edge of a bruise trailing from her chest towards her hip. I swallow and quickly drop the shirt and busy myself rinsing the cloth. The water turns a disgusting brownish color as it carries away the traces of blood and some of the dye. Her skin remains a mottled blue, only scrubbing will remove the dye entirely. Stripes of rust wash away on her forearms and her shoulders, which I bare only to check for other wounds. The scratches on her hands and fingers are thin and already sealed. The bruise I'd discovered on her hip also appears on her collarbone and another on her right upper arm, like she'd been smacked with the broad side of a sword. My brows furrow as each stroke of the cloth wipes away blood that, besides what's in her hair and her hands, doesn't appear to be hers. Whoever this stranger is, she made her attacker bleed.

I turn towards her face, gentling my touch further, as I'd already discovered the bump on her head. As the cloth sweeps across her brow, the blood-soaked strands of hair part, exposing a second spot on her crown, and the source of the blood in her hair. An open wound found, I reach towards my cabinet for a healing tincture. It won't close the wound—she needs a healer's hands for that—but it will slow the bleeding and start cleaning it of any impurities. Her nose scrunches at the touch, but she doesn't wake.

Finally, I attempt to wash her face. The dye remains stubbornly glued to her skin, but enough is washed away that her features finally appear. A dainty nose, full lips, soft cheeks leading to high cheekbones. At worst, and even as blue as a blueberry, I'd call her objectively pretty, especially combined with what I remember of her startling caramel-colored eyes.

I rinse the cloth one last time and gaze at my guest. The rug is covered in stains that sluiced deep into the fibers. It haloes around her as if tendrils of color are crawling from her skin. She's in the center of the pretend cocoon, like a fairy tale creature waiting to be awoken in one of the ancient stories my people used to tell. A goddess waiting for worship at her altar.

She looks so familiar.

She sighs and shifts on the floor, twisting to her side. But pain must stop her, as she whimpers from the jarring movement, and she quickly rolls onto her back with a wince. Her face is still scowling, pursed in discomfort. That is an expression that looks commonplace, one of irritation and anger. *When have I seen this woman so angry?*

And in that moment, her features align, and I instantly realize who is lying on my floor, nearly dropping the dirty cloth on her face.

This stranger, this battered woman, is Enna, the now-Pitiful Princess, and my people's greatest threat.

Fuck.

Chapter 3

Unknown

I blink my eyes open, disoriented and groggy. I'm lying in a bed this time, not the cold forest floor, covered in linen sheets smudged with blue. The window confirms it is still evening, and a flickering candle by my bedside casts a warm glow around the room. But the candle is powerless against the darkness and the shadows gathered in the corners, obscuring the rest of the chamber. Unmoving, I cast my gaze down my body, doing a visual inspection. Vaguely, I remember doing the same thing not a few hours earlier, as the details of my first unceremonious revival floods back. I was lost in the woods, with little memory, covered in dye and blood. And then I found a cabin. I flick my gaze to the wall behind me, my neck jarring. The painting of the handsome man has been covered, but a recovered memory tells me I met him in this house.

But he didn't harm me. He *tended* to me. I'm still wearing my own clothes, but the rust stains on my skin have been cleaned. I'm blue, but that's no surprise. It will take vigorous scraping to get this damned dye off my skin. Although my stomach grumbles, removing the dye is my first need. I'll never be able to leave this cabin unless I can remove the trace magic that will attract Lumadh's predators.

I still my slight movements. Lumadh is my country. I remember that! Cracking a wide smile and hoping more nuggets of memory will come to me, I try to sit up, and a dull muscle ache follows. I shuffle until I'm resting against the back wall and gingerly inspect my scalp. My hair was recently wet as it dried in crunchy curls. There's a tacky spot on the top of my head, evidence I was bleeding, but it's started clotting, meaning it isn't all that serious.

Except whoever got me into this bed didn't seal it. *Damn.* I hate sealing my own wounds. The smell of burning skin always makes me nauseous. I delicately tap the spot and bring my fingers to my nose. It smells of the arcanis plant mixed with echinacea, two ingredients in an expensive healing paste that can ease infections. We don't have easy access to them, that I remember too. I'm assaulted by jumbled memories of sealing wounds, washing blood, splinting broken bones after battles. *Or we don't have access to healers*, else I wouldn't have such vivid memories of doing it myself.

At least I remember how to seal wounds, as I must do to this one, but the paste gives me a little time before I must care for it.

Voices outside the door halt any further investigation.

"Of course it's a trap," a masculine voice snarls. That's likely my handsome savior. *Did I fall into a trap? Is that what took my memory and dyed me blue?*

"Gods, you're paranoid," a woman answers. "Looking for monsters in the shadows."

"Not in the *shadows*, Allanagh. In my bedroom."

I blink and dart my gaze around the room. *What monsters are here hiding in the dark?* My fists clench where they rest on top of my hips. I wish I had my daggers.

"Your guest has awakened," the woman—Allanagh—says. There's a smile in her voice.

Something thumps in the hallway, followed by the man's deep grunt. The door careens open, and he stands scowling in the threshold. His green eyes, guarded and watchful, meet mine.

He *is* more attractive in person. The beard hid too much of that sharp jawline. The tunic at his neck gapes open, displaying tanned skin that looks smooth to the touch. Maybe once I'm clean, he'll let me inspect *him*. In the hallway, Allanagh laughs. Without taking his eyes off me, the man reaches behind him and shoves. Footsteps sound in the hallways, getting quieter as Allanagh walks away.

"You're awake," he says, his tone measured.

I nod. *Obviously*. Allanagh already confirmed that, and my eyes are open.

"What are you doing here?" He stalks closer to the bed, arms outstretched as though I'll leap from it.

I sweep a blue arm down my body. "Enjoying your hospitality, of course."

He blinks and frowns. I want to press my fingers into the grooves of his mouth and smooth them out. "How did you find this place?"

"Luck, mostly. I was looking for a town, but I found your cabin first. Thank you for the help." I offer as bright a smile as I can. He tended me and used a valuable commodity on me, I don't want him to regret it, especially if I want to get to know him better.

"Luck." His scowl deepens, which seems impossible. "You expect me to believe that?"

"You don't have to." I shrug, swallowing a wince when it irritates the sore muscles in my neck. "But it's the truth. Where are we, by the way?"

"In one of my homes in Olthion." His expression doesn't waver. "With soldiers less than an hour's ride away."

Well, that's nice, but not relevant. The nap brought back some clarity and the few new flashes of memory tell me I'm handy with a sword. I certainly don't need a soldier's protection. *Except someone struck me in the head and dyed me blue*, I remind myself. But I disregard it. *That was probably a fluke.*

While I've been mentally conversing with myself (which seems to be a habit rather than something my amnesia brought on), my handsome savior looks to be hyperventilating. Maybe he thinks I need the soldiers for protection *now*. Despite his stance and palms revealing his lack of experience with weaponry, I can still see the taut, corded muscles in his arms; together we could stave off any attack.

"I don't think we'll need them," I say, smiling at him. He could really use some stress relief if a few minutes of silence make him uneasy. "Where is Olthion? Somewhere in Lumadh? Or did you name your home? I've never named my home, at least that I remember. But I don't remember *any* homes." I purse my lips. "Or who I am. Or even where Lumadh is. Is it here? Oh, also I didn't catch your name."

"No, it's—no." His face goes from irritated to panicky to shocked within a breath. "Allanagh!"

⸻ ◆ ⸻

Callum

Allanagh stands over my favorite kettle in my kitchen, preparing tea as if nothing is amiss, snagging dried leaves and roots from jars of colorful ingredients we've collected together.

I loom over her, bracing a hand on the aged wooden shelf above her. "She doesn't have her memory?"

"It *exists*," Allanagh says, ignoring my rather threatening presence to pull down three cups, elbowing me out of her way. Her healer's signet rings clack against the pottery as she runs her pale fingers along the inside of the cups, imbuing them with healing magic. "And you're not threatening in the least."

I scowl down at the third cup and the person Allanagh expects to drink it. "What did you do to the brew?"

She shoots me a look as she pours out the tea, setting the third cup aside and starting a new pot. "It should promote clarity of mind, but you're irritating me so much I might put in *constipation* instead."

I grimace. Allanagh's touch magic is intent based, which means it's heavily influenced by her own feelings. An annoyed Allanagh means I'll be drinking a sludge instead of something soothing. I heave out a breath, wishing she wasn't stingy with that hybrid lily tea that soothes my nerves. Unfortunately, she'll only prescribe it during sleeping hours.

She slams a cupboard closed, her short blonde hair puffing up in irritation like a dandelion. "No lily tea for you. You'll overdose."

Grumbling, I reach for the bottle of my favorite rum sitting on the counter and pour a generous amount into my tea. If I must wallow in whatever sour feelings Allanagh put in there, at least I'll be pleasantly buzzed. "So, she's lying."

Allanagh's expression turns reflective. "I mean, I can see flashes when I try to read her. She, and by extension me, just can't access it. She doesn't know who she is or who you are." She eyes me up and down. "Which might work out for you for once. You could finally get laid."

I roll my eyes at her crassness. "First, she's an invalid, and I'd feel like a predator taking advantage. Second, she's the mastermind behind the defeats of our people for the last ten years." The Prolific Princess, cutting her teeth on battlefields the minute she hit her majority at eighteen.

"Interesting that her identity wasn't *first* on the list," Allanagh says slyly as she leans against a nearby shelf. "But it's just like a one-night stand. You meet a stranger, have some fun, and then leave in the morning. For all I know, I've bedded princes, princesses, beggars. The surprise is part of the fun."

I finish my tea and reach for Enna's cup, pouring a liberal shot of rum in it. She doesn't deserve Allanagh's brew. "You can read their minds," I remind her. "None of it is a surprise."

She raises her cup in a mock toast. "The surprise is for them! When I leave the next morning."

I slump onto a bench beside the kitchen table and cover my face with my hands as the teapot squeals. "What do I do? I can't take her back to Lumadh without someone trying to murder me when I cross boundary lines—"

"Maybe *we* should institute that policy. All strangers shot on sight. Your father would love the brutality of it, even if it goes against his 'civilized battle' strategy. And it would have kept you from being in this situation."

I ignore her. "And I can't keep her here because she'll murder me once she regains her memory." Our war strategy has an elegance to it. Unlike the Valenthians who take advantage of our civility, who lurk in the shadows and launch surprise attacks. Or, at least they had, before the summer. They're no better than barbarians.

"You could abandon her in the forest," Allanagh suggest. "There's nothing *requiring* you to care for her."

Patterns form in the blackness of my vision as I press hard against my closed lids. "She'll find her way back and murder me then."

Allanagh hums. "You don't think she'd just go home?"

I let out a sarcastic laugh. "She's a Valenthian, Allanagh. Murder and mayhem is what they do, or else we'd have negotiated peace a decade ago." I'd been proposing it for years, but Father said peace was impossible until the Valenthians were put down. Once they were thoroughly defeated, they'd have no choice but to negotiate with us. We just hadn't had the opportunity to *put them down* in quite some time.

Allanagh slides beside me and yanks my hands away from my face, looking apologetic about the abrupt touch. "I know you think your father does no wrong, but this could be an opportunity to see the war from their perspective."

I rear back. "From their perspective? Allanagh, you're doing the healing when our troops return, all superficial because the Valenthians kill any of our injured rather than let them heal and fight again. You think there's a chance for peace there? Don't be absurd. She'd kill me as easily as negotiate with me."

There's a hint of uncertainty in her eyes, as if she were hiding something. "That's not what happens. It isn't the Valenthians that—"

"What are you talking about?" *Because Father always said—*

She cuts off my inner thoughts before I can finish them. "Of *course*, your father. That... Look. Your time with Enna could be the chance for the war's end, like you want. *Without* Darroch leading it. You could... usher us into peace."

I restrain a scoff. She makes me sound like a pacifist. While I'd like peace, like any sane person, which obviously doesn't include my brother Darroch, the reason isn't all that altruistic. It was my chance to display my talents in the art of negotiation and diplomacy. And in peace times, we could focus on non-combat skills for once and I could truly shine.

She scowls, obviously overhearing my thoughts. "Fine. If you're already dead, you might as well have some fun, Callum." She closes her eyes and tilts her head up towards the ceiling, as if listening to Enna. "She'll be into it."

"Stop being—wait, she would, she is?"

Allanagh smiles like a cat, lips curling over gleaming white teeth. "She thinks you are gorgeous and wants to know if you're clean shaven all over."

I blush. "Yes, well. I'm a better man than that. I won't take advantage of an amnesiac." The kitchen is silent except for the soft sound of Enna moving around upstairs... doing whatever an injured amnesiac does in a strange house. "When do you expect her memory to return?" I finally ask.

"Depends on whether the cause was magical. You said she hit her head, right?" At my affirmation, she shrugs. "If it was a physical injury, it may never fully heal. But if it was magically induced, I or a more talented spellcaster may be able to reverse it."

"Can you figure it out?"

"Possibly." She takes a sip of my spiked tea. "You know my powers are stronger when I'm touching someone. I can treat the head wound and start searching."

Frustration bubbles within me as I bang my head against the table, resting my cheek on the cool wood. I have to find a solution soon. I can't let Enna leave and I can't let her stay either. "That's the top priority. Once we know, I can figure out what to do with her."

Allanagh looks skeptical but then smirks. "Bring Darroch here and let them go at each other."

It's a tempting idea: they could fight each other and solve one of my problems. If Darroch kills Enna, Olthion will rid itself of an important enemy and gain leverage in negotiations with Rian. And if Enna kills Darroch, my power will only increase in the kingdom's eyes. It's a win-win situation.

"No, no, no. They won't be killing each other, but..." She makes a crude gesture with her hips gyrating them forward.

"What is that?"

She stops and puts her hands on her hips, the clinking of her rings echoing in the silent kitchen. "Don't pretend you don't know what sex is, Callum."

I shake my head, trying to push away the image of my brother and Enna together. "What is your obsession with sex and my brother?" I shiver at the thought and stalk to the kettle, taking it off the heat. Finally, the shrill sound of its screech stops.

Allanagh waggles her brows. *They look like two caterpillars dancing*, I think meanly, hoping she hears it.

"Those are my two favorite things," she says, ignoring my clever insult. "Big muscles and a small brain? It's a perfect combination. He can throw me around and there won't be anything in his mind to distract me from his body."

I pause, my curiosity getting the best of me. "Does that happen often?"

"One time, I was straddling this priestess, and I fell into her deep memories where she had a traumatic experience with a bunny. A bunny, Callum. I could barely keep from laughing, and she thought it was at her body and..." She trails off, giggling. "So yes, a blank mind is a sexy mind. Like Darroch's."

I cover my ears. "Never mind."

"You asked. And you look similar enough that I'm sure she'd find him attractive too."

My nose wrinkles, unable to hide my outward disgust no matter she can hear my inward revulsion. "Doesn't that mean you think I'm attractive?"

"Gross." She pretends to gag.

A thump sounds upstairs, halting our teasing. Allanagh and I both stare at the ceiling.

"She's looking for a weapon," Allanagh says.

"Son of a b—" And I run upstairs to stop the Predatory Princess from gaining another unearned advantage.

Chapter 4

Allanagh and I reach my bedroom simultaneously. The Purloining Princess is kneeling beside a chest of drawers, digging through my clothing. She's completely comfortable in my room, looking as though she belongs here. Her back curls and her leather tunic drags upward, revealing another slip of taut blue skin. She doesn't stop her search when we arrive.

"Do you have a knife I can borrow?" she asks.

I'm rooted to my spot in the doorframe, unable to move or look away. "Why?"

She turns, gesturing vaguely to her head. "To heat up and seal the wound. Although, I'll need some lumia powder to line the blade. I'll replace it as soon as I... remember where to find it again."

What kind of backwards healing does Lumadh provide? Rather than fearing her people's barbarism, I want to comfort her and guide her towards a different, civilized path. I shake away the thought. The pretty and amnesic enemy is still the enemy. "That's what Allanagh's for," I respond slowly.

Enna's pouty mouth wears a hint of a mischievous smile. I swallow Allanagh's theory that Enna was interested in me; that smile is pure danger. Before she can say more, I push Allanagh ahead of me; she can distract Enna while I run for help. Allanagh scowls and elbows me in the stomach.

"I'm a healer," Allanagh explains, drifting closer to Enna, showing off her signet rings.

"That's fantastic! I'll never turn down a healer's inspection." Enna stands, her body ascending like a graceful cat. But when she takes her first step towards Allanagh, she stumbles.

Involuntarily, I race forward and catch her by the hips to keep her from falling. I tell myself that letting her fall again would either keep her here longer or jar her memory back, two things I'm not ready to deal with. But I've been lying to myself for years, so why stop now?

Enna directs that impish smile up at me. "That's the second time you've saved me from breaking my nose on this floor. How lucky for me you were here."

I fight a blush as Allanagh mimes something behind Enna's back. I can't even understand the finger movements, but it's surely sexual. Refusing to meet Allanagh's gaze, I focus instead of Enna's caramel eyes ringed in blue dye. "Once Allanagh heals you, I can draw you a bath to remove the rest of the dye."

"That would be wonderful. I can't remember the last time I had a bath." She wiggles her brows at me. "Get it? Because I lost my memory."

Allanagh groans. "That was terrible."

The Playful Princess drags her hands up my chest, one side of her mouth ticked up in a way that should not be so sultry. Her delicate wrists and slender fingers wrap around my tunic laces in an imitation of how she clung to me before passing out earlier. In a whisper, she says, "I'm still waiting to learn who my savior is."

With hands on my chest and her eyes locked on mine, my body responds. Quickly, I look away, frustrated at my body's betrayal. When I finally feel under control, I clear my throat and pray *Allanagh* suffers from amnesia and forgets this entire exchange. "C-Callum."

"Thank you, Callum." Enna releases me and losing her touch feels like ice water dumped on my head. After a brief hesitation, I keep my hands on her hips... just in case she fumbles again. With agile fingers, she unlaces her leathers. My hands drop from her as if scalded.

"What are you doing?" My voice cracks and I curse internally. Father had taken me to more than a dozen spellcasters as a child to boost my confidence. I'd lived through them spitting in my mouth to give me a confident tongue, gluing peacock feathers to my back to force a poised stature, and shoving acorns in my shoes to make me dexterous. But, as is more obvious than ever, it hadn't worked.

"She's a healer, you said? I'm not going to waste the opportunity to heal everything, so we need to check for all my injuries."

"I already did," I say, flexing my fingers and almost reaching for her, before slipping them into my pockets. Allanagh coughs until I admit, "At least, I checked what I could without disrobing you."

Enna continues to unbutton her shirt, slowly revealing her bare shoulders. As blue breasts spill out, my gaze shoots to the ceiling. "And that's how faewisp bites get infected." She puts her hands on her hips. From the edges of my vision, I can see jiggling. "Do you want me to get infected?"

"Of course not," Allanagh answers when my tongue won't untie itself. "The trousers too, then."

Enna bends at the waist, her chocolate brown hair just sweeping the floor as she drops her pants and then bounces back up. She hisses, and my eyes stray back to her. Her hair falls in waves around her angular face, the loose locks curling just above blue-tipped nipples atop perky breasts. My face flushes, but I can't control my straying gaze, tripping down her toned body, over the dip of her stomach, and further. The bruise on her chest and hip, the one likely from the flat edge of a sword or gigantic stick, looks a ghastly black against the light blue on her skin, and the attraction feels even more inappropriate.

"Natural brunette," Allanagh mouths behind her.

You're awful, I think loudly, hoping she catches it. I shift closer to Enna, my hands outstretched in case I must catch her again. "Are you alright?" When I notice where my hands are positioned, I shove them back in my pockets and refocus on the ceiling.

"Moved too quickly," she says, sounding unconcerned. "What kind of healer are you?"

Allanagh moves towards her, blocking any further view of Enna. "A touch healer," she says. She makes sweeping movements as she no doubt inspects Enna's body.

"We don't have *any* of those where I'm from," Enna says. And then she grins. "Look at that. I remembered something else!"

"You'll be a fount of knowledge, I'm sure," Allanagh says dryly. "Well, the head wound was the extent of it, and that mark along your chest. I also lessened the muscle strain."

Enna stretches her neck and raises her arms high. "That's great. Better than I ever remember feeling." She lets out a gusty laugh. "I've found sanctuary, allies, and relief from faewisp bites. Perhaps whatever bad luck took my memories is changing for the better."

Allanagh turns and looks at me pointedly, but directs her instructions to Enna. "Callum's bathing chamber is down the hall. You can walk without a chaperone, but it's certainly better to be cautious."

Enna peers around Allanagh and my gaze strays to her against my will, though I keep my attention above her neck. She cocks a dark eyebrow at me. "Will you be joining me in the bath?" she asks playfully.

"It's just through that door, the last one on the left," I tell her.

She sighs. "That wasn't what I asked, but alright. See you in a moment." She strides into the hallway.

Allanagh cocks her head and watches her leave. "How specific was that spell for dyeing all those nooks and crannies? I mean, the precision to get it all the way in between—"

"So, it was a magical malady then," I ask, ignoring Allanagh's crude commentary.

"Yes," Allanagh says, all business now. "It looks almost a literal veil over her memory. Some places are thinner than others, but it's all covered."

I trudge towards the bed as I hear the faint sound of water running down the hallway. The sheets are streaked blue but smell faintly of the arcanis plant and petrichor. I sit on the edge and lay back down, perpendicular to where her body rested. She's the first person besides Allanagh to sleep in this bed.

"I don't know what to do with her," I say, directing my confession to the ceiling.

Allanagh slips beside me and mirrors my position. "Not planning on letting her and Darroch work out their aggression on each other, then?"

"Stop putting foul images in my head." I stare at the wood slats on my ceiling. "Did you catch anything else in her head I should worry about?"

"That you *should* be worried about? No. That you *will* because you're you, probably. Hidden or not, there's likely lots of dangerous information in her head." She slowly rests her head against my shoulder, giving me enough time to move away but I let her stay. "And more information could trickle out, like it did today."

"I can't believe they don't have touch healers. And they seal wounds with heat?" I shiver. The small ripples of her old scars flash through my mind. Other images of her body as she flounced around the room flood it too and I shake my head to wipe out the visions.

Allanagh, thankfully, doesn't comment. Being best friends with a mind reader means I rarely have any privacy, but Allanagh never uses what she learns to hurt me. Instead, she follows the thread of my conversation rather than the unraveling of my thoughts. "Imagine if all the Valenthians in Lumadh are stabbed in their necessary organs. They'd seal the wound in without handing the internal damage." She snaps her fingers, the sound loud like a bang in the quiet room. "Immediate death."

I review the conversation we just had with my long-time enemy. Enna didn't falter in revealing that tidbit, a fact that we could easily exploit. I stand up and pace from wall to wall as an idea forms. "If she reveals more information like that..." I hesitate for a second, torn between the potential advantages and the dilemma of exploiting her memory loss.

"We *could* receive an incredible benefit. We could finally overcome them and negotiate peace after their loss."

Allanagh leans up on her elbows. "Having sex with her is taking advantage, but manipulating her trust and faulty memory isn't?"

I don't dignify that with a response, because she's not wrong. "Father will love it. It could turn the tides for us." At some point, Lumadh will set its sights on us again and meet us in battle, and any influence can help.

Allanagh scoffs. "Seems a wasted opportunity, focusing only on the strategy of it. Instead of getting information from her, you could get something *else* and not pander to your ass of a father."

I pause in my pacing. "Is the 'something else' sex?" I don't even comment on her opinions about Father. He has his reasons for acting and treating me the way he does. If Enna's presence changes that, then that can only be a good thing.

"Yes. That wasn't my best euphemism." She sits up with a groan. "So, you'll, what? Befriend her, gather as much intel as you can while you pretend to find the counterspell, and then shove her, alone, over the boundary lines still amnesic?"

I nod. No need to speak aloud when Allanagh already heard it from my thoughts.

Her brows knit together in a frown. "It sounds like something your father would do. Manipulating her, abusing someone's vulnerabilities."

"...And?" That's why it will work. I'll gain more respect from him by behaving how he always demands I do, maybe even take Darroch's place by his side.

"I don't think it's going to work out how you think," she says. But then she sighs and crosses the room to me, wrapping me in a hug that I don't shy from for once. "If you're certain, and your mind apparently is, go to the bathing chambers, learn from Enna, and see what comes up."

"Is that another euphemism?" When she nods, I scowl. "Stop that. Will you make sure she doesn't hit her head again?" Gods forbid she regains her memory from it. It would be just my luck.

Allanagh closes her eyes, a sure sign she's focusing on Enna's thoughts or she's irritated with me. It could go either way. Finally, she says with a leer, "She wants you to wash her back."

I push her towards the door. As Allanagh leaves, I swallow the images that followed her revelation and gather the sheets for cleaning. Anything to distract myself from the naked woman in the next room and what I plan to do with her. And that isn't a euphemism.

⸺◆⸺

Unknown

I fiddled with the dials and levers in Callum's bathing chamber until water pooled from the bottom of the large copper basin. A table close to the wall holds a few pots with sweet smelling herbs. I toss a few that smell the nicest in the basin, something floral that reminds me of springtime with something dark that makes my nose quiver but in a good way. As I slip into the warm water, the door behind me creaks open.

"I was hoping you'd join and make sure I don't hit my head again." I crane my neck hoping to see Callum's muscular form, but it's the healer, Allanagh.

She rests against the closed door. My first thought is that she's too far to reach if I needed to subdue her. I remind myself these are allies that healed me and offer her a forced smile.

A subtle crease marks her forehead. "Rarely is a beautiful woman *disappointed* when I walk in on them in the bath."

Leaning back in the tub, I give her a quick inspection, now that the head injury is no longer distracting me. She's probably a few years younger than me, mid-twenties, with a petite but lithe frame, muscles honed likely from grinding herbs for her poultices and pastes. Short blonde locks frame her round face, her piercing blue eyes like twin blades. Despite her diminutive statute, her movements fill the space, like a quiet storm. "You *are* lovely," I tell her regretfully. "But not the savior I was hoping for."

Allanagh tilts her head like a curious bird. "How do you know we're your saviors and not, as a *random* example, your mortal enemies, planning on slitting your throat tonight?"

I dip my fingers into the bathwater, swirling the bubbles the springtime scent created. "Seems silly to waste healing paste on me if you're planning on killing me."

"Maybe we have an odd moral code," she says, a faint smile playing on her lips.

I don't believe it. Healers have magical oaths to fulfill, meaning Allanagh likely can't harm me. And Callum looks more like an advisor. Advisors would set someone else on me rather than risk the damage to themselves. *And* arcanis plants are rare. If their intention was to harm me, they wouldn't waste the time or supplies to heal me. But in case the memory loss dulled my intuition too, I flick my gaze around the room. There are at least three things within reaching distance I could use as weapons if I need to. I may be overconfident, given someone had taken overpowered me recently, but there had to be an explanation that wasn't 'I'm an unskilled novice in protecting myself.'

Allanagh's gaze tracks mine and her smile widens. I want to amend the title I've given *her* in my head, but she'll know the minute I do.

"Perhaps not," she says, clearly agreeing with my mental determination. "Speaking of odd moral codes, why the immediate and overt interest in a stranger, savior or no?"

There's a squeak outside the chamber. She slaps her palms against the wood, and I can hear Callum's soft grunt as he's knocked from the door.

I scrub away at the blue dye, which continues to cling to my arms. "Have you ever had a near-death experience?" I ask idly.

She shakes her head. Flashes of disjointed memories burst through my mind. A man seals a burn on my shoulder with a red-hot sword, the tented placket of his pants grinding against the steadily dampening front of my covered cunt, and then he kisses me fiercely. Another man gazes up at me from between my legs, blood in his hair, but his lips shiny as I force his face back down. Another claws at my hair as I go down on my knees for him, a long wound trailing up his bare leg.

A mischievous smile spreads across my lips. "Near-death experiences remind you that you're alive. Why not experience life through some energetic post-battle sex?"

Allanagh's blonde brows are at her hairline. "One of those was wearing a Naithair uniform," she mumbles under her breath. But it echoes in the silence of the bathing chamber as she confirms what I didn't dare think she was.

"This is Olthion, yes?" I ask. The name is still meaningless to me; Callum didn't explain whether it is a city in the territory I know instinctively is my own, Lumadh, or a neighboring country. Allanagh's tone tells me Naithair is likely an enemy of one, or both, of them.

Allanagh nods, her eyes locked onto the water's surface, a subtle glimmer of either embarrassment or desire in her gaze, a consequence of the memories she watched.

A thoughtful quiet settles between us, interrupted only by the gentle splashing of water against the edges of the bathing tub and the harsh scratching sounds as I attempt to scour off my skin.

Slyly, I ask, "And how long have you read minds?"

Allanagh laughs then, before wincing. Her expression while examining my sexual exploits was clearly one of lust, as now she is undoubtedly embarrassed now. "My whole life. I suppose now I'm the unsubtle one."

I rinse soap and dye from my cheeks. "I assumed you weren't trying to hide it when you announced I was awake before you'd even entered the room."

"I'm surprised you heard that," she says.

I shrug; given she's a mind reader, there's no need to tell her my hearing is incredibly sensitive. She should already know that, since I do.

She stalks closer to the tub, a gleam in her eye. "You're not upset that I've been poking around in there?"

"I'm used to it. My cousin has the skills, but they're weak." I've trained myself to filter out thoughts I don't want him to accidentally pick up on. I grin with delight. "And you must be my good luck charm, as I've only just remembered that!"

"Me or Callum," she says. Hesitantly, she adds, like it's a secret, "Mind reading is a unique trait. Aside from myself, your cousin is the only one I've heard of."

Callum squeaks again from the hallway.

Perhaps it *was* a secret. But my own secrets matter more than Olthion's right now. I burst to a seated position, sloshing water over the sides of the tub. "Can you read what happened to me?"

She settles on the floor beside me, wriggling until she gets comfortable on the bare floor. A pale spot reveals that a rug normally rests there but has been removed recently. "I've never seen anything quite like this," she says. "The memories are there, but they're veiled by a powerful magical barrier. It's as if someone wanted to keep them locked away."

Mystery enemies. Maybe I'm not as lucky as I thought. "Who did it?"

She hesitates before responding, a ripple of uncertainty crossing her face. "I can't unravel the specifics, but it was undoubtedly a powerful enchantment by someone. It *could* have been a protective measure, or an attack."

My stomach swirls with disappointment, but I swallow it down. "An attack sounds more likely. Why else drop me in the woods for the predators to eat me?" At least I know whoever did it must have been powerful, and I wasn't subdued physically by someone else. "Can you see anything else in my mind? Like my name?"

She nods, looking relieved. It must be because she has the answer to that one. "Your name is Enna."

"Enna," I repeat, savoring the sound as if it holds the key to my identity. But the word is meaningless, two dull syllables that say nothing about who I am and why someone attacked me.

Allanagh's gaze meets mine. "I wish I could offer more. Such powerful magic surpasses my abilities."

I sigh as I scrub the last of the dye off my legs. Knowing my name must be enough. For now. "Maybe keeping you and Callum around will spark more memories. I know I'm from Lumadh, that I have an irritating cousin, that I have significant survival skills, *and* that I've had a lot of experiences." I waggle my brows in her direction.

Allanagh laughs, lust dancing over her expression. "Keep me in mind for that next near-death experience, will you?"

Chapter 5

Callum

"I can't believe you gave her our secrets!" Just as I'm about to continue sniping at Allanagh, two consecutive sneezes interrupt me as we pass the row with cooking spices. "We're supposed to be getting them from her."

It's the morning after Enna invaded my cabin (and life). Allanagh told me Enna's hearing was sensitive, and I can't risk the Prying Princess overhearing anything else. We're in the chilly garden outside as I work through my plan and Allanagh gathers herbs.

"First of all, I gave nothing away," Allanagh says, dropping to her knees to pull up sprigs of lavender on a bush she planted.

I snap my gaze to the windows, squinting as if I could see Enna peering through the openings. "You told her we didn't have mind readers," I whisper.

She ignores me, as usual. "And second, *we're* not getting secrets from her. You are, assuming you get 'permission' from the King."

"He'll see the merit," I protest, crossing my arms around my chest to stave off the morning freeze. It doubles as a comforting measure, as Father rarely appreciates my ideas. Him taking my suggestion last week was as rare as dragon's tears. But if I can show him I've found Enna and can gain useful information from her, he won't see my success as a fluke. For once, time in his presence won't be a confrontation with someone who only sees me as a disappointment.

Allanagh holds out a pungent bundle of herbs, but I gesture to my hands hidden in my armpits. She rolls her eyes and shoves them into her overstuffed basket. "Why are you checking with him, anyway?" she asks. "If you're going to exploit her, just do it. The King can't absolve you of your own moral quandaries. It's not like he cares about his own."

I run a hand through my hair, the curls damp in the morning dew, before shoving my hands back around myself. "You know why."

Her lips purse. "What do you intend to do with her while you're checking with *Papa*?"

"I can't bring her inside the castle," I say immediately. "That would give her access to my secrets instead of the reverse. But I don't want her getting loose elsewhere in Olthion by leaving her alone here." With all I know of her, she'd not sit patiently waiting for me to return when she could be out wreaking havoc on her own.

Gathering her baskets, Allanagh stomps towards the door. "*Fine*. I'll take her to Liaf, and we'll wait for you there."

"But she could be recognized," I murmur as we enter the kitchen, staring up at the ceiling. The kitchen is below the bedroom, and I can't have Enna overhearing.

Allanagh withdraws various pots to store her gains and pulls out a mortar and pestle, not even attempting to be quiet. "She's still asleep."

"Are you kidding me? Then why the need for secrecy away from the house?"

She smirks when she finishes cutting the last of the herbs and storing them. "We didn't. I wanted company in the garden."

"Thanks." I toss myself onto a hard wooden chair. "I'm trying to keep us safe from any of her Valenthian schemes and you're playing games."

"The only one playing games is you," she says, dragging out a new pot of minced herbs. "She's been sincere so far."

I cross my arms around my chest. "You said she routinely sleeps with the enemy. And she threw herself at me last night. That isn't playing games?" No woman has desired me for who I am, only as a stepping stone to Darroch or Father.

Allanagh stops and glares down at her concoction. "Sometimes I wish we had the magic for time traveling. Then I could revisit the past and kick your father in the crotch for the complex he's given you."

I shake my head, knowing with my luck, the spell would involve getting hit over the head with a clock and never being born. "You know I have allergies from the fennel," I say, trying to change the subject. Fennel featured prominently in Oige stews, which didn't help my training any. "If you wanted me out there in the garden with you, you could have asked. I might have said yes."

Allanagh shrugs. "You owe me for babysitting in the city,"

"You're a mind reader, not a seer. You didn't know I'd ask," I say under my breath, relieved that the tension that always appears when talking about my father is broken.

Again, she ignores me. "She won't be exposed. With her memory, she's a blank canvas. Only a few would know who she was, right? It isn't as though she has some particularly memorable battle style or something."

Not that Allanagh would know, she's never been on the battlefield. Her time in the healing tents means she only sees the aftermath. But then again, I haven't been in even *mock* battle since my demotion and eventual departure from the Oige. "I recognized her," I say mulishly.

She scoffs as she grinds down the herbs and mixes the blend into some sweet smelling oils. "Because you study those field drawings Nerwin did before he died like they'll be on a test."

She freezes and directs an apologetic expression towards me. But the reminder of my failure in the Oige doesn't sting as much as it used to. Still, Allanagh reaches for my hand, but I'm not comfortable with skin contact today and recoil.

She sighs and says, "But unless you *do* plan on taking her before your father, no one else would recognize her. Not even Darroch, I bet."

That isn't surprising. Darroch can barely recognize himself in the mirror. A thump sounds upstairs, suggesting Enna has awoken.

"Here," Allanagh says, handing me a thick mixture inside a tin pot. "Hair dye."

I take the peace offering while I stare up at the ceiling, as if I can see Enna's movements. "You can't apply it?"

"You're the one who thinks it's necessary," she replies matter-of-factly.

With a swallowed curse, I go upstairs holding the pot like a shield in front of me. If Enna has regained her memory, I could throw it at her and run.

Enna is wearing a dress of Allanagh's, something she must have borrowed. But with her taller height, the dress that normally falls just above Allanagh's calves now sways well above Enna's knees. Without the blue dye covering her skin, she looks even more beautiful with a healthy glow. My throat tightens as she turns to face me and the dress twirls, revealing more tanned skin.

"Good morning, savior," she says with a smile. "I heard something about hair dye?"

I tuck the confirmation that she can hear as far as the kitchen away to consider later, ignoring the endearment and the fluttering it creates in my stomach. "Yes. I want to take you into town."

She glances at herself in the small handheld mirror Allanagh must have given her. Her fingers trail over her reflection. "And I need to be disguised for that?"

I step closer, holding out the pot. Allanagh would have told me if her memory had returned, but I remain out of reach just in case.

"As a precaution. You never know who might try to harm you." My voice catches slightly, and I clear my throat.

"Don't worry, savior. I'd protect you from any harm," she says. Her eyes gleam teasingly as she brandishes a letter opener.

I imagine her in battle, holding her sword aloft and charging forward, her long hair whipping behind her. My guilt rises until I remind myself that if Enna were in my position, she'd be doing the same thing. She probably *has*, given her success in battles. That I finally can show myself as valuable to Olthion is at the expense of Enna's trust is... fine. She's the enemy, she deserves no trust.

"Although you're lucky you're cute," she says, gesturing with the letter opener. "Or I'd be irritated you want to subject me to any more dye."

I offer a forced smile as I slowly take the letter opener from her and trade it for the hair dye. Lying and manipulating her will be more difficult than I thought.

Especially as she drops herself to kneel before me, clearly at work manipulating *me* instead. She peers upward, exposing the graceful line of her neck as she shuffles forward on her knees. My tongue sticks to the roof of my mouth when she smiles coyly at me. "Can you apply it?" she asks softly. "I might miss a spot."

I cough and take another step backward, my tongue thick in my mouth. Something else is thickening right in front of her face, something unseen except in the morning when I wake. I feel my cheeks heat. "A-alright. Turn around," I demand gruffly.

Gods, I hope Allanagh isn't listening to this.

The Playful Princess doesn't move, instead biting her lip and staring at the beginnings of a bulge in my pants. With all the dignity I can muster, I stalk around her. I'd assumed having an enemy on their knees at my mercy would be thrilling, but it doesn't feel... right. With her battle hardened history, the more likely scenario is her above me. My mouth dries and I struggle to clear the images forming in my brain, of times when Enna would *ever* be above *me*.

Remembering my reason for keeping Enna with me, I force myself to apply the concoction to her hair. The touch isn't as upsetting as I expected. The room fills with the scent of herbs and dampness. As the dye transforms her dark locks into a rich shade of red, she makes soft, pleased sounds with each rub of my fingers.

I can't tell what game she's playing, but I won't let her take advantage of it. Enna couldn't be attracted to me; she must want me off kilter to learn *my* secrets instead. The entire idea is ludicrous and Allanagh must be wrong. She's never read a Valenthian's mind before. Although they look like us, we're practically a different species.

When I finish, I race from the room to rinse my fingers in my bathing chambers. Another mirror rests against the far wall. My reflection looks hungry, disheveled though I've done nothing more than run my fingers through her soft hair. But the red on my fingers, flecks trailing up my forearms, bring to mind blood. I close my eyes as I scrub it off, trying to focus on the necessity of this plan. When my fingers feel raw, I dunk my face into the red tinged water, staying submerged beneath the surface until the dye stings my eyes and the burn of my lungs is greater than the image of Enna burned into my mind.

Once I've returned to her, she's gazing at her reflection in the mirror again. A faint smile crosses her lips when she sees me. "How do I look?"

My eyes meet hers in the mirror. "Different, but it suits."

"Brown was better though." She touches her newly dyed hair. "Don't you agree?"

My cheeks heat again, but still I nod.

Enna

The three of us descend from Callum's cabin into the nearest city, only a half mile away. It definitely was luck that brought me to Callum rather than some other person in the city. How many strangers would waste healing paste on an intruder?

Although his friendship with a healer could make it less meaningful.

I can feel Callum's eyes on me, his attentive presence unwavering, even as we stand before the city. I'd think it was because of my teasing him this morning, but the nervousness began well before that, when he suggested I disguise myself.

He must know something I don't, since I feel like I've arrived in a world turned upside down. Even without my memory, I know this place is unlike any city I've ever seen before. I expect to see cramped cobblestone streets bustling with merchants hawking their wares, children rushing in between the stalls squealing with laughter. That must be what I'm used to in Lumadh. But instead, the city feels austere, *empty*, even though it is clearly well-organized. Simple houses flank each other, laid out in uniform precision. Our walk remains deserted, with only the occasional passersby who are too absorbed in their own agendas to even acknowledge our presence. Only when we approach the center of town does the atmosphere shift to something somewhat familiar. Despite the dismal-looking buildings, there is at least a small crowd that appears to be enjoying themselves. In the distance, I hear the call of training drills, from what must be this city's military.

Callum marches us quickly through the town square, sticking to the edges and not engaging with anyone. Once, when a child nears me, he flinches, though I can't tell if it's fear for me or a passing child from me. My eyes narrow and

I glance at Allanagh, whose hands tighten on the knapsack she carries over her shoulder. Something tells me they both know more about me than they're admitting. I blink away the thoughts, just as I do when my cousin is around, lest he pick up on something I don't want.

To distract my wandering mind, I clasp arms with Callum, who squeaks when my skin brushes his. "That was brilliant, to disguise me," I tell him.

His cheeks color with a slight blush as his bright eyes meet mine. For a moment, I fantasize about seeing those flushed cheeks as I hold his head between my legs. Allanagh fans herself and winks at me.

"Yes, well," he stutters out. "It only seemed reasonable. For your safety."

"My clever savior," I tell him, trying to tamp down any curiosity about *why* my safety is so important.

Maybe I'm an important asset to the kingdom, I think as the castle looms closer. It sits just beyond the city, encircled by a moat and open drawbridge. The presence of such a massive monument suggests Olthion is a country akin to Lumadh. Towers pierce the skyline, rising upward and capped with flags covered in unfamiliar symbols. The stone walls are a stark white. It must be magic that keeps them so pristine. A flash of memory tells me the castle I know best is a black and dark as the night sky, nothing like what's before me. I mentally amend my ideas as to who I might be, with my memory of another castle so poignant and this city feeling so strange.

I tear my gaze from the castle back to Callum and his darkened cheeks to ask, "What plans do you have for me this morning?"

"I have a meeting... to determine what to do with you, at... at the castle," he says, wearing a subtle smile. One hand nervously picks at the hem of his shirt. It looks like faux leather, similar to what I was wearing when I awoke here, but there are no holsters for weapons or cross hatching for sword piercing protection. He's no soldier, that's for sure. Although he's strong and lithe, the muscles feel all wrong where I grasp him.

I squeeze closer; better to focus on the pleasure of his touch rather than attempting to unravel the mystery of who he is with Allanagh around. After all, I've got to figure out who I am first. I playfully wiggle my eyebrows at him. "Something fun, I hope."

He clears his throat. "Well, there's the matter of your memory. We need a... spellcaster to unravel the amnesia."

I smother a shiver. The mere mention of spellcasters evokes a deep-seated wariness within me, likely stemming from my missing history, and I can only guess at what my issue is. I'd rather figure out the solution alone than engage with a magical practitioner. Allanagh's magic is fine, but flashes of memory tell me magic has irritated me often in the past. "Is there another way besides involving a spellcaster?"

Allanagh opens her mouth, but Callum shoots a sharp glance her way. "We need to know the person who spelled you to discover how to remove it. Only that person... for mental spells, you repeat what was done to you, but in re-verse," he says. He looks shifty. Maybe his experience with spellcasters is similar to mine. "And we can't know *what* they did without determining who did it," he adds.

I nod, tucking the information away. "But it doesn't work that way for physical spells?"

Allanagh elbows Callum from his other side and quickly says, "Magic is transferred through tangible items. Want to be the best baker in the city? Find a spellcaster to cover your hands in flour, then you'll bake delicacies. Want to learn a new language? Find a spellcaster to stick a key on your tongue, and the knowledge will be unlocked." She glances at Callum before finishing, "Removing those kinds of spells doesn't require a... reversal. Simply another spellcaster with another tangible item."

My lip curls. I suppose I'm lucky mental spells don't work the same way, or some spellcaster could decide that dunking my head in honey was the best plan. And then instead of predators after me like with the Oros' dye, it would be bees. But reversing a mental spell sounds troubling, particularly if the tangible item is the dye again. I swallow the thought. "How does your healing touch magic work, Allanagh?"

"Transferred through my hands. That's the tangible item." She wriggles her fingers, her smile turning lascivious. "Imagine how fun near-death experiences with me could be."

Callum breaks into a hacking cough, and I quickly rub his back. When he regains his voice, he clears his throat and says, "There may be someone at the castle with knowledge of who did this to you."

He must be someone of importance to traverse the castle so freely. Unless Olthion doesn't keep to the formalities of rank. "Do you have contacts at the castle?" I ask, keeping my tone idle.

He shrugs, his body trembling slightly where we connect. But there's a muted pride in his voice as he says, "Yes."

I open my mouth to tease him again, but two figures appear from a side street. Callum's body stiffens at their arrival.

The two men wear leathers similar to what I woke up with, but in the wrong color. My gaze flits over their forms. The first, a pale lanky figure with disheveled blond hair, looks barely strong enough to hold a sword. He's likely a lancer, I reason, built for nimble movements. The second, more muscular and bald with warm bronze skin, has the gait of an archer. They must be in the armed forces for this place, Olthion's soldiers.

"Well, if it isn't the quitter," the blond sneers, eyes locked on Callum.

Callum's flushed cheeks reappear, but this time it's mottled and angry looking. Callum must not be the advisor I thought he was. No soldier would address their strategist that way or else they'd be looking at a battle on the front lines without support. My senses hone in on the potential threat.

"Finally crawled your way out of the library to see what real men are like?" The second one, who towers over us both, leans closer. "I thought you'd had enough of us after failing the Oige."

My lip curls back in a sneer, fists clenching at my side as they make their veiled threats.

The blond snorts meanly. "Didn't fail, remember? Gave up to avoid the embarrassment of being the first member of—."

Just as I'm planning on intervening and knocking some manners into these boys, Allanagh steps towards them with a charming smile. "Boys," she says, her voice deepening lustily. "Is this any way to greet an old friend?"

The men shift their focus from Callum. He lets out a loose breath and I squeeze his arm. Whoever these men are, they aren't friends of *his*. But Allanagh is the mind reader who lives with these people. I'm willing to let her handle this. I am supposed to be acting discreet, after all.

"Were we friends?" the blond asks slyly, running a dirty hand through his hair. "I remember *trying* to be, but you had to run back to that little prin—"

"I remember you falling into your cups last time," Allanagh interrupts. "Which kept you from falling into me."

The bald man laughs. "That's true, Sid. Allanagh had to fix your misshapen head, and you slept on the floor."

Sid scowls. "At least Allanagh would'a bedded me, Garbhan," he says mulishly. "I don't remember you getting that far."

Garbhan leers at me. "Always been more partial to redheads. Who's this fiery beauty? A spellcaster friend of yours, Allanagh?"

But for Callum's flinching earlier, I'd have kicked these two somewhere sensitive. His demand that I disguise myself tells me I'm trying to remain inconspicuous. After a long look at Callum, who nods, I step forward with a confident grin, ready to play. "I'm—"

"Cadhla," Allanagh and Callum say together. Sid and Garbhan blink in unison at the interruption.

"Right. Cadhla," I repeat, frowning. I look to Callum and Allanagh for further clues on how to respond to these not-quite enemies but certainly-not-friends, but neither give me any guidance. "No spells here," I finally say. "Just enjoying good company."

Sid and Garbhan exchange glances before a malicious expression reappears on their faces.

"Good company... with Callum?" Sid asks, sliding closer to me. "Sounds like you don't know the meaning of the word."

Lying low doesn't mean I need to let them insult my savior. "Callum has kept me quite satisfied," I say, reaching back for him and interlocking our arms again. He winces as the two men watch the movement.

As Sid opens his mouth to say something that will no doubt be insulting, I grab Callum by the chest and press my lips to his. It's a simple thing, more a peck than anything else. But as he shudders against me, I can't resist taking advantage of the attraction building since I saw his painting. The desire that sparked when I saw him yesterday has grown stronger throughout the day. I kiss harder, my tongue swiping against his lower lip, arching my back to press my breasts against his lean frame.

One man makes a sound low in his throat and it reminds me of where we are. When I pull back, Callum's cheeks are red and lips wet. "Quite satisfied," I say, dragging my thumb over his bottom lip. His breath hitches and sends a swoop down my middle.

Allanagh steps between us and presses her hand against my low back. "Come along, Cadhla, Callum. We've got places to be."

As we walk away, I peer back at Sid and Garbhan, who look as confused as I did when I first awoke here.

***

Callum

I leave Allanagh and Enna in an alley behind the castle, where they won't be accosted by any more of my childhood bullies. Sid and Garbhan could have revealed who I was and stopped my plan in its tracks. But Allanagh's quick thinking at distracting them saved the day.

And then Enna... The Puzzling Princess kissed me, when she didn't have to. When there was nothing in it for her.

Her actions this morning felt like teasing me, trying to break me, but this was unnecessary kindness. The feel of her soft skin too overwhelmed me to see how my former tormentors reacted. But I know the town will be buzzing with tales of "Cally getting kissed in the square" for weeks to come.

As I make my way through the castle's servants' wing, still feeling the tingling sensation on my lips from Enna's touch, I can't help but wonder about her intentions. Was she teasing me earlier or was there genuine sincerity in her actions?

The soft sigh of satisfaction she emitted wasn't feigned, at least not that I could tell. She kissed me *and* called me clever. That's the first time someone has done either in ages. Her eyes shined at me too, like I was valuable and desirable. Maybe her touches this morning weren't a game, maybe Allanagh's assertions that Enna was sincere were real too. *Not that it matters*, I remind myself.

That thought ends my lingering smile. Almost morosely, I slip through the side corridors until I find the throne room where my father will be. The door opens as I arrive, and Carrin and Brogan stumble out.

Allanagh and Enna may have escaped confrontation with more of my childhood tormentors, but I won't be as lucky.

Brogan sports a bloody lip that Carrin has pressed a handkerchief to. "He didn't need to hit me this time," Brogan says.

"You suggested an ambush. You know he doesn't like that. It goes against our military *tradition*," says Carrin.

The two of them certainly loom over Father, but *his* physical prowess doesn't matter. He's respected for being King. And he wields that respect with an iron fist. And a literal one, as evidenced by Brogan's face and my own memories.

Brogan scowls, wincing as it pulls on his lip. "But if he were a little less inflexible, it would get him—"

Carrin presses a hand against Brogan's chest when he notices me, his eyes narrowing with malicious delight. "Cally, you're looking... well-rested."

"Carrin, Brogan," I say through clenched teeth. Unlike Sid and Garbhan, slimy second-rate soldiers who barely passed the Oige themselves, Carrin and Brogan are skillful warriors. They're highly ranked, more intelligent, and could crack even Darroch's head between their meaty palms. They had once, before he'd locked them in the dungeon as a prank. *I* manipulated them into going there while he handled the actual execution, but they disregarded my part after successfully escaping. Darroch earned their respect for supposedly outmaneuvering them, but not me.

Then I was their sole victim. And the instructors rewarded them for it. The Oige demanded we adapt to the constant strain and injuries, forcing us to develop resilience. All it developed for me was a healthy dose of fear of physical touch. The physical attacks had finally ceased when we hit majority and they could take their aggression out on our enemies, instead replaced by a barrage of uninspiring taunts.

Carrin raises a thick auburn eyebrow, exchanging a glance with Brogan. "What brings Elric's spare to the war room?"

Brogan laughs, a guttural sound I used to hear in my nightmares. "Yeah, you know wars are planned there, right? For people who will actually get to fight?"

I know more of our military history and tradition than the two of you combined, I think. But the words remain stuck in my throat.

Carrin cracks his knuckles, smearing Brogan's blood over his fingers from the handkerchief. "*Cat* got your tongue, Cal?"

Brogan snorts, hitting his armored knee with a meaty hand. "Oh my Gods, cats! Car, do you remember when we dropped that cat into Cally's tent when she was in heat, and she sprayed all over him?"

Carrin glares at Brogan. "That's why I mentioned it."

And you're higher ranked than I am, I think. *Once I get information from Enna and stop this war, your reign over me will end. I'll be the one laughing.* My fists clench, a feeble attempt to stave off the anxiety and irritation that claws at my insides. "Is the King alone in there?" I ask with as much dignity as I can muster.

"Fuck you," Brogan says.

But Carrin only laughs, his smile wicked and malicious "No, no. It's good. Given his current mood, the King will *love* hearing from him. Good luck, Cally." Carrin touches Brogan's chest again. "Let's head to the healer and get you some lily tea. We can forget all about this day."

As they saunter away, Brogan feints toward me, as if he's going to hit me himself. To my internal shame, my body betrays me, and I flinch. The echoes of their laughter linger, as does Brogan's parting statement to Carrin, saying "I wish we could forget about Cally."

He's not the first one to think that. But I push those feelings aside and steel myself for what lies ahead: proving them all wrong about me. Starting with Father.

Chapter 6

Enna

After Callum leaves us, Allanagh takes me to a nearby pub. Although calling it a *pub* is a stretch. It's an open courtyard covered by large swaths of fabric running from building edge to building edge. She directs me to a corner table and two tankards of ale are dropped in front of us along with a boule of bread and a cutting knife.

I trace the rim of my cup, my eyes flickering across the varying patrons, all in quiet conversations. No one is familiar, but that's not surprising since I'm not from here. But nothing about the pub or its atmosphere feels familiar either. *Maybe I'm not accustomed to visiting pubs in Lumadh.* I purse my lips. *Maybe I need to stop thinking of this as a pub, and Olthion as* anything *like what I'm used to.*

As I'd expect from someone who regularly read minds, Allanagh answers my unasked question. "We're not... allowed true social gatherings in the city. There's a proper pub outside the city limits, near Callum's cabin, but it's not something we talk about. One of the rowdier practitioners spelled the knowledge of the location inside a locket, so no one can find it if they haven't already been."

I catch glimpses of men who must be warriors, stern-faced and all wearing clothing similar to what Sid and Garbhan sported, and a handful of women wearing dresses like Allanagh's. "Why must it be a secret?"

"Our public life... should be about efficiency and discipline," she says, her slender nose wrinkling. "It's irritating, but what can you do?"

Leave, I think. *But where would they go? To Lumadh? To... somewhere else in this world I've forgotten? Are there even open borders?*

"Not officially," says Allanagh. She leans forward, her voice lowers. "I've heard of people who have breached the borders or hidden in the border ranges. No one knows what happened to them, though. Given where they went, we're all guessing..."

I lean in and mirror her posture. "Guessing what?"

She runs her finger across her throat, expression somber. But a mischievous smirk spreads across her face as she waves at the newcomers entering the courtyard. "Although personally, I always thought that was a bit of propaganda. Lucky there's no other mind readers here, or they'd pick up on my treason."

"Lucky," I repeat grimly. I eye the newcomers. They are all dressed the same too, in red armor, while Callum's was black. "Does everyone serve?"

She speaks from the side of her mouth, still directing a smile outward. "Yes, unless they fail out, then they're expected to provide for the country in other ways."

A man Allanagh waved to ambles towards us. His uniform has four bands embellishing his shoulders. I wonder if that means he's higher ranked. Callum's black outfit didn't have any bands at all. "What does Callum do?"

But the man interrupts any answer to my question. "Good evening, Allanagh, gorgeous friend of Allanagh," he says. He's stocky with an impish smile, likely my age. Meaning he'd be Callum's age too.

"Nolan," Allanagh says with a purr. "Will I be seeing you tonight, or does Darroch have you running drills until dawn again?"

Nolan flicks deep brown eyes in my direction before responding. "You might. King's got us changing the plan after midday training." He directs a sensuous smirk at me. "Will you be there too? Allanagh knows I'm good to share."

Callum's soft smile and bright green eyes replace Nolan's charming russet brown face before me. "Not tonight," I tell him, not unkindly.

He puts a big palm near my hand and leans against it. "You could always watch me run drills. That usually convinces women to spend the evening with me."

I tiptoe my fingers over his hand until I reach the bread knife and clutch the handle in my hand like a dagger. "Not tonight, I said."

His smile falls, but only slightly, before he appears to rally. "Pity. Allanagh, I look forward to seeing you later." He leaves and we watch him join another table.

I take a small sip of the ale. It's bitter and tastes like something thick congealing in my throat. Holding back a grimace, I watch Allanagh's stare intently at the men and women present in the room. "Seems free love is common here, too," I say.

That's something that feels familiar, at last.

"Another open secret," she replies.

I chance another bid for information, since my last was disrupted. "Callum seems more reserved than the rest of you."

Allanagh glances at the entrance, as if expecting him to walk in. "He's not really had the opportunity."

"How? You want to talk about gorgeous, I mean, hello." I waggle my brows suggestively for emphasis. I'd certainly watch *him* do training drills.

Allanagh huffs a laugh. "It's more of an *internal* problem, if you understand me. In a world that expects him to be a warrior, he's made himself an oddity... by not. And he's always been overshadowed by Dar—his brother's more traditional successes and his father's massive demands. He dropped out of training just to avoid 'officially' failing them. But it just made it worse." Her expression shifts to a mix of empathy and frustration. "His personality is a consequence of that. Along with his excessively high self-expectations, based solely on the idiotic opinions of his father."

I study her face. This is the most serious I've seen her. She really does care for him. After pandering to Sid and Garbhan, who clearly upset him, made me curious.

"He's my best friend, and they wouldn't stop unless preoccupied," she says in answer. She leans in again, and I wait for the next almost-secret she might reveal. "Look, you have no expectations of him. I know it's a circumstance of something bad happening to you, but... you could be good for each other."

"I like him, Allanagh. I've made that clear." I tried to seduce him just this morning. All I did was make him uncomfortable. He might have liked the kiss, but he needs to initiate if there's ever to be a next time. I'm not going to push him.

"He needs a little pushing," she says, wistfully. "In his soul, Callum craves the recognition *truly* he deserves. But he won't believe his worth unless someone convinces him. He needs someone who will help him realize he's more than simply the shadow he's cast in. "

I can't make him discover his worth when I'm trying to discover who I am. I need the information from the spellcaster and to go home, with or without Callum's name on my tally. All I say is, "You're a bit of a poet, Allanagh."

She reaches across the table and touches my hand. "I'm not saying you should neglect your own issues to handle his. Gods, no. That would be awful for you both. All I'm saying is... maybe don't let him hide away. And otherwise, just be yourself."

"The self I'm not fully aware of," I say skeptically.

Allanagh sighs, her gaze momentarily distant. "I have a good feeling about it." She takes a large gulp of ale when her face loses its color. "We need to—"

A commotion breaks out, cutting off her demand mid-sentence. With a loud thud, a burly man, one of the few not wearing a military uniform, slams his tankard down, sending ale spraying across the nearby tables. The room erupts with movement as every man in uniform stands up, reaching for their weapons. My own hand instinctively reaches for the hilt of my daggers in the holsters by my hips. I curse under my breath. My daggers are missing, and my holsters hidden with my leathers somewhere in Allanagh's bag.

Allanagh grips my wrist, her nails like claws. "We can't be here."

I rise from my seat, one hand clutching Allanagh's, the other holding the bread knife. We weave through the crowd, my gaze fixed on the unfolding brawl, searching for potential threats. Only the non-uniformed man is causing trouble, but others seem prepared for a fight. The agitator's loud cries for fairness compete with the grunts and strained efforts of two soldiers as they try to forcefully bring him to his knees. As I glance sideways, I spot a man exploiting the ruckus. He slyly trips Nolan, provoking Nolan to emit a fierce growl and immediately launch himself at the offender.

And then it's as if they are all predators and prey combined, as the room explodes into fights.

With a swift tug, I drag Allanagh through the crowded space between Nolan, the original instigator, and a trio of men locked in a fierce struggle for available weapons.

A flicker of fear crosses her face. "Move!" she screeches.

Only my sensitive hearing allows me to hear it over the din. I spin, dropping her wrist to hold my forearm out protectively. But the assailant isn't after me. A thin man, his eyes filled with fury, lunges towards her. His own weapons remain holstered, his hands curled as if to choke her. Leaping in front of her, I deflect the blow with the flat of my blade. I deliver a swift barrage of kicks to his weak spot, sending him crashing to the floor with a loud thud.

"Foul woman," he snarls, curling protectively over his crotch. Like a spell, the words cast a silence over the tavern, broken only by the labored breaths of the former fighters.

"Is that a woman?" someone mutters from behind us.

I don't stay long enough to figure out who speaks, or why my gender would be a factor. "Come on," I command Allanagh, racing towards the courtyard's opening. We emerge into the midmorning air and sprint hand-in-hand down various alleys, running towards the castle. When we finally reach the alley where we met Sid and Garbhan, we stop.

Allanagh bends over, hands on her thighs, heaving out breaths. "Thank... thank you for..." She straightens, her fingers digging into her rib. She likely has a stitch from the run. "Yes... yes, that's it. A... a stitch. Not used to all this exertion outside a bed... a bedroom. And thank you for... for protecting me." She gulps in air until her breathing evens out.

I examine the blunt bread knife I'm holding before letting it fall to the ground with a noisy clatter. "Former lover?"

She winces. "Something like that. I may have ditched Rayan for Callum a few too many times." And by the earlier reaction when we were in this alley, Callum seems to inspire irritation and rage in other soldiers. "Yes," she answers. "But don't tell him."

"About a man trying to attack you when you were unarmed?" Heat pools in my stomach, a comfortable form of anger.

Allanagh directs her gaze to the building behind us, another utilitarian house without personality or feeling. "I don't care about Rayan. I can handle him. Don't tell Callum about the... incident."

"The bar brawl between some drunken idiots?" It was the first thing that felt familiar about that so-called tavern.

"That wasn't a bar brawl. We don't have brawls." My brows raise but, as expected, she answers my unanswered questions. "Fighting in public goes against our codes of discipline. Only soldiers fight, and only each other as so-called skills test. That was a distraction. Because that man was no soldier."

"He was wearing—"

"The clothes of a layperson, someone who failed out. Yes. But his mind revealed he's from Naithair." She frowns.

"Probably brought by Rian to cause trouble and get the others expelled."

Expelled from service, reducing the army's recruits, my mind supplies. *Underhanded battle strategy but strategy, nonetheless.* I tuck away the question of *who is Rian* deep within, instead focusing on the tavern's reaction to me. "Should I be concerned about the attention I got at the end?"

Allanagh rubs her wrist. "I need to check. See there's any lingering... suspicion." She leaves the alley without further explanation.

As if awaiting her disappearance, a figure appears from the shadows under a cotton window awning. I grapple for the knife as they stalk into the light. It's a man, tall and thin, wearing what looks like an overlarge blanket over a black tunic and pants. I shift into a defensive position. I've already destroyed my opportunity to have a low profile, but I won't attack him until necessary.

He tucks his chin, his slick black hair slipping off his shoulders. "*This* is the grand plan you wouldn't share with Tear? You're shadowing me again? Do you know how worried Tear's been? I received a raven only yesterday in a panic. Do you even know what Mouric's intentions are as you waste time here going after the sword yourself?" He stalks closer, his nearly-black eyes trailing over my face as I tighten my grip on the knife. "Did you... *dye* your hair? Idiotic plan or not, you could have at least come to me for a glamour."

I furrow my brow, not lowering the knife. "Who the fuck are you? And Tear? And *Mouric*?"

He rears back, his dark eyes wide. Footsteps sound from behind us. His ears must be as sensitive as mine as he cocks his head towards the sound like a bird, before stalking backward and vanishing back into the shadows.

Allanagh stumbles into the alley, clawing wisps of her sweaty blond hair from her face. "No one thought much of you, other than a bit 'uppity' for behaving like a man should. But... don't tell Callum."

I nod, my eyes still focused on the shadows where the man vanished. Allanagh follows my gaze. "Are you alright?" she asks. "Did something else happen?"

Can you not see it? But her eyes remain guileless, only concerned. Something about that wraith-like man must disrupt her mind reading. The man that knows me. "Nothing," I finally tell her. "Just... ready to have my memories back."

She purses her lips. "You should leave town sooner rather than later. Immediately, if possible."

That's the best advice I remember hearing.

Callum

Father sits on his lavish throne, his gaze intent on the map spread across the long table before him, an expression of glee on his face. It's unclear whether the source of his joy is because he just hit Brogan or something else. Ever present at his side is his shining sword, one that appears to glow under the harsh candlelight. He doesn't look up when I enter.

Knowing Father's disdain for time wasters, I speak the moment I breach the doorway, deciding to start with Enna before moving to my plan for Rian, to build on my success.

"I've found something, or, rather, someone. An opportunity," I begin, my voice steady despite the anticipation tightening my muscles. My fingers stray towards my lips, but I shove them in my pockets.

Before he can comment, I draw a long breath, already prepared for his resistance, a constant presence in my life. "Enna, from Lumadh... she has amnesia. I believe we can use her to gather information about the Valenthians. She's already provided several pieces that could be of tactical importance." Father still doesn't look up, but I'm undeterred. "What she recovers could be what we need to force peace. Those missing memories are—"

His gaze flickers towards me then, his expression turning stern. "Information from a woman without her memory? Do not waste my time, Callum. You do enough of that by merely existing."

I swallow hard, my throat dry as dust as I press him, for *once* not taking his immediate 'no.' "You're... misunderstanding me, Father. It's Enna—"

"Yes, the bitch is missing, though I do not know how you learned of this. Darroch and Rian are reuniting in anticipation that the Valenthians believe a Netherin kidnapped her and will seek reprisal. They will be left with no *alternative* but to respond to my battle demand."

The Lumadhans stopped accepting Father's battle proposals this summer, after he'd deceived them into thinking he would agree to a peace summit, another one of my ideas. Despite accepting the invitation, he dispatched troops to the border, intending to escalate the meeting into a forced skirmish. The Valenthians decimated our troops and have shown no willingness to meet or engage in a direct conflict ever since. But Father hadn't cared about the loss. He hadn't cared that he'd lied to me, making me believe he'd finally listened to me in negotiating peace. His only concern was that his meticulously chosen battle strategy had been ruined, preventing him from pursuing the organized conflict he loved.

Father grins, his green eyes lighting up with a delighted gleam that is only seen when discussing war. "Our swords will be wet with blood within the week. Finally!"

Not that his sword will be used, I think as frustration tightens my jaw. He hasn't stepped foot into battle himself since Darroch and I hit majority, but he never explained why. And he's barely listening to me, as usual. And while the Lumadhans might not agree to another pitched battle, her knowledge could still get him what he wants. "Yes, and this is our opportunity to act strategically now that she's within—"

Father raises a hand, cutting me off, the large cut gem in his insignia ring blinking in the light. "Strategically? Callum, do not play at war, as you lack the foresight to understand its intricacies. Leave such matters to those whose sword has been wetted in battle."

I fist my hands at my side and try to salvage my proposal. "This could be a turning point, in both our fight with the Valenthians and Naithair's overreach. Enna—"

He interrupts again, his voice dripping with disdain. "Enough. I've wasted far too much magic on you without success to spare any more time in your presence now. I deigned to consider your proposal last week, and it says little for your plans that they were over before they even began."

I hesitate, my mind racing to understand what he's implied. Darroch and Rian are working *together*, he'd said, meaning the need for my plan has vanished. But that wasn't my fault.

Anger gives way to anguish but I hold it back. Being criticized and denied is familiar to me; how I handle it reveals my character. If only Father understood that.

"Then we should formalize the alliance between us," I urge. "Rather than let Rian withdraw his support at his whim and leave us fighting the Valenthians alone like last time. I know you... in your wisdom, chose not to engage in negotiations with the Valenthians last summer, but now we have the chance to attempt it with our own people."

"Alliances are for children," he says, snorting. "Much like pinky promises and reading for pleasure. Real rulers understand only blood, fear, and information can shift the balance of power in war."

"Father—"

His eyes pierce through me, a judgment that cuts deeper than any blade. "Go, Callum. I am meeting with Darroch in moments and do not wish to have such an occasion sullied by your ramblings. Attend to your books and let those more capable handle the affairs of the realm." He returns to the map and my opportunity disappears, just like Enna's memory.

Dismissed, I turn to leave, shuffling down the hallways. Defeat gnaws at my stomach, a familiar ache that accompanies every attempt to prove myself. The Oige was my first missed opportunity. Darroch and I had graduated from section one at age eleven. And while I took top marks in the second section's problem-solving tests—showing skills in resource allocation, preventing enemy infiltration, and limited civilian casualties in the mock battle strategy game—most of the physical skills eluded me. I was unable to transfer into section three when we turned sixteen, as required. Apparently *Darroch's* proficiency in weaponry, mounted combat, agility, and strength compensated for *his* limitations in problem-solving, as he transferred just fine. Father demanded I withdraw rather than fail out, which meant I couldn't enlist. And since the son of the King cannot be a tradesman, I am no more than an un-ranked member of Father's court.

After last week, I'd thought Father was finally recognizing my skills have value, but I was mistaken. Again.

With every step taking me from the castle, the disappointment turns to determination. He may have dismissed my ideas, but it doesn't mean I must. The decision forms: I'll continue my plan with Enna alone. It isn't as though I have anything to lose. Once I've shown the merit in it, Father will be forced to recognize that I am worthy of his atten—to be included in our warfare strategizing, perhaps even to enlist. Alliances might be for children, but *information* is for kings.

I find Enna and Allanagh outside the castle, in the alley where I left them. Allanagh meets my gaze, her blue eyes mournful. With a knowing look, she lets out a weary sigh. I'm thankful Enna's presence keeps her from saying she told me so.

Enna greets me, a wide smile on her lips. "Did you learn anything useful?"

With each step I take towards them, the weight of guilt and false intentions press down on me, but I force them away. "Not from the castle," I admit. "But no matter. There are only so many spellcasters who could have done this."

Enna, crimson hair shimmering in the reflected sunlight, reaches for me but stops before her fingers can touch my chest. She flicks her eyes at Allanagh before peering up at me. "Will you give me a list?"

I stare into her trusting caramel eyes. "Better. I'll join you."

Chapter 7

Enna

Allanagh stays behind as Callum and I begin our journey. We're searching for a "truthteller," a type of practitioner that can look beyond the magical block on my mind. Their skills in truthtelling should overcome the other spellcaster's magic and get to the truth of what happened.

We leave directly from the city after Callum's visit to the castle, stopping only for a few minutes at Allanagh's nearby home for extra clothes. She keeps a stock of Callum's there, and lent me a few more dresses, along with the knapsack she brought from the cabin. She filled it with various healing tinctures and my leathers, which I changed into the moment we were free of an outside audience. Not that I care about the audience, but the color of my leathers, and perhaps even the gender wearing it, tells me I would bring unwanted attention. Which made Allanagh's request—that I withdraw Callum from the shadow he placed himself within—seem even more confusing.

It was at her urging that I let him accompany me. I couldn't say no. After all, she was offering me a veritable treasure chest in that knapsack.

And he *is* gorgeous.

Callum and I start east, towards where I woke up, though he attempts to hide that fact. He carries the map to the truthteller, but I'd be a poor soldier if I couldn't determine our direction from the landscape. He's taking us towards a kelpie's hollow, but Allanagh added two small daggers to the bottom of the knapsack that will come in handy in case Callum doesn't realize what he's walking us into. I eye the sword in his holster. It needs a scabbard, the metal looks rusty, but a sharp pointy thing is still a sharp pointy thing.

The forest cradles us as we venture deeper, the pixies and faewisps and snorlix chattering around us. The first few hours are silent except for those sounds.

"Are you *sure* the truthteller lives this direction?" I ask, breaking the silence that enveloped us. A kelpie whinnies somewhere in front of us, towards the gulf and nearby ocean. Kelpies are tricksters and manipulators. I can't imagine a being known as the 'truthteller' would want them nearby. The constant lies would probably grate on whatever magic they have.

Callum nods, pulling out the map and holding it close to his face. He shoves it quickly back into his pocket and fixes his gaze on a distant point beyond the swaying branches. "Their cabin is to the north."

I stutter to a stop. "The north?"

He nods again, silhouetted against the shifting backdrop of swaying creeper vines. "Yes, the north." He points to the moss that clings to the trees. "The moss is a natural compass. I'm surprised Valenthian soldiers don't know that."

I tuck away the revelation that I'm a 'Valenthian,' along with the confirmation that I'm a soldier. "That's a myth." I sneak closer to him, sticking a hand in the knapsack. "We're going east."

The creeper vine lifts a tendril towards his shoulder. He bats it away absentmindedly, too focused on frowning at me in irritation. "No, the moss grows on the southern side of the trees. We're traveling in the opposite direction, towards the north, where the truthteller is."

The vine grows bolder, two tendrils reaching out like fingers, ready to wrap around Callum's throat. I leap forward, withdrawing the daggers and slashing the vines as they claw towards his skin. He screeches, the sound mixing with the vine's own squeal. The vine shrivels back into itself as I pull him farther from it.

His gaze flits from the daggers in my hands and the vine behind him. His fingers fumble at his own sword, withdrawing it clumsily.

"It's finished," I reassure him. So much for gentle handling, though he certainly didn't want his neck severed. "It won't try again. It knows our scent and will avoid us now that we've shown we can hurt it."

He blinks, his green eyes owlish, before he finally appears to understand what I've said. He slides the sword back into its holster, arms shaking. "Thank you," he says, staring at me. He chews on his lip as though he's working out a difficult puzzle. "We're going east?"

"And towards a kelpie," I add helpfully, offering him a playful smile. It doesn't diffuse the tension. Instead, his shoulders slump. "North is that way," I tell him, pointing with a dagger. His eyes catch on it and widen, and I shove them into my own holsters. The holsters are made for my own specialty daggers, but these substitutes still fit.

With a frown, he starts off towards the north, leaving me to trail after him. I remember Allanagh's description of this place, and how Callum didn't fit into it. *But why would Olthion make him feel so worthless?* Because he couldn't finish some school? To a society that focused on efficiency and work, why create a man so emotionally fragile that a simple mistake would undo him? That's not efficient.

"You'd need to be incredibly familiar with the forest to recognize the vines," I say when I catch up to him, sparing a few seconds to take the cut vines with us, just in case. I could make a bow from them later. They wrap themselves around my wrists like bracelets.

"I should have recognized them," he bites out. "I know every plant in Olthion. It's the least I—" He sighs, biting his lip again.

"The least you what?"

"I'm the smart one compared to—" He cuts himself off, resentment radiating from him. "The one inclined for strategy, diplomacy. The subtler aspects of warfare. Even if I've never taken part in a mission, I should know how to travel the forest without getting strangled by a plant or wandering into a kelpie nest."

"Kelpie hollow," I say softly, placing a hand on his arm. He flinches and I remove it, gentling my tone further to ask, "Did you ever even study survival skills?"

"We were supposed to," he says, the lines around his face deepening. "I... That training happened in section three."

And you left before then. I frown. "It's unrealistic to demand perfection in something you've never studied."

His hands twist together until he drops them to his side and makes tight fists. "Not for me. Not for my family."

"No one is perfect," I tell him.

"My brother is." There's vulnerability in his eyes. "Or people think he is. The embodiment of physical prowess—skilled with a sword, charismatic, the epitome of a warrior. The ideal..." He scowls and starts walking again, continuing in the right direction. "This way? We don't want to waste time. Gods forbid I do something *right* and find the truthteller."

I remember Sid and Garbhan's taunts from this morning. The complaints Callum had about his brother's talents when he didn't know I could overhear him in the kitchen. Allanagh's hints about his brother's 'traditional' talents. "Fuck that."

He stops, pulled from whatever internal musings he was falling into thinking about his failure today. "What?"

"You made a mistake. Who cares? Worth isn't defined by perfection, but by *work*. You haven't seen a creeper vine before, but won't forget what they look like now, will you?"

He tilts his head, the lines in his face deepening.

"Your brother didn't become *strong* without mistakes," I continue. "He worked at it. Probably got hit in the head with a few swords?"

"Yes," he says, a small grin forming.

I yank up my left pant leg and point to the burn on my calf. "This happened when I walked into a hollow. And only *now* I know what not to do."

His eyes hold mine for a moment in an unspoken exchange before he nods again. "Are you ready to continue forward?"

I smirk as I drop my pant leg back down. "Absolutely."

Callum

A small part of me is concerned that giving Enna the map may trigger a memory and remind her she's in enemy territory. But the bigger part of me is worried about walking into a kelpie nest. Hollow. And the Proficient Princess does know better how to survive in the wild. Growing up amidst endless conflicts against my people must have honed those skills.

But despite my initial reservations, Enna's continued presence has started to change my opinion of her.

Why would a Valenthian, known for their unsophisticated ways and barbaric nature, try to comfort me after my failure? She should have scolded me for almost getting choked by a plant. That's what an Olthion general would do. Or worse, demand a warped form of Enna's proposed lesson in learning from our mistakes: letting the vine choke me until near death and only *then* destroy it, to prove that suffering begets wisdom. I keep a curious eye on her as we travel, now in the right direction. With the map in hand, she maintains a steady pace, meticulously describing everything that catches her eye.

"That's poison," she says, pointing to another plant.

Besides the creeper vine, there are none I don't recognize, and I feel vindicated that my knowledge isn't as limited as I'd originally thought. I don't tell Enna that I don't need her running commentary. Her eyes light up with each identification she makes, clearly excited her memory remains with her.

And there's always a chance she may let something important about Lumadh slip out unintentionally, of course.

The forest continues unfolding before us, a mosaic of sunlight filtering through the dense foliage. As midday approaches, Enna's gaze snags on a cluster of vibrant flowers, their petals a riot of colors. "Those are…" she trails off. "Well, damn. Either we don't have those in Lumadh, or I've hit the limit on my memory."

"These are incredibly rare hybrid lily blooms," I explain, feeling a touch of excitement that I can redeem myself from the poor showing earlier. "They have healing properties when brewed. Not for physical wounds, but emotional ones." They form the base of the tea all the soldiers drink, and the one Allanagh doles out to me so stubbornly. "Tradesmen cultivate them in greenhouses not far from my cabin. I never thought I'd see one in the wild."

She crouches beside the plant and runs a finger down the petals. "Healing plants in general are rare in Lumadh. We certainly have nothing for emotional wounds."

"Really?" I shiver at the delicateness of the touch as she continues to drag her fingers over the petals.

"I have deep memories of emotional grief. Unfocused, but a part of me," she says quietly. "I'm sure if there was a plant to help, I would have done whatever I could to reduce the pain."

"Who?" I ask in the same gentle tone.

Her brow furrows in thought. "My brother, I think. A long time ago. He put his faith in the wrong person." Her brother Liam, I knew, had disappeared ten years ago, and she'd taken over command in his stead. It had never been confirmed that he'd died, but we assumed it. Or else Enna had usurped her brother's leadership position and dumped him in the wilderness. That's what we were taught about Lumadhans: they were ruthless and merciless, which is why we must be even more ruthless and even more merciless.

But then Enna smiles, a coy smile like the one she gave me this morning and last night, all traces of sadness gone. "Allanagh was right, you truly are my good luck charm. Being around you keeps triggering more memories."

The thought doesn't fill me with the joy I'd hoped it would. Could I truly tell Father the best way to stop the Valenthians is by targeting their organs because they have no touch healers, or inflicting emotional trauma to slow them down? When I've seen the scars of her skin and the pain in her eyes? When she tried to make me feel worthy earlier?

Allanagh's voice echoes through my head, that *this won't work out how I think*. I scowl internally. If making me sympathetic to the barbarians we've been fighting for centuries is how it *will* end, then perhaps Allanagh is right after all.

Enna cocks her head, like a fox with a rabbit in its sights and leaps to stand, all teasing gone. "Thank the Gods, a stream! I've only just gotten used to my own image. Being a redhead all day was going to give me anxiety."

She takes off, and I chase the crimson hue of her hair through the trees. She stops before the stream, barely more than a trickle. Her hearing is more sensitive than I could have imagined if she heard it that far away. As I arrive, she unlaces her shirt and I quickly stumble over an unearthed root.

"Must you?" I know I sound like a scandalized matron, but Enna's comfort in nudity is more than I can handle. I've barely held myself together from her touches and the visions of her body. Guilt aside, she is unaware of my identity. Once she realizes we're on opposite sides of this centuries-long skirmish, she'll want nothing to do with me. Unless it's to remove my head for getting to see her nude form without real consent.

Enna raises her brows. "I'm not staying a redhead, if that's what you mean."

"No, must you remove your clothes?" I flail for an excuse other than 'your nude body makes me pleasantly uneasy and you won't want to share it with me once you know the truth about me.' "...Won't you be exposed to potential faewisp bites?"

She kneels by the water's edge, her fingers gingerly touching the surface. "The dye will stain my clothes if I get water on them, and I'll be damp and wet all day." She looks up at me through lowered lashes. "Do you want me to be wet all day?"

I clear my throat and crouch beside her. "What if I help? Lean your head back and I'll rinse out the dye. I am the one that applied it, after all."

She answers by shifting, and I can see the ghost of a smirk as she turns away from me, displaying her neck and letting her hair fall down her side. My gaze lingers on her silhouette for a moment before I cup the water, bringing it to her red locks until a cascade of crimson-tinted water carries off the artificial hue. Behind her, I see her hands skim over her face, the distorted reflection in the water. Only a short time later, the dye is gone and the chocolate color returns.

She replaces my hands in her hair, squeezing out the remaining water, the locks curling. Then she stands, staring down at me and grinning. With the sunlight flickering through the trees, haloing her body, she looks like a wild goddess, some creature of the woods. She's only missing a crown of wildflowers. Leaning forward, her fingertips hover just above my cheek, not making contact. She's been doing that, teasing me with touches that never come, ever since she kissed me this morning. Because I'm not normally fond of physical contact, I tell myself that I don't miss it.

"Shall we continue?" she asks quietly.

I nod, my tongue stuck to the roof of my throat.

As the sun begins its descent, we press on through the forest, following the path marked on my—Enna's—map. She's been watching me since the stream, those caramel eyes fixed on me. Not my body, not the teasing way she had yesterday and this morning about my looks, but looking through me. Like there's something there she's trying to catch. I'd call it unnerving but a small part, the part that fades each time I bring Father another failure, appreciates that she sees something of interest in me.

Before the sun sets, I take the knapsack from her in search of supplies for a meager dinner. But Enna smirks and tells me she plans to hunt for our supper, pulling out a makeshift bow she's created from the creeper vine tendrils she'd been wearing around her wrists. I swallow various thoughts about that, starting with *when did she do that* and *what was I doing that I missed it* to *how distracting is she?* Her smile looks forced, like she's afraid I'll say 'no' to her hunting. Unsure why I would, I gesture her forward.

The smile turns sincere as she crouches low, her lithe figure blending with the dappled sunlight. She holds the makeshift bow in her hands. Arrows carved from slender branches, another thing I never saw her do, rest against her thigh. Her eyes, sharp and focused, scan the underbrush.

I watch with a sense of anticipation as she moves with a stealthy determination. It's rare that one gets to see their enemy this way, as the predator they are. A rustle to her left, barely perceptible to my senses over the chitters of the pixies, signals her quarry. I can't see what she's found; I just hope it isn't a snorlix. The spikes always looked unappealing.

Enna's movements are deliberate and her fingers cradle the bow as she draws it taut, the arrow poised to slice through the air. The release is swift and sure, the arrow finding its mark with a soft thud. Enna's exhale echoes the quiet triumph of a skilled predator. She approaches her fallen prey and kneels beside it, revealing a hare. When she looks at me, eyes dancing with success, I feel compelled to clap. She laughs in response.

"Never have I been applauded for catching dinner. That I remember, at least," she says. Her hands move with practiced efficiency as she field-dresses the hare. "I should keep you around. I could do with some worship."

My cheeks flush at the memory of my thoughts about her at the stream. "It was definitely impressive," I manage to say.

She raises her gaze to meet mine and tilts her chin challengingly. "We *all* have our strengths."

I stumble away to search for kindling.

Chapter 8

Callum and I work together to build a fire, gathering dry wood and arranging it into a small campfire. While he arranges the logs, I use my knife to sharpen sticks for roasting our dinner. His makeshift fireplace was as good as any I'd seen in the woods, but I keep that to myself. I don't want him to think I'm pandering to him. He'd already run off when I'd tried complimenting him earlier. *Thanks, Allanagh. Great advice.*

He reminds me a little of my sister, I realize, as I retrieve flint and steel from the knapsack. I'd forgotten her too. Her face still eludes me, but I remember how I felt about her: she was sensitive and shy, but incredibly smart. I remember telling her that she wasn't lesser, just different, when she delisted from the army. I couldn't sit through a dignitary meeting without forgetting all of import that was reported. She couldn't hit a target if it was a foot away from her.

The fire cracks, born of Callum and my joint effort, as more memories tear through my brain. I know I'm a soldier and a damn good one. My sister practices diplomacy the way

I study swordsmanship, but we both attend the same war councils. I flick my gaze down to my faded leathers, a nod to my past. I can't help but think about how our roles have reversed. Here I am trying to play diplomat with a potential enemy. If the memories are true, I most certainly serve on the opposite side of Callum's country. *Am I the enemy to these people? Is that why he disguised me? A 'Valenthian' in the land of another creature?*

"What will you do with the organs?" Callum's question pulls me from my internal alarm. If I'm his enemy, he's treating me kinder than I'd expect.

But someone did this to you, my musings remind me. *Maybe you aren't an enemy, but a spy that was discovered.* That seems unlikely, unless I've vastly overestimated my own skills. *You could be a traitor and that's why he's helping you, because you turned on your own people.* That seems even less likely. *Maybe* he *did it and his guilt is overwhelming him. But why would Allanagh try to push us together if so?*

Callum's expression tightens the longer I fail to answer him and continue having an internal conversation with myself. I silence my inner voices and refocus on Callum's question.

"Out here, I leave them," I say, trying not to betray the conflicting thoughts running through me. I glance at the small pile of organs—heart, liver, and kidneys—I set aside during the dressing process. "They're too small to bother with, not worth the effort."

A thoughtful expression crosses his face. "I... might have an idea."

I watch as he fashions a makeshift grill from the sticks I'd pulled from the pile of kindling to sharpen into more arrows, placing it to the side of the highest flames. He arranges the organs and looks up at me with a faint grin. The self-doubt from before has all but vanished, and it's a good look on him.

As the organs sizzled over the fire, an enticing aroma fills the air. If the organs had been any bigger, the idea wouldn't have worked, as the sticks would have caught fire and crumbled well before the meat cooked. I don't tell him that, instead saying, "That was very clever."

He blushes, his green eyes darkening.

We sit beside the crackling fire, burning our fingers on the delicate offal as we wait for the hare to cook. He hands me the last kidney. I try to keep our fingers from touching, but he grazes them. When we've finished the small offerings, Callum stares heavily into the fire.

"Do you remember anything else?" he asks, breaking the weighted silence. "Anything about your life before waking up in the forest? Like... where you were going?"

I hesitate, spinning the spit to give myself time to answer. Any of my theories about myself could be damning. I've only *just* gotten him to stop flinching in my presence. But at the same time, I can't keep hiding my memories from him, not when he's abandoned his regular life to help me.

"Mainly bits and pieces, glimpses of people, the clang of swords and battle," I tell him. "Nothing about who did this to me or why."

He frowns, his gaze flickering for just a minute. I remember all he's done for me, all he intends to do, when I could be anyone. A Valenthian that wears the colors of a different command.

"I have a sister," I offer. "I remembered her too." He makes a quiet sound, which I take as encouragement. "She is soft and kind. Not a warrior." The unspoken comparison to him lingers in the silence between us.

"She sounds familiar," he says, tossing a stick into the flames. "Let me guess. She's the disappointment in your family of warriors."

"Because she can't fight? Of course not," I say firmly, though I know my words are more for Callum than a true memory of my sister. "Her skills are different, but still necessary."

His gaze flicks to mine. "Which are?"

"Diplomacy, keeping me from running into a situation without the knowledge to overcome it." Although the little I know of myself is that the latter is more of an *aspirational* goal for her. I cast my memory back, trying to find something to give Callum. "We have a council that meets with... Lumindar, maybe. That's another country, I think, not a city in Lumadh. She attends it every single time." My brow furrows as I try to pierce through the veil blocking my memory. "I don't know if she's part of it, or goes for fun, but I remember her reporting it back to me—to us, because I would get it twisted, or forget by accident when I attended." Frustration creeps in as I struggle to remember more details, giving myself a headache. "I'm sorry, Callum. That's all I've got."

His focus is back on the fire, his lips pursed. "No, thank you, that's helpf—interesting." He offers a forced smile.

I frown. "Is it different here?"

"We rarely partake in diplomacy, if that's what you're implying," he says, scowling. "You'd think alliances would be valuable, but no. They're seen as a game, a tool for manipulation. They're for children."

Which Callum has said is where his talents lay. I'd already guessed as much, given his breakdown earlier today and Sid and Garbhan's teasing. He clearly prides himself on his diplomatic abilities, yet they hold little value here. He'd be an advisor in Lumadh. Of that, I'm sure. What I remember of the war councils is that we're a peace-seeking country. Given the many disjointed memories I have of fighting, our battle skills are a necessity, not a choice. A demand to protect ourselves from an aggressor. It doesn't appear the same here. The few memories I've recovered of Olthion tell me it isn't a place to be proud of. Maybe this is Allanagh's plan, for Callum to spend time with someone who understands the value of his skills.

"That's a damned shame," I say.

He meets my gaze, his green eyes widening in surprise. I shuffle closer and hold my hand out over his heart. I won't touch him without permission, not knowing what I know now, not when I've realized his reactions aren't born of something as simple as shyness. He doesn't seem to realize that he inches forward, meeting me until the tips of my fingers press against his chest.

I can feel his heart beating, fast and irregular. I'd noticed the rapid pace each time I'd touched him before, the subtle hitch of his breath. But there's no fear in his gaze, or discomfort, just need. For reassurance. For someone to recognize he has value. If I wasn't already troubled about who I am to Olthion, I'd burn it to the ground for the emotional suffering they've given this sweet man.

"We need the diplomats to keep us sword-types from running the pointing ends through things when a compromise would have worked," I tell him quietly. "They're two sides of the same coin. Without one side, what do you have?"

He blinks at me but stays silent.

"A glob of metal."

He huffs out a laugh and I use the success to push him a little farther, bringing my other hand forward slowly until it lingers just above his shoulder. My brows raise in question, and he nods, almost imperceptible if I weren't so close to him to notice. I touch his shoulder gently as warmth winds through my core, settling below my pelvis and tingling.

"You are valued, you know." I drag my hand from his chest towards his neck to toy with the dark hair at the nape of his neck. "You're smart and clever and good. Gods, Callum, you—"

He wets his lips, and I want to taste them. "I what?" he says, sounding dazed.

I smile at him, and it looks like he can't help but smile back. It's a soft thing, a bit overwhelmed, like the look he gave me at the stream when he stared at me as if I was some magical creature come to answer all his wishes. "You helped a stranger, someone who could be anyone, trusting that I won't take advantage of it. You're going out of your way to discover what happened to me." I huff a disbelieving laugh. "You're a good person, Callum."

With a blink, he rises and distances himself from the fire, as my hands drop to my side.

"I'll take the first watch," he says gruffly, leaving me to finish cooking the hare and wonder what I said wrong.

⚬◆⚬

Callum

When I'm sure she's asleep, what feels like hours after that moment at the fire, I can finally breathe again. I'd managed to keep from engaging her again, even when she tried to pull me back in with the meat she'd cooked.

I lean against a tree and shield my face with my hands. I can't make sense of my own feelings towards her. All I know is that this plan has become more complicated than I ever imagined. And entirely too quickly. Enna, the Persuasive Princess, had pulled me in, had said everything I'd wanted to hear, had made me feel worthy. Until I'd ruined it.

I could really use some of that hybrid lily tea right now. It's been several weeks since I needed any besides to sleep. I should have known what thoughts would crest after meeting with Father.

Would she still think I was a good man if she knew why *I was helping her?* She's a soldier. She might understand. She might comfort me, hold me again and tell me that there's nothing to be guilty for, that seeking an advantage in this world doesn't make me a bad person. She was a Valenthian, that's what they did after all. *Right?*

She could even be... proud of it. My cock twitches at the thought. Something true, not the milquetoast pride Father couldn't even be bothered to offer. Something meaningful, from someone powerful enough to understand it. I remember her body standing over me at the stream, asking for worship; I remember her hands in my hair, telling me I was smart and clever.

My cheeks flush, her face in my mind, and I'm hard. I peer around the tree; Enna is still sleeping. My cock strains against my pants and I push the heel of my hand against my groin, hoping it would be the end of it.

It isn't, it does nothing good.

It does everything good, because it feels like fire and I want...

Before I can talk myself out of it, I untie the laces and take my cock out. The coarse fabric brushes against it and it feels good too, a little pain reminding me this is real. I wrap my palm around my shaft and squeeze, barely relieving the pressure and only increasing my desire for more.

I imagine Enna with me, standing over me as I kneel before her. She'd lean towards me, her thumb lightly brushing against my cheek, before finding its place on my bottom lip, like after she'd kissed me.

Gods, that *kiss*. I hadn't even let myself think about it. Her lips against mine, her breasts pressing against my chest. I give one slow, experimental tug to my cock and my eyes roll back in my head. It's been so long, but I can't... I can't stop myself now.

My eyes close and Enna's before me again. She'd push her thumb between my lips, and I can almost imagine the taste of her. I have no idea where this imaginary vision came from, it's never one I've gone to in the past, but I don't care. I'm on my knees before her and she's telling me I'm good and letting me touch her. *That's* power, her power shared, power that feels better than anything I've felt before.

My hand blurs as I squeeze up and down, tight enough to sting. I'm almost choking on my tongue as it builds, this feeling of pleasure and power that Enna has over me, even in a vision. I'm gasping, hoping to the Gods that Enna is still asleep, thrusting into my fist. The glide is almost painful, and I bite my lower lip to keep from making a sound, chewing the skin hard enough to draw blood. I cover my mouth with my other hand and, Gods, that feels agonizingly good too. The strokes come faster, harder, my hand twisting around the shaft until fire licks at my low back, embarrassingly quick had I not been alone. With a bitten off groan, I stutter as a bright whiteness flashes over my vision. I see Enna, her face and that fucking coy smile, and I can't stop—can't stop seeing her face, can't stop the heat of pleasure.

Until I'm alone again in the dark of the forest. The power and pride seep from me, cold like the release on my fingers, leaving me alone with my usual self-loathing.

Chapter 9

We pack up as soon as the sun rises. Callum won't meet my eyes and I wonder if I went too far yesterday. If Olthion doesn't appreciate the softer skills, my reminding him likely didn't help. That's why we need diplomats like him. To balance out our—my—impulsive nature and prevent the stabby-types from making rash decisions that could lead to disaster.

Keeping my gaze fixed forward, I steal glances at him as we walk. Although the man needs *some* reassurance, he'll likely crumble under the weight of his own high expectations otherwise, I need to stop pushing him. Pushing him to be comfortable with me, pushing him to acknowledge his own skills. Soon, I'll probably push him all the way back to his cabin. And there's an itch under my skin that doesn't want that. The thought of being alone on this quest makes my skin crawl, and I can't shake off the unfamiliar feeling of needing someone by my side, as though my being alone is what put me in this position in the first place. Which is... odd.

We're close now, the map confirms we're a stone's throw away from the truthteller's den, when a faint sound disrupts the silence—a distant rhythm of metal clashing against metal.

"Wait," I whisper, my hand shooting out to grasp Callum's arm. His muscles tense beneath my fingers. I'd chastise myself for touching him without his express permission if I weren't concerned for his safety. "Hear that?"

But I don't wait for an answer, swiftly guiding him behind a broad tree trunk. My fingers make shapes I don't recognize, muscle memory from other times I've needed to be quiet. They must be signals, silent communication when needed. I shake off the slowly-forming memory, pressing a finger to my lips. His eyes hold a question, but he stays silent, trusting. At least I have that.

I edge forward and part the foliage for a clearer view. Before us is an army training group, all wearing the leathers of the soldiers I'd seen in town.

"Enna," Callum hisses, panic sharpening his voice. "Close your eyes."

I hesitate. I'm the one to give orders. Another memory bursts forth, one of violence and volume, my calling out commands.

"Trust me," Callum murmurs, desperation threading through his demand.

I realize I must trust him, or I wouldn't have let him guard us last night. My eyes fall shut, the sight of the soldiers seals away. The image lingers, though, imprinted on the darkness: the glint of sunlight on steel, the uniformity of their deadly dance, wearing those colors. I've seen those movements before. My blades have struck theirs.

In that moment, my world narrows to the sound of his voice, the pounding of my heart, and the unseen mystery that dances just beyond my closed eyes.

Callum

I curse under my breath, the slip of memory grating like a stone in my boot. There was an ancillary training ground, hidden away in the dense folds of this forest – how could I have forgotten? But then again, I never had cause to visit; my path had veered sharply from the soldier's road long ago.

"Enna," I whisper sharply as I reach for her hand. Any hesitation for her touch must be smothered by necessity. Enna cannot see those men, she cannot remember. "Can I guide you out of here with your eyes still closed?"

Her lips twitch into an amused smile. "Lead the way, Callum," she says, and there's a lilt of challenge in her tone.

I nod, swallowing the awkwardness that lodges thick in my throat. Carefully, I take her hand and step forward with tentative assurance. We weave through the trees.

Then, a scream from the training camp—sharp and shattering—pierces the forest. It claws at the sky, a harrowing sound that turns my blood to ice.

Enna's eyes flash open, wide and wild. She wrenches her hand from mine and darts ahead.

"Enna!" My own voice is a distant echo, drowned by the clamor from behind us. I sprint after her.

I can barely keep up with her, but fear gives me speed. My breath is ragged, catching in my throat as I lunge forward and seize Enna's arm, yanking her back just shy of the clearing.

"Callum, wh—?" she begins, but her words hang suspended as we both grasp the gravity of the scene.

A soldier has collapsed on the ground, blood seeping into the earth. Despite the years they've mocked me, labeled me a pariah and a reject from their ranks, I can't restrain the gnawing twist of empathy at the grim vision.

A raw brutality becomes apparent: one of the soldiers dealt a blow too fierce for training. The victim lays dying, his life pooling beneath him but no one even stops to render aid. Instead, voices rise in a cacophony of discordant suggestion—one barks about an eye for an eye, a reciprocal stabbing as just recompense for excessive force. Another counters, suggesting a promotion for the to-be-murderer, extolling the virtues of ruthlessness on the battlefield.

The words strike like arrows, embedding themselves within me. These are the teachings of the Oige. My chest tightens, a maelstrom of anger and sorrow fighting for dominance. The men—Father's men, Darroch's men—speak of punishment and prowess, without an ounce of compassion among them. That's what we have been taught.

"Warriors without mercy," I murmur, the taste of the words like ash upon my tongue. "That's all that matters."

The injured soldier's gasps for breath are faint but unrelenting, calling out over the soldiers' argument. I don't know what possesses me, but I make to step forward, every fiber of my being screaming to intervene, to offer aid. None of these men would do the same, for me or for their soldiers in arms. *Are you proud of this, Father?* But Enna's hand clamps down on mine, her grip unyielding.

"Let's go, Callum. There's nothing for us here," Enna says, her voice steady yet carrying the weight of unspoken understanding.

But I remain, watching the soldier bleeding out, coughing and sputtering, and the men all standing beside him, ignoring his final moments. If I overcame my concern at them seeing me with Enna, or if I were a stronger person, I'd have leaped into the clearing and helped that man. Like Enna, who raced towards danger without a second thought.

Finally, the injured man stills. A commander, one I recognize, barks orders to dispose of the body and for the remaining ranks to return to training. A healer passes out a large canteen and each man takes a swig. Lily tea, I'd bet. I suppose it's a comfort they *might* have felt something towards their comrade, had they not drowned it in tea.

"Damn it, we *could* have done something," I hiss, feeling the sting of helplessness clawing at my insides. Allanagh gave us her standard healing kit for Gods' sake. "We have all the healing tinctures a soldier needs."

Enna's hand on my arm is firm, no false comfort in her voice. "It wouldn't have made a difference, Callum. That kit is for scrapes and cuts, not... not anything serious."

Surprise jolts through me, followed quickly by an unsettling mix of relief and anger. I remember Allanagh's claims, that what my father said wasn't always the truth. *Are* we *the barbarians then?*

"I suppose I should feel lucky I will never be abandoned like this," I say bitterly. "A benefit to being a weakling suited for diplomacy."

"No, Callum," Enna counters sharply, her eyes dark with a sorrow that mirrors my own. "I won't press you on your worth again, but know that you wouldn't be left behind.

Soldiers carry each other home, dead or alive. We don't leave our own behind—not like this."

I can hear the bittersweet pride in her voice: that she remembered something new but that these were the circumstances underlying her remembering it. It's a stark reminder that while I failed to become one of them, she did not—could not—forget what it means to be a true soldier.

⎯⎯◆⎯⎯

Enna

I press forward through the dense underbrush, my shoulder brushing Callum's arm in a silent bid to bolster his spirits. It isn't touching him, but reminding him I'm there. After his first experience with death, it likely wouldn't take much for him to hide away again. If not for my recent realization that I've fought those men, or their similarly-dressed comrades, I'd have leapt into the clearing with him. That's what pushed me to run towards them when I heard the death scream, muscle memory at helping a fallen warrior. But seeing what had happened, realizing how these Olthion soldiers treat each other, it only made me more committed to the regain of my memory. To get home and away from a society that would allow such a thing.

It's midday that we reach the marked location on the map. I can feel it before we see it, the air shimmering with an otherworldly energy, some tingling magic that lingers in the air. A worn path leads through towering trees, moss crawling on all sides. I almost point to tease Callum but stop myself before I drive him away again. That he only closed down briefly after the soldier's death is probably luck. After last night, I could see him abandoning this entire quest.

"Come on, we're almost there," I murmur, glancing over my shoulder. His face is a canvas of conflict—anger and sorrow warring beneath the surface.

The path opens into a small clearing, uncovering a modest cottage at its center. Luminescent pink flora gives the stones a painted, ambient glow. Only then do Callum's eyes shine with a blend of excitement and reverence. Feeling lighter at his joy, I take a deep breath and the forest's enchantment seeps into my very being. It could have been beautiful... if not for the magical interference. As we step into the clearing, I clutch the daggers in their holsters.

"Be careful," I tell him. "That enchantment may be affecting us already."

"Only with the truth," a voice murmurs, their ethereal tone resonating through the mystical woodland. It comes from the surrounding air, male and female and not, childlike and aged and not. In the open threshold of the dwelling stands a figure cloaked in head to toe black. The only feature seen within the black hood are their glowing eyes, ethereal and timeless.

Callum shakes off the daze and moves to stand by my side in a sweet show of solidarity. "Why would one famed for the truth hide themselves?"

"Because only the truth matters," they answer. Their eyes stare into me, making me suppress a shiver. "You seek knowledge from us."

Callum digs into his travel pack, pulling out a hunk of quartz. My brows raise; Callum must have more experience with spellcasters than I'd ever imagined. "We bring this gem, for you to reflect the truths we seek," he says in a hushed tone.

The truthteller lifts their gloved hand, and the quartz flies from Callum to inside the open door of the cottage. "Such an offering is acceptable, and we will give you your truths. But know this: the truth you receive may not always be the truth you demand."

Callum and I exchange a glance. I take a step forward, to ask, "You don't provide us with the truth?"

"When a truth is sought, we will reveal it. However, if the truth within your being is more urgent, more pressing than the truth sought aloud, then that is the truth we will impart, regardless of your request."

Callum nods slowly, clearly understanding quicker than I do. "You will tell us what we most desperately want to know, not necessarily what we ask for."

"Yes, Callum of Olthion," the truthteller confirms. "Now, what truth do you seek?"

I pause, glancing at Callum. He brought me here to find the spellcaster that veiled my memory. But I can likely figure that out on my own; like he said, there are only so many spellcasters in the world. More important is what brought me here, a commander of some sort in the world of another army, one I have visions of facing in battle. This is my opportunity to determine who outmatched me. *This* is the truth I desire most. And if this being already intends to tell me what I want most, I won't waste time with questions that won't be answered. "Tell me the truth of my past," I answer. "I want to know who did this to me. And why."

The truthteller laughs, a deep, grating rasp. "Those are extraordinary requests, Enna of Lumadh. We will only answer one. Be specific."

"They're the same," I say, stalking closer. It isn't as though I asked for my life story, simply information on who did this and how they overpowered me. "What happened to me is something within my past, and how it was done and why are entwined."

The truthteller raises a glove covered hand and cuts off my further demands. "Although the threads of truth weave a complex tapestry, and the answers you seek are coiled within, the demands are too great. You must choose."

I swallow a growl. The urge to shout at them, shake them and demand the information rather than these riddles, is so overwhelming I bite my cheek to stop myself. My problems with spellcasters must stem from them acting like assholes. "*Fine*. I want to know who overpowered me and brought me here."

The truthteller turns their attention to Callum. "And you, Callum of Olthion. What knowledge do you seek?"

"I'm only here for Enna," he says softly.

"That is the partial truth," the truthteller says, their voice a rasp. Their intense gaze seems to reach into the depths of our souls. "Your agenda cannot hide here."

He jolts, eyes darting to me and wetting his lips. "There's no agenda other than Enna's."

A sudden darkness falls as shadows crawl over the clearing, dark spindly fingers creeping towards us.

"Don't anger the practitioner," I hiss. He blinks, taken aback, and I force down the irritation. It isn't his fault. "Just tell them the truth. It can't be that bad. And then we can get my answer *and* yours."

His eyes skim across my face before he turns back to the truthteller. "Truly, there is no other information I need to-day."

The truthteller nods, the shadows retreating from where they came. "That is the truth. You need only what we will tell you. Recall our warning, Enna of Lumadh and Callum of Olthion." They withdraw a clear faceted gem from the depths of their cloak, not the one Callum offered but something that reveals light from within, and lift it to their lamplight eyes. A gentle hum comes from the earth beneath our feet.

The air shimmers as the truthteller spins the gem, reflecting light in all directions. Images and sensations appear before us, but nothing looks or feels familiar. Callum's hand reaches out towards mine, causing me to startle, but I immediately tighten my grip, refusing to let him pull away now that he offered himself to me.

Amid the spectral display, a voice calls out. "Enna," it whispers, a haunting echo of some still-forgotten memory.

"The practitioner Eodez of the Briste Mountains overpowered you by erasing your memory, Enna of Lumadh," the truthteller says, hiding the gem away.

Like a candle winked out, the images and sound vanish, leaving us standing outside the clearing, on the path that now leads nowhere.

⬥

Callum

"I mean, yes, that's the truth, but it isn't what I asked," Enna is saying, her voice filled with frustration, as we leave the southern forest towards the Briste Mountains. The mountains aren't far, near the border between Lumadh, Olthion, and Lumindar, but the inconvenience has gotten under her skin. Enna's not wrong to be upset, but the truthteller had already shown their wiliness in how they responded to me. Of course, I was there for more than simply Enna; I just hope Enna doesn't ask me about the slip or my so-called mysterious agenda they revealed.

"*That's* what I demanded," she continues. "*That's* why I didn't ask about who spelled me because why waste my time? The memories are coming back, I don't need it reversed. I need to know who did this to me, as in had it done! Meaning I asked what I most wanted to know."

She whips her head around to face me. "That's what you wanted to learn too, right, Callum? You didn't ask anything, but wanted the same information I did, right?"

I open my mouth to cast forth some excuse, the words tangling on my tongue. The truth was, I wasn't ready for her to know that just yet. I wasn't actually lying when I'd said her agenda was mine. Knowing who spelled her *did* help me, it gives me more time until her memories are returned. Because... I want that time with her, as I work through the surprising conflict between duty and desire, logic and emotions.

But the truthteller's warning rang... true. There apparently was something I desired to know more than Enna's demands. Because while the truthteller spoke aloud to Enna, they also spoke within my head. They told me *"His validation is not the one I should be seeking, nor is it the beacon that should guide my quest."*

I can assume the *he* the truthteller referred to, given whose approval I have always sought. I glance at Enna; *is she whose validation I should seek instead?*

Thankfully, Enna doesn't stop to let me respond, instead stomping forward and continuing to complain, her hands splayed towards the sky. "That gem was clearly reflecting all kinds of truths," she hisses. "They could have given us a little more!"

She keeps up the exasperated remarks as the forest thins and the mountain range looms above, its craggy peaks disappearing into mist-heavy clouds.

"I just can't believe it," she growls. "All that way for nothing."

"It wasn't for nothing," I tell her, trying to reassure her. "We knew we needed to discover who did it to unravel your memories."

She grunts, and I fear she knows I'm lying, that any talented spellcaster could remove it, but that would mean finding one and revealing my Valenthian companion to them, something that would get me thrashed—or worse—if it got back to Father. Not to mention, Enna would know of my duplicity.

"Perhaps this Eodez will give us more," I offer. "And tell us who overpowered you when... when they explain how to retrieve your memories." I knew the name from my studies, a being who existed before there were divisions between the Valenthians and Netherins. Eodez wouldn't get involved in any of the battles, refusing to pick sides. It's curious that Eodez would help another person harm Enna.

She snags my shirt sleeve, not touching my skin. "You're right. I'm sorry. This was a good idea, Callum. I'm just sorry you went all this way. You... you don't need to continue on with me. You've done more than enough." She points with her free hand somewhere to the right of us. "If you go south from here, you'll be heading toward your cabin, and I can head to the mountains alone."

"I—" I blink down at her. How do I tell her I need to keep going with her, when I can't explain the reason?

She releases me before I can come up with a response, assuming my hesitancy was the answer, and instead offers a slight smirk. "I told you that you're a good man, Callum."

The wind picks up as she continues the march forward. I don't need to be an outdoor expert like Enna to know it's signaling an approaching storm. It feels like a manifestation of the swirling confusion inside me. My conscience prickles with the continued awareness that I'm exploiting her, the guilt settling hard in my steps. *Am I no better than those soldiers, who cared nothing for their comrade?*

Already I've learned enough to prove myself to Father, damn the truthteller's revelation. I'd never known Enna's sister was involved in tactical planning; we never even knew she *had* a family outside her missing brother. And we only knew of him because he was the general before her. If Father or Darroch knew about a sister, they'd suggest focusing all forces on kidnapping her and using her as a hostage against Lumadh. Knowing they have no hybrid lilies to cool their emotions, it would likely be a devastating blow.

My turmoil echoes in the weather. The chilled air hints at the elevation we're going to encounter. Just as we begin our climb, the raindrops shift from a hesitant drizzle to a relentless torrent. Enna bounds upward like a graceful doe, unaffected by the scraggly ground and mud-slicked path beneath our feet. As I attempt to keep pace, I stumble on a loose rock, landing hard on the unforgiving ground.

"Damn it," I mutter, tasting a bitter mixture of dirt, rain, and embarrassment. The cut on my leg, courtesy of an inconveniently placed rock, stings with an intensity that matches the relentless rain.

Enna rushes to my side and drops to her knees, concern etching her wet features as she inspects the gash between the ripped fabric of my pants. "Are you alright?"

"I'll survive." I try to inject a casual tone in my words; Enna walked around for miles with a head wound until she found my cabin. I ought to have the ability to handle a cut while I limp up a mountain.

Enna looks as though my survival might be optimistic. She scans our surroundings through the gray haze, her eyes narrowed. "There," she says, pointing towards a small alcove in the rocky terrain. "We'll take shelter until the storm passes or you're well enough to continue."

She doesn't hesitate in touching me now and with shared effort, we stumble towards the safety of the cave. The inside is damp and musty, but dry, and that's all I can hope for.

The minute she deposits me on the ground, she wastes no time in collecting damp twigs and leaves to fashion a makeshift fire. I settle against the cool stone, grateful for the reprieve from the rain. The space is narrow, each flash of lightning illuminating the small area. If we keep Enna's fire lit all evening for warmth, we might not even have enough space to sleep on either side of it.

"I know we both want the answer to my amnesia quickly, but racing up the mountain isn't the way to do it," she says, her tone teasing. "Shoes off."

I huff a laugh, wincing as the movement jostles my leg. I force it down to unlace my boots. "Yes, it was my curiosity that got the best of me. Not more evidence of my limitations."

Once the fire is lit, she rummages through her knapsack, shooting me a sidelong glance. "I think you just want me to tell you how great you are again," she says lightly, crouching beside me. She pulls out a flask with a label in Allanagh's handwriting and a large swath of cloth. "And, I'm sorry, Callum, you'll need to remove your pants."

I swallow the spit in my mouth, coughing and irritating my leg even more. She clutches at my back, holding me up.

"We'll have to remove them anyway," she says, as if that's a reasonable follow up, pouring Allanagh's concoction on another slip of cotton she's pulled from the knapsack. "To get dry. I'll keep you covered, I promise."

That was certainly *part* of it. I close my eyes and start yanking my pants down. I can almost feel her stare, the Prying Princess who has somehow decided I'm attractive enough for her. There's a pull within me, deep in my middle, that wants to expose myself to her just as she had offered her skin to me.

Thank the gods for the pain in my leg or my body might betray me again. Once my skin is bared to the damp air, she quickly lays the sheet over my lap. I can finally open my eyes. She smiles reassuringly.

"Now, this might sting." She barely lets me prepare for it when she presses the soaked cloth against my wound.

A sharp inhale escapes my lips. The sting was as promised, but it soon fades and a blissful numbness follows.

"It's not a bad thing, you know," she says, as she wipes more ointment on my leg. "To want validation."

"I never said it wasn't."

"But last night, you got upset when I—"

I shift my leg away. "Validation must be earned," echoing the sentiments of my Father. Unsaid is that I've never, apparently, earned any. Until she offered it. The truthteller's rasping voice repeats through my head like a refrain.

As she sighs, I focus my attention on the dirt ground, avoiding any glimpse of her expression and the disappointment that seems always directed towards me.

She turns back to the fire as I release a heavy breath, feeling sorrier for myself than I should, given I saw a man die today and am manipulating a woman trying to treat my wounds. She spins around, hands hidden and eyes alight, and asks what sounds like an innocent question, "Do you like surprises?"

Before I can answer, she moves as quickly as the wind and presses something against my numbed wound. Not numbed enough as a bright pain bursts through the skin and I clench my jaw to hold in a scream.

"What the fuck!?" All the thoughts I'd had when I first met her surge through me. She *did* care about the truthteller's remark about my false intentions, and this is my punishment. Here I thought I was manipulating her, but she's been playing me, getting me somewhere private to murder me. Instinct has me shove her away, and she slips onto her back, a dagger falling from her hand and skittering somewhere in the dark.

She sits up quickly and holds up her hands as my stuttering heart eases to a less manic pace. "I didn't think that through," she says. "I assumed you didn't like the warning, given how you reacted to the healing ointment."

"I don't like pain. What a surprise," I say under my breath, hissing as the pain slowly ebbs. "Why did you *burn* me?"

She gestures to my leg. "We don't have a touch healer and I will *not* do something as crude as sew it like they do in Lumindar. This is the only way to seal it."

More proof of their brutality, I think meanly. I bite my lip, the surge of adrenaline slowly fading. "Must you seal it?" I finally ask. "Couldn't you have bandaged it? Instead of aiming to liquify my skin."

"If you wanted to walk tomorrow, yes, I did." She tilts her head back, as if remembering something new. "We don't have many healers, and none like Allanagh, so we've all learned in the field healing. A bandage could get infected, especially if you keep moving and reopening it. That could lead to death. And I'm always game to prevent that."

I look down at the closed flesh, which seems to shimmer in the fire's light. "I see. In that case, thank you. But... please remember to actually warn me next time."

"I know better now," she says with a laugh. "If I come closer to hand you the healing ointment, are you going to shove me again?" Her smirk shows there's no offense, yet it doesn't ease my guilt.

"Of course. Yes, please."

She passes me another jar, one full of greasy smelling goop.

I keep my gaze on the burn as I tell her, "I'm sorry for pushing you."

"It's fine. Good instincts, if you thought I was coming at you." She rubs her shoulder and smirks at me. "And you're wrong about not having any strength."

My stomach clenches. "I hope I didn't hurt you."

The smirk turns into a full grin, a wicked gleam in her eyes. "I know how you can make it up to me."

That look will be my undoing. "How?"

"Rub lanolin into my aching muscles."

The sheet on my lap moves from the sudden twitch of my hardening cock.

Chapter 10

I was teasing him about the lanolin, though my feet would need it if we walked much longer without a break. The pretty blush when I'd asked was enough. I couldn't push him too far, as it wouldn't be fair to him: my selfless savior, who had already done so much just to get me answers. Even if they aren't the answers I wanted. *Thank you kindly, truthteller.*

But as charming his bashful expression is, he won't be able to avoid touching me tonight. With the rain still beating down outside our tiny cave, we needed heat. Since Callum's modesty kept us both mostly clothed through the late afternoon, our clothes stayed slightly damp and chilled. As the evening freeze begins, I can't continue catering to his delicate sensitivities any longer.

"We'll need to sleep together," I tell him after we've finished the rabbit jerky leftover from last night.

He's still lounging against the stone wall where I'd dropped him when we arrived. Those green eyes look fearful, like a deer with a wolf in its sights. "Excuse me?"

"We'll freeze if we don't," I continue gently. "I didn't push on the clothing thing, and we've stayed in these wet things all afternoon, but this is necessary. For our safety."

Some emotion flutters over his expression before he bites his lower lip and asks, "You mean we're sharing a bed for heat conservation?"

"Yes. What did you think I meant?"

The fire illuminates another of his charming blushes. "We refer to it as something else in Olthion."

My curiosity piques, but a sudden gust blows through the nook, kicking up the fire and hurtling a trail of icy rain over my body. "Look, it's nude Enna or snuggling. I wouldn't mind both, but I won't be greedy."

He laughs then, a stuttered, nervous thing. "Huddling for warmth makes sense."

I said *snuggling* but fine. I'm trying to be less pushy, after all.

"And," he says, wincing as though someone is forcing the words from him. "Drying our clothes makes sense."

My lips curl as I watch him take off his still-damp tunic. "Do you want to be the big spoon or the little spoon?"

He pauses, the shirt halfway over his head. The lean form I've felt over his clothes is more truth than his sullen claims about lacking 'strength.' Defined muscles bunch over his arms and chest as he moves, a wiry strength in the set of his broad shoulders. A smattering of hair dusts his chest and a dark line of it trails from his navel to the sheet still covering his lap. "What about spoons?" he asks.

My eyes spring back to his face by the time he tosses the shirt to the ground. "The little spoon and the big spoon. That has to be a phrase that crosses over from Lumadh.

When two spoons are placed in a drawer, one spoon cradles the other." I start to mime it before he holds up a hand.

"I understand. We can simply lie side by side."

I'm already regretting my internal promise not to push him. But I'll follow his lead and see how it goes. As I undress, I turn away to shield his modesty and take our clothes to the far corner of the alcove. When they're arranged, I plunk to the ground beside him and lay on my side, putting him closest to the fire.

His hand flutters above my waist, his body just skimming against me from behind. "Won't you be cold?"

My skin breaks out in gooseflesh, but that's more from his fingers grazing over me. "I'll manage." The proximity will help and maybe I can use the extra dress Allanagh gave me as a blanket, or convince him to share the sheet I—

His hand slides between us, dragging over my low back before yanking up the cloth covering his crotch and draping it over our hips. Then, he shuffles himself forward and pressing himself hard against my back.

I hiss at the heat emanating from his body, the burn of it almost unpleasant against my chilled skin. "Are you sure you're comfortable with this?"

He stiffens against me, his hand squeezing my hip. "I'm not a child."

"I never said you—"

"I'm not afraid of the female form, or your—" He cuts himself off, sounding frustrated. "I'm trying to be respectful of you and your... body."

I turn around to face him, our skin brushing against each other in the dimly lit cave. With the fire behind him, I can only see the outline of his hooded eyes and sharp cheekbones. I keep my focus on his face.

"It's *my* body though," I remind him.

He holds me closer, baring his teeth. I can't help but imagine them nipping at the juncture of my neck. He sounds pained as he croaks out, "And I shouldn't be look—"

My inappropriate libido wanes. Dealing with this is exhausting. "There are two parts to this, Callum. I choose who can see my body, and they can choose whether they want to." Pushing on his taut chest, I try to put more space between us, but he holds me firmly. I take it as a good sign. "You have *my* permission," I tell him. "But I was ignoring the second part of that and for that, I'm sorry."

The look he gives me is all sorrow. "It's not... that's not... that's not the issue."

"Then what is?"

"You don't know me," he almost shouts into the quiet cave. One hand leaves my side to gesture vaguely at the small space between us. "You shouldn't be so... cavalier with that. I could be anyone."

"And?" I prompt.

"And you should be more concerned about that. You can't give consent if you don't know who I am," he explains, a touch of anger in his voice. "I could be taking advantage of you, or luring you into a false sense of security to steal secrets from—" He cuts himself off again, a muscle ticking in his jaw. "It's not safe."

"I assume Allanagh tells you everything, right?"

He doesn't answer, his eyes focused on the cave wall as though he's thinking through something painful.

"If she does," I continue, "she would have told you my penchant for 'celebrating life' after battles. And that those celebrations were not dependent on me having any specific knowledge of the partner."

He growls. "Yes, but—"

"No." I'm quick to interrupt. Better we deal with this now before I spend more time worried about this man's inflated sense of modesty. I already let myself stay uncomfortable today because of it. What else might I accidentally do? "Look, if you have an issue with my body, that's one thing, and I've already stopped teasing you about it. But if your issue is that I can't choose who can look at it, because you think you know better, because you're a so-called stranger from a different country, then—"

"I don't," he whispers. I throw him a filthy look, ready to start my screed again, but he continues before I can, "I don't have an issue with your body. Or... seeing it."

"Oh." All the fight drains out of me. "Well, good then."

"I'm simply afraid you'll regret letting me look at it," he admits.

I shift closer into his arms, but he squeezes my hips before I can fully envelop him. I'll have the indent of his fingers on my skin and none of the fun of getting in there. "That's incredibly unlikely. But if you're that worried, just don't do anything that will make me regret it."

He laughs, sounding helpless. "I'll... I'll try."

The fire cracks behind us as a hesitant silence engulfs us. We should really watch the flames, and the alcove entrance at my back, in case—

He interrupts my spiraling thoughts. "What now?"

I think about bringing up his low self-esteem issues, but maybe that's too much emotional discussion for a single evening. And, even though I promised myself I'd let him initiate, I can't help but ask, "Do... you want to kiss?"

He laughs again and presses his cheek to the top of my head. Given the hysterical tone in his voice just now, I won't tell him I was serious.

———◄◆►———

Callum

The first light of dawn pierces through the entrance of the cave. Rubbing my eyes to adjust to the bright morning light, I wake up to find Enna nestled against me, her head resting on my chest. Thank the Gods she'd stayed somewhat facing me, or I'd be pressing my cock directly into her back. As it is, it greets me merrily under the sheet, a little flag reminding me it's morning and a beautiful woman is in my arms.

"How's your leg?"

Her voice startles me into releasing her, shuffling to the side and angling my hips as far away from her as I can. "I'm ready to continue, if that's what you're asking." I clear my throat to disguise the tremble in my tone.

She sits up. The part of the thin sheet that had migrated up her chest during the night falls to her lap. My gaze shoots to the rough-hewn roof of the cave. From the corner of my vision, I see her neck stretching upward to see what holds my interest, before she shrugs.

"We really should have taken turns sleeping. Someone or something could have attacked us," she admonishes before her lips curl into a smirk. "But I can't say I minded spending the evening in your arms."

I cough. "Yes, well. I put up wards on the entrance when I stepped out last night." When I hobbled outside to use the necessaries and attempt to clean myself in the pooled rainwater while she gathered clean water, I shoved the few stones I had left along the threshold.

She stands, tossing me my clothes and shimmying back into hers. "Clever. If I had known, we could have avoided the sleeping shifts. We'll be able to repeat our snuggle session nightly."

"I—" I clear my throat again, unable to tell her we need an enclosed space for the wards to work, lest she think I'm implying something else. "Do you think we'll make it to Eodez's today?"

She chuckles, a soft sound that echoes through the cave. "You'll admit it sometime, Callum. I'm going to find breakfast. Do you want to join?"

Once I've got my pants on, I stand and test my injured leg tentatively. "No, I'll pack up." Better to have some alone time to recenter myself from how off kilter I feel with her.

"Don't put out the fire," she says as she stalks through the cave entrance, taking her arrows with her.

I shove my stiff shirt over my back, revisiting the discussion from the night before, the conversation looping over and over. I should have kissed her last night, when I'd had the chance. She'd said my identity didn't matter, after all. She'd seemed to have meant it and meant that she wanted me. Then I could put her out of my mind and continue forward, without the distraction of my fantasies. Like my hands buried in her chocolate hair, or running my tongue over her sun-kissed skin.

Or the fierce desire to watch her, to let her use me.

By the time I finish my self-flagellation and gather our meager belongings into the knapsack and travel bags, Enna returns, holding something in her cupped hands. She kneels by the fire, dropping her quarry and constructing something with sticks.

Hunger overcomes my libido as my stomach growls in anticipation and I sit beside her, watching her toss dried leaves into the makeshift pit to stoke the flames. "What is it?"

She glances up, an impish spark in her eyes. "I found a nest nearby. I'm going to use your offal trick from two days ago and cook some eggs."

My body warms, not from the heat of the fire but the slow burn of pride. My cock twitches and I admonish it internally. While I don't get praised much, getting hard each time it happens from now on will be inconvenient. Although... I watch Enna putter over the fire, deftly turning the eggs as she prepares them. Something tells me the reaction is born more of Enna's praise than anything else.

"What deep thoughts are running through your head this morning?" Her taunting voice interrupts my woolgathering.

"Only how skillful you are to have caught and cooked our breakfast so quickly," I lie.

She laughs. "There you go again, praising me. But no clapping this time?"

Desperate to keep the subject far away from what was really in my head, I clap politely.

She pulls the eggs from the heat, gently tossing them to the cave floor to cool. Her caramel eyes peer at me through the long locks of her hair dangling in her face. "You can do better than that, can't you?"

Intent on teasing her just as she enjoys teasing me, I slide to my knees and applaud loud enough for the sound to ring all around us.

"That's what I was hoping for. You look gorgeous on your knees," she says, a soft smile on her face. "Excellent work, Callum. You did exactly what I wanted."

And then awareness strikes, just like one of her arrows finding its mark. All those thoughts that have been spooling around my heart find sudden clarity. That reassurance I'm looking for, that demand to prove what I am, comes from the yearning for praise from someone more powerful than myself, someone who I could give myself to without fear of embarrassment or mistreatment. My choices have been shaped by that desire: every book I read, every meeting I attended, every action I took in the kingdom, all following this instinct to find someone powerful to value me. The truthteller's words suddenly make sense. It wasn't my father; it wasn't the citizenry. It was all building toward *her*.

Gods, I *really* should have kissed her.

She reaches for the eggs and tosses me one that I somehow catch, distracted as I am on my knees before her. As we both peel open our prizes, she comes to sit by my side and we lean against the cavern wall to eat.

"I remembered something else. Well, two things. The first is about where I live. I have connections to a castle too, if you can believe it," she says, laughing lightly, as if it's a ludicrous thought. "And the castle has—"

I stop her, even knowing she might have valuable information about the castle's construction. We don't even know where the Lumadh stronghold *is*. But I ask instead, "What is the second thing you remembered?"

"My favorite color."

"Which is?"

She knocks her shoulder into mine and I don't shy away from the smile in her gaze. "Green. Like your eyes."

Chapter 11

He kisses me then, something tender and soft, unsure. His heart pounds loud enough to hear over the quiet sounds of our mouths moving together. I knit my arms around his back and let him take small sips from my lips, like he's savoring me, like he's trying to keep from becoming overwhelmed. He pulls away with a shudder, but there's no embarrassment or vulnerability now. Instead, his eyes glitter like fire. I was right to let him initiate.

"Was that all?" I ask. It's a taunt, a challenge.

He tilts back my chin, a dark smile on his lips. Then, he slants his mouth against mine, desperate and hungry, all the yearning I knew was under his skin bursting forth and laying claim to me. I part his lips with my tongue, but he's not idle either, and he wrenches a moan from me as he nibbles and sucks on my tongue. It's a clashing of lips and tongues and teeth, two feral creatures at war. But this was no war I could let him win. I shove him backward and he skids to his knees again, staring up at me. He looks as debauched as I feel and we've done nothing more than kiss. I card my fingers through his long black hair and he leans into it, nuzzling my palm.

Breathless, I ask the question I hope I know the answer to. "Do you want me?"

"Yes," he says, his voice a deep growl.

"Then prove it."

But he doesn't move, and his expression changes to one of fear. There's a swooping sensation in my stomach, like I missed something vital and whatever I do next will set the tone for anything else with this gorgeous, complicated man. I watch him on his knees, the intensity in his eyes as he looks up at me.

And I know now what he needs.

My fingers lightly brush against his jaw, before settling gently around his throat. He gazes up at me in awe as the rabbit thrum of his heartbeat stutters against my fingers. His pupils are blown and he swallows, I feel it beneath the meat of my palm. "Is this what you wanted?"

He nods. "But I'm afraid that you'll regret—"

My free hand covers his mouth and his eyes widen. When he's quiet, I curl my fingers around the nape of his neck, petting the hair there. With a sigh, I lean down and kiss him. Once, twice, three times until his mouth reaches for mine again and I must pull myself away before I get too hungry for his lips when there are places other than my mouth I want him to kiss. My cunt clenches just imagining it.

I brace against the wall, hissing at the cold. He reaches for me again, as if to save me from the temperature and I can't resist smiling down at him. But he retreats to his position on his knees when I press him back. And then, agonizingly slowly, I unlace my pants and pull them down, kicking them somewhere near the entranceway. My tunic goes next and his eyes are a physical thing on my body. The shy glances he'd stolen last night and the first day are forgotten. This is a stark inspection, his eyes tracing every inch of my bared skin, like he's memorizing it. When I can't bear to remain untouched any longer, I take his hands and place them over my breasts. His eyes fall shut with a pained exhalation.

He does nothing more than cup my breasts, long enough I suspect I'll need to instruct him. I push my chest harder into his hands to urge him on when, beneath lowered lashes, I see him tilt his head and kiss a mark into the sensitive skin on the underside of my breast. I make a soft sound at the sensation. He pulls away, green eyes wide, but must see the pleasure in my hooded gaze as he returns, licking upward until he sucks my nipple in his mouth. My cunt clenches again and I stare down at him as his own eyes flutter and pleasured groan pulls from deep in his throat.

Emboldened, he drags open mouthed kisses down my stomach, his hands following until his fingers take hold of my hips. He stares up at me, for permission perhaps. I give him none, cocking a brow. He's proving this to me, after all.

Shuddering, he grazes his fingers over to my inner thighs, the rasp of his calluses kiss against the sensitive skin there. Gently, oh so gently, he presses my back against the wall. My breath catches at the feel of the cold stone again. He looks up, face studying me for any disapproval. A slow smile unfurls from his pouty lips at whatever he sees there. He ducks his head, pressing his face against my mons and trembling out another deep moan. I feel myself get wetter just at the sounds he makes. Then his hands quiver at my thighs, his breath coming in pants.

My lips pinch as I watch him unravel. I want him uncomfortable in a good way, not unhappy and upset. "Callum, look at me."

Obediently, he adjusts his position, still leaning against me but angling his head to meet my gaze. The green in his eyes is eclipsed by black and he looks like he might cry.

"Do you want to do this, Callum?"

"Yes." The word is fractured, broken. "But I... I don't—I..." He trails off, dropping his gaze to the floor.

Understanding dawns and I hook my left leg over his shoulder, leaning back and spreading my hips wide. "Does this work?"

He stares at what I've exposed, his mouth dropping open. "Yes," he repeats in a whisper. His fingers tremble as he touches my cunt gently, petting at my curls.

I softly reply, "Please." It's not a prayer, not a plea, but gentle encouragement to urge him onward. And then he buries his face between my legs.

The first swipe of his tongue against my slit is searingly hot and I feel as though I might go into shock between the scorching sensation at my front and the chilled stone at my back. He moans, loud and lewd as his jaw works against me. I widen my legs as far as I can, grabbing his hair like reins and maneuvering him exactly where I need him to be. My hips roll, rutting against his tongue. He groans against me, a sound born of pleasure and need and I feel him shuddering.

I wriggle against him as the expected fluttering feeling builds in my belly. The movement pushes his tongue harder over my clit and he laps at the sensitive nub over and over, but it's not quite enough.

"Your fingers," I hiss between breaths.

He moans again, and one hand coils around my hip to slide between my legs from behind. Two fingers dip into my opening, thrusting lightly, and caressing at a spot deep within me. As those nimble fingers and questing tongue come together, a delicious tension builds, starting at the tips of my toes and ending at the top of my head. And then there's fire licking at my belly, centered on the pulsating heat of his tongue and fingers between my thighs. Everything breaks, and I'm coming, my cunt clenching, thighs squeezing his head, back arching as he drags me over the edge.

My legs give, and I slip to the floor, taking him with me. I land half on his lap and his arms capture me, one hand cupping my head from knocking into the wall.

"Thank you," I tell him, curling my arms around his strong shoulders. "That was wonderful."

"No," he says, his face slick with my release and his green eyes rapturous. "Thank you."

———◆———

Callum

The sun climbs higher as we make our ascent up the summit where we'll supposedly find the spellcaster. My interlude with Enna's body delayed us some, but the melody of her groans is one I'll never forget. She wanted to return the favor, and I wanted her to, but I'd already sated myself by touching her. With a coy smile, she'd kissed me again and then extinguished the fire while I'd cleaned myself up.

"You don't want to spend another day here?" I'd asked.

"With you? I'd rather find ourselves a bed. Or a comfortable sleeping mat." The Passionate Princess had grabbed the laces on my tunic and pressed close. "Don't worry, we'll have a repeat. And soon."

I was worried, but not for the reason she thought. The world fell away when I was touching her. And when it had ended, and she'd looked down at me, I knew I was ruined. She made me feel more confident than any of Father's misbegotten spells. And damn my Father, damn Olthion, Enna's presence is all I need to fill the gaping hole of need within me. Her memory's return threatens to end that, unless I prove to her I'm as valuable as she thinks I am. Then I could return with her to Lumadh and we could overpower my father together. Her people's brutality mixed with my knowledge of Oltion's weakness. Another win-win plan.

I simply needed time, time for her to desire me as much as I desired her, for this to have meaning. And then my reasons for helping her, my first manipulation, and my identity won't matter. She'll forget I was her enemy, a worthless man in Olthion, and instead maybe see me as I see her. As something fundamental.

"Are you sure?"

Her playful voice draws me from my gloom, and I ask, "What's that?"

"Are you sure you want to carry everything?" She gestures to my body, where her arrow drapes around my chest and the knapsack joins both of our travel bags.

"Yes. That way you can focus on the map."

Enna raises her brows and I don't need to be Allanagh to guess what she's thinking. We haven't looked at the map since leaving the truthteller. But I can't tell her the actual reasons I've taken her burdens. While I long to push her hair to the side, feeling its silky strands between my fingers, as my lips trace a path down the curve of her neck, I can better prove my value this way. To let my actions prove I'm worth it, even if my identity isn't.

She opens her mouth to respond, a wry look on her face before she halts. She holds up her hand, cocking her head to the trees on the right of the path. After a moment, she shoves me to the left, dragging me behind a large boulder. She twitches her eyebrows and makes figures with her hands, but I can't understand what she's saying. Scowling, she rolls her eyes and mimes sealing her lips shut. I nod in acknowledgement.

Together, we peer cautiously around its edge. A group of figures appear from the depth of the trees. Two men and two women, and two of them are dressed in leathers that match Enna's. Enna frowns as they draw nearer, as if she's attempting to uncover who they are. My heart stutters in my chest at the risk they pose.

I lean close to her and whisper, praying the answer is no. "Do you recognize them?"

She winces, slapping a hand over my mouth. The reason becomes clear, but by then it is too late. One of the strangers spins towards our boulder. He must have as sensitive ears as she does.

"Come out before we make you," he growls. He's reed thin, with sandy blond hair, wearing two bows over his shoulders. His tunic has a hint of green and the bows on his outfit remind me of delicate wings, earning him the uncharitable nickname 'Grasshopper' in my mind.

After releasing me, Enna takes a deep breath, squares her shoulders, and emerges with her arms outstretched. "Good afternoon, all."

"Drop your weapons," Grasshopper says.

Enna turns slightly, catching my eye and nodding. She tosses her two daggers to Grasshopper's feet. I ease her makeshift bow from my shoulder and drop it to the ground with a thud. When I withdraw my sword, the woman not in Lumadh colors stops me.

"No, doesn't look like it's anything but decorative," she says, sniffing with derision. She's as pale as milk, with a shock of blonde hair bundled tight to her head. I dub her Faewisp. "He can keep it, not like he knows how to use it."

The other woman titters at Faewisp, but Enna's hands clench at her sides. I inch closer to her, but Grasshopper swiftly reaches for one of his bows, pointing an arrow at me with a menacing glare.

"Watch yourself, pretty boy," he says with a scowl, his voice dripping with contempt.

The other man, dressed in Enna's colors, takes deliberate steps forward, coming to a halt just inches away from where Enna dropped her daggers. He's a head taller than me and as stocky as a bear, with umber skin like a kelpie's silky hide. Combined with his lumbering form, he becomes Oros, the biggest predator to me, given he may know Enna from Lumadh. Oros rubs his scruffy black beard and stares down at her. "Do I know you?"

Enna tilts her head up and stares challengingly at him. "Probably."

My stomach clenches as my worst nightmare comes true. Her memory has come back, or this Oros will tell her exactly who she is and I won't get the chance to show her I'm worth taking with her.

Oros' eyes narrow at Enna before a toothy grin spreads across his face. "I thought so. Brendan, stop pointing at my kinfolk." He snaps thick fingers and Grasshopper drops his arrow to aim at our feet while I release a relieved breath.

"Name's Oisin. You a deserter, too?" Oros—Oisin hooks his thumb at the woman wearing the leathers that match his. "Me 'n Cathal left when that Mouric sent soldiers to the General's peace summit and slaughtered two of her guard. She should'a cut him down right then, but took us on that merry chase instead. You involved in that?"

The relief is transformed to dread. Oisin may not know Enna, but if he mentions the *name* of 'the General,' I'm as good as done for. Especially since he's just revealed what is likely classified information. The Netherins only know that the Valenthians are infighting. Darroch's intelligence said Enna's people drew first blood and peace was never on the table. I huff internally; that's what we get when we put Darroch and 'intelligence' in the same sentence. If I'd been in charge of that fact finding mission, we'd have gotten something true.

Enna responds while I start to panic. She crosses her arms around her chest. "No. I left at the same time. When the General did... that. Why stay if she can't even handle her own house? Only a poorly run regime would allow that."

A feeling similar to hysteria starts to consume me. Will Enna realize she's just insulted herself? For all I know, she's the Patriotic Princess and might stab things when she learns of the insult to her and her country. Like me.

"Damn right," Oisin says, his blue eyes lighting up. He turns to the second woman standing behind the others, who, in my spiraling panic I hadn't gotten to name yet. "See, I told ya. And right after that disaster with Olthion. She should'a learned."

Cathal rolls her eyes, tossing her red hair with a scowl. Oisin turns back to Enna, his face lighting up with a boyish smile. I shift closer to Enna, one hand braced to grab her. Or stake my claim. Or push her if she swings my sword in my direction, whichever is needed.

"Don't you worry about Cathal," Oisin says. "She didn't so much desert as get stuck in the medical tent and I sprung her. She'da probably have gone back if not for Aoife."

Faewisp wiggles her fingers at Enna. She'll remain Faewisp because she's already irritating me like a pesky insect. Enna looks from Faewisp to Cathal, her eyes taking a long drag over her body. She then unclenches her fists, leaving me curious about the thoughts that occupy her mind.

"I'm Cadhla and this is Finn," she says, tilting her head towards me. Grasshopper's hands move like he's going to take aim at us again and my own fingers stray towards my sword.

Oisin slaps me on the shoulder. The unexpected pressure causes my knees to buckle, and he lets out a chuckle. "Tell your man not to worry about Brendan. If he'd really wanted to hurt you, you'd be bleeding by now."

"Why are you out here?" Faewisp asks, her nose still high in the air.

I fist my hand on Enna's low back to keep the irritation off my face. She turns and raises her brows in question. I look back at her, my own brows furrowing. *Is she suggesting I take the lead and come up with our alibi?*

I straighten my back, puffing out my chest and gripping the hilt of my sword. Faewisp and Cathal's eyes follow the muscles tensing and untensing in my forearm with the movement. Even Grasshopper's gaze narrows on me and a sneer forms.

"We ran away together yesterday," I say. "Our families didn't approve."

Faewisp claps her hands under her chin in mock excitement. "Is it true love?" Her tone is snide.

Enna runs her hand down my arm until she entwines our fingers. "Damn right."

A smile bursts from me involuntarily, no matter I know it's part of our cover story and I could still be in trouble here. "We'd heard the Mountains were abandoned and thought we could make a go of it living out here. We didn't expect company." For some reason, Enna smothers a smile at that, but I ignore it, instead tipping my head at Oisin, who is clearly the leader. "We'll be on our way shortly and you needn't worry about us."

Oisin rubs his beard. "You're welcome to stay with us. Kept Aoife's tent just in case, but she and Cathal don't show no signs of stopping. Would be nice to reminisce about home. Cathal don't indulge and Brendan's a Netherin."

"And Fae—Aoife?" I ask. She stands beside Cathal now, the two leaning on each other, and blows me a mocking kiss.

"Not sure *what* she is," Oisin admits. "But what d'ya say? At least for a night."

I look at Enna, who says nothing. I can't interpret any of her facial cues, either. While there's the risk that Oisin inadvertently exposes something about Enna, prolonging the time before Eodez discloses Enna's past can only help me. I'm stuck between two poor options, but I'll choose the one that has more time to prove myself, *and* covered sleeping arrangements.

"That would be accept—" I start, wincing when Enna squeezes my fingers tight enough to rub the bones together. "I mean, no," I quickly correct. "We planned on making it to the summit today and surveying the land. But your generosity is appreciated."

Oisin's face falls, but he nods. "Understood. But be warned... you go another few hours northward, you'll meet the spellcaster."

Grasshopper holds out Enna's daggers, hilts first. She releases my tender hand to grab them, shoving them in her holsters while I flex my fingers.

Enna juts out her hand to Oisin. "Thanks for the warning, but I'm not worried about a spellcaster."

He laughs and shakes her hand hard enough to jostle her. "Spoken like a true Lumadhan."

Before we can retreat, Grasshopper stalks closer to Enna, sniffing audibly. "You smell of Oros," he hisses, his hands tightening on his bows. "I thought you said you just arrived on the mountain."

Enna's expression turns fierce at his remark, her body tense and poised to attack. But there's too many of them, no matter how skilled she is. I adjust my posture again, standing taller than the weedy Grasshopper. Untested in battle or not, I ought to be capable of squishing him beneath my boot. Darroch certainly would. Strength is all Netherins respond to. And with Enna's praise still simmering in my blood, I feel like I could take on one hundred Grasshoppers.

"We did," I growl.

Brendan's thin face contorts into a snarl as he glares at me, his eyes full of hostility. "Then how'd you meet the Oros already?"

Enna shoots me a glance, but before I can attempt to decipher her expression and fix this, she loosens her stance and answers, "Finn's family *really* didn't approve of us," letting them fill in the rest.

Grasshopper squints, as if scanning both of us for answers, before finally giving a curt nod.

Oisin diffuses the tension with another chuckle, though this one is forced. "No worries, Cadhla. Brendan's nose's better than ten hounds together. No predators on the Mountain as good as him." Meaning we don't need to worry about trace dye on her skin as they won't attempt to hunt Enna down.

"Are there any Oros in this area?" I ask. It's likely Eodez used the dye from the creature's fur when spelling Enna, which means we're even closer to the answer than I thought. The pit in my stomach grows.

Grasshopper grunts, his focus locked on the sword at my waist before Oisin's cough has him respond begrudgingly. "An hour west, towards the lake."

Enna reaches out and grabs onto my hip, soothing the turmoil within me. "You know, Oisin, I think we will take you up on that tent." As she smirks in my direction, all my worries about spending more time with these people evaporate. "Does it have a sleeping pallet?"

Chapter 12

Enna

Oisin's crew have created a scattered base about a mile from where they found us. And there's a tarn lake a stone's throw west of the boulder we'd used as an unsuccessful hiding place they use for washing. I'll blame not hearing the trickling water on Callum. He was to blame for the looseness in my muscles, after all. Why not give him credit for a dulling of my senses too? The morning left me so relaxed that I was oblivious to even the slightest rustle of leaves. And I barely noticed Oisin coming upon us.

That hadn't happened before when I've fucked other strangers, that I *recall*. Although Callum and I haven't exactly fucked yet. But that opportunity was rapidly becoming the only thing that occupied my thoughts. I'd already been interested in taking him to bed, and that was *before* he'd gotten on his knees for me. My desire to meet this Eodez and uncover the mystery of my memory is strong, but having Callum at my feet and at my mercy—finding sanctuary before me—wasn't something I was going to let pass by me without exploring it first. *And* then I return home.

"That's Aoife's tent," Oisin is saying when I refocus on our surroundings. He points to a simple A-frame tent made of a deep brown canvas, which is slightly taller than me and will require Callum to hunch over if he wants to stand. Despite its cramped size, it will certainly offer more comfort than sleeping on the ground. Especially if the pallet is big enough for two. Callum's lip curls at the sight, but he stays silent.

"That will work," I tell them both, prompting Callum to drop the knapsack and travel bags by the tent's open flap. I see him swallow his complaints and I run my hand over his sinewy arm before turning back to Oisin. "Can we help with anything?"

Oisin slaps his knee. "See? Already feels like home, the generosity of the Lumadhans." He bumps Callum, who lets out a soft grunt. "These Netherins could learn a lesson or two."

I link arms with Callum, pulling him away from Oisin's elbowing range. "I don't know about that. This Netherin has been very helpful. He left his family and home for me, after all."

Oisin cocks his head. "Think love might'a had something to do with that. Our resident Netherin Brendan won't do a damn thing unless he has to, and, woe, he's not my type."

A small smile emerges without my consent. It's not love, but there is an undeniable allure to Callum. It's good to know others recognize it too. I'd been proud of how he reacted earlier, coming up with the cover story and standing up to Brendan's misbehavior. Maybe he just needs a few more orgasms to gain confidence, then he could *lead* this country. I trail my eyes over Callum and imagine giving him another one, a real one that wasn't untouched this time, inside our newly obtained tent. "Did you need something, Oisin?" I ask idly. "Or will my Netherin and I have some time to help each other first?"

Callum's cheeks darken at the euphemism, and Oisin looks uncomfortable. "Tell you what," Oisin says after a moment. "Take some alone time with your Netherin and we'll hunt up supper together in a little while. Got a deal?"

I hold out my hand, and Oisin shakes it again. "Deal."

Oisin plods away and I tuck inside the small tent, Callum only a second behind.

"They're going to think we're having sex," he whispers.

I raise a single brow. "Aren't we?" I'd promised him a sleeping pallet at the very least, and this tent had one.

Callum drops our bags by the interior tent flap. The sleeping pallet dominates the small space, the long edge of it pressed up against the back canvas wall. At the head is a thin, knobby blanket that looks well used. "Not here. They'll hear us," he says, gingerly sitting onto the pallet. Dust kicks up, and he wrinkles his nose.

I drop beside him and lean against his shoulder, tipping my head upward to stare at his strong jawline. "I stopped for the pallet, you know. I don't care if they hear us."

His eyes darken and he runs his finger down a loose tendril of my hair, gently tugging. "They don't deserve to hear you."

Warmth pools in my belly at the growl in his voice, the confidence in his tone, the implication that he deserves it, that my self-conscious Netherin is realizing his value so quickly. I stand and face him, resting my hand on that jawline I'd been so enamored with. "What if we did something different?"

Even with disapproval in his eyes, he leans into my touch. "What?"

My tongue wets my lips and those eclipsed green eyes track the movement. "I'll touch you this time."

He leans forward, pressing his face into my stomach with a soft groan. "I've never... never done that before."

I pet his glossy hair, the strands like silk under my fingers. "Do you want to?"

"I've thought about it for ages, fantasized about it." A tremble runs through his body and I can almost see him in his bed at home, hand wrapped around his cock, eyes rolling back in his head as he imagines someone there with him. "I never... never thought I'd have the opportunity."

I sink to my knees and spread his legs. "Then let's take it while we have it."

He sounds drunk when he says, "But they'll hear *me*."

"Then you should be quiet."

Before he can offer any more insincere protests, I find the laces on his pants, the string taut with his cock straining against the fabric already. I withdraw it from its cloth prison, hard and fully swollen, longer than my hand and slightly curved. Tracing a thumb and finger up and down the shaft, I take a minute to appreciate that velvet softness I haven't yet been able to experience. Gods, that will feel incredible whenever we can finally break in this sleeping pallet.

I kiss the leaking tip, and Callum stifles a groan, shoving his hand over his mouth. He tastes salty but clean, something almost surprising after two days in the wilderness. He stutters a breath, his stomach jumping and I release his cock to rake my fingers up his thighs and over the taut muscles of his abdomen.

"Callum," I say teasingly. "Have you earned this?"

He releases his mouth, placing his hands back on the pallet. His eyes sweep across my face, lingering for a moment on

my lips before darting down to take in the rest of my body.
"I—"

"You have," I assure him. "*You* deserve this." And I can't
deny the burning satisfaction I got when he nods like he
believes me.

Unable to deny *him* any longer, I open my mouth and
let him slide over my tongue, the underside dragging against
my lower lip. His hips snap up instinctively, and I gently tap
his thigh in warning. He fists his hands into the pallet and
I reward him by cupping his balls with my fingers. As his
breath speeds up, I lick stripes up and down his cock with
the flat of his tongue, teasing him until I've tasted every inch.

I look up at him from under my lashes and his abdomen
jumps, but he doesn't thrust again. His legs quiver, the palpable tension in his legs revealing his urge to move. I smile
around his cock. He *does* deserve this, and he deserves to have
this exactly how he's pictured it.

This time.

I take one of his hands, carefully unclawing it, and place it
in my hair. He makes a soft questioning noise and I look up
at him under my lashes. As I wiggle my brows, his face lights
up with amazement. With a shaky gulp, he covers his mouth
again. Then, he gently pulls me closer, forcing my mouth
to draw his cock deeper within. My cunt pulses with each
slow pump until he gains confidence and unsteadily drives
his shaft into the back of my throat. I let it rest there for a
second, breathing deep until I can swallow around it. His
white-knuckled fingers tremble against his face, desperate to
muffle any potential sounds.

I hope he gets over his aversion to being overheard, because I'm about to become desperate for him under me
again.

I release him, drooling and feeling almost drunk myself as I gasp heaving breaths. My tongue laves a spot directly under his cockhead before I take it back inside, sucking it to the back of my throat. His thighs tense and his balls tighten in my hand as I do it again and again, my eyes watering. His fingers twist into my hair, not hard enough to hurt but enough to expose how restrained he's attempting to be for me and how easily I can make him lose control. There's a bitten off sound behind his clenched fingers, my name. I shiver as more desire than I thought possible pools in my belly, each thrust getting me wetter and wetter for him. All too soon, he shudders, his cock pulsating into my mouth. He pumps through his orgasm, and I swallow his salty release. His expression is dazed, two pink spots high on his cheekbones and the imprint of his own hand over his mouth.

His eyes refocus and trip over my face, one of his hands brushing away wetness at my eyes. He frowns. "Any—" His voice is hoarse and he swallows. "Any regrets?"

I rest my head on his thigh and lick my lips. "Only that we can't keep going. What about you? Did it live up to what you've imagined?"

His frown unravels into an obscene grin, the confidence I'd hoped for appearing easily. "Much better."

"Next time I want your hands by your side," I tell him teasingly.

His eyes shine with anticipation, and I know he doesn't think it's teasing, that he wants me to take control. "You might need to tie my hands down."

"Would you like that?" I ask as a sharp smile forms on my still-wet lips.

Oisin's shadow looms over the outside of the tent. "You, uh, you free yet, Cadhla?"

With a disappointed sigh, I kiss Callum's bare stomach under the tunic and it quivers. "Be right out." After wiping my mouth, I brush the strands of hair away from my face and make my way towards our bags.

Callum laces his pants and watches me retrieve my makeshift bow and daggers. "I don't trust Grasshopper or Faewisp," he says quietly.

I freeze in my unpacking, one hand deep into a travel pack searching for my leftover arrows. "Who?"

"Brendan and Aoife," he says, irritation coloring his tone. "Even Cathal could be a problem."

I imagine them from Callum's perspective, who likely didn't assess their risk level by scrutinizing their bodies and movements. Cathal favored her left leg and there was a bandage peeking out from the leathers under her tunic. Since Oisin didn't let the Lumadh healers finish before taking her away, she's likely no stronger than a lamb. And Aoife can't be too skilled, leaving an unknown risk with a weapon. She may not think Callum can use the sword, but even a poor fighter can get a stab in. The only unknown risk is Brendan. "Ah. Cathal's fine. As for the other two, those are both creatures who only bite when threatened. Don't antagonize them and you should be fine."

"I don't antagonize people." He folds his arms over his chest, the muscles twitching and distracting me. "I'm worried about you out there with them. You should stay here."

"I said I'd help, and I mean to keep my word." I lean down and give him a smacking kiss. His lashes lower and I almost consider telling Oisin to come back later. "But don't worry, I'll be back soon. I'm one behind you in the orgasm tally. And I intend to collect."

His cheeks darken and an sheepish smile blossoms over his striking face. "I'm at three, all told. That first night, after you'd been so complimentary, when I took the first watch, I, well..." He trails off and bites his lip.

My mouth drops as another wave of lust rolls through my body. "Really? And you didn't wake me?"

"Cadhla?" Oisin calls.

I stand and stalk the three steps to the tent flap. Before I duck through the opening, I jab a finger at Callum. "This conversation isn't over."

***

Callum

While I enjoyed Enna's mouth more than I could ever say, it's too risky to remain here longer. I can't fathom why I thought differently. I'll blame Enna's mouth, Enna's body, just Enna. Enna could learn *anything* from Oisin, and I should prepare myself for it. She likes my body at least, maybe that will be enough to keep me around a little while longer once she realizes who I am. I should have asked Allanagh if she saw any of Enna's conquests last longer than a night or two.

I dawdle in the tent as long as I can. While I try not to wallow, Faewisp, *Aoife*, drags her fingers over the canvas, cooing at me and suggesting I join her and Cathal at the lake. To drown me, most likely. But I'd think myself as dim as Darroch if I take them up on their offer. Once they finally leave, I slip outside, watching the sun's rays slowly dip under the horizon.

Brendan is sitting on an overturned log in front of his tent, a knife in one hand and thick stick in another. It looks like he's whittling stakes. I acknowledge him with a nod and he grunts.

"Sit if you want," he says, kicking the low rock beside him. They've made a circle of various detritus around an unlit fire pit. I perch hesitantly on the rock while Brendan sharpens the sticks and watches me.

"Old sword you got there," he says.

I touch the hilt. "Family relic." It's true, he just doesn't need to know which family. Or that it's one of the ceremonial swords Darroch and I got when we started the Oige. Father is obsessed with swords, has been for as long as I can remember, his in particular. The Oige apparently used to include much broader weaponry training before he took control. One demand of training was to keep your sword on you at all times, even when not on duty. Darroch advanced to a soldier's series when he graduated section three and enlisted, but this sword remained faithfully with me, when I'd remained behind and withdrawn. I kept it because even a dull sword can have its uses, though I've not needed to wield it. *Yet*.

"Why didn't you take yours with you instead?" He gestures with the knife. "Lots of predators out here and the standard soldier series is more lightweight. Better handling."

"We left in a rush. I only grabbed what I could," I say, trying to cobble together the right lie. I attempt to remind myself that I owe him no deference, and he doesn't scare me.

"Mmhmm. Now see, I think you don't have one," he says. A single drop of nervous sweat beads on my forehead at the potential revelation. He continues meanly, "I think you're a useless dropout, and *that's* the only weapon you've got."

For a moment, I'd feared he'd belatedly recognized me, or recognized the sword and realized he'd seen me around the training grounds on the way to the castle. I breathe out a sigh of relief as his guess misses the mark. But while I may still be a stranger to him, the hostility in his voice suggests that he's itching for an argument.

All the times I let the other recruits insult me, when I'd told myself that disengaging was the mature choice, when it was really due to fear that Father couldn't spell out, race through my mind. And I have two choices: what I always do, or what Enna would do. I counter, "Why do you care?"

"I'm just making conversation," he says. The tone of his voice sounds like someone who is attempting to act innocently but doesn't know the true meaning of the word. "Oisin seems real interested in your woman staying with us. Meaning you and I could become... close friends."

Not if I can help it. I'll follow Enna where she wants, but spending more than one night with these people will be like playing a game with no winners. "How considerate," I say sharply. "If we're doing introductions, you can tell me why *you're* not carrying your issued sword. Or are *you* the dropout?"

"That's not your concern."

I hold out my hands. The power I felt kneeling before Enna seems to have lingered, inflaming the release of the desires that had built up every time someone pushed me and I didn't respond. "Looks like we're at a stalemate. Though I'm at least carrying a sword, which says something about the differences between us."

"You know nothing," Brendan says, the stick in his hands snapping.

"I know more than you," I mutter.

Brendan stands and looms over me, as my hand tightens on my sword's hilt. "I served directly under Darroch, son of Elric, you fucker. Who did you—" He cuts himself off and stares at me aghast.

I slowly rise, inwardly cursing. Given his past experience with Darroch, he would most likely notice the similarity in our appearance. No longer am I Finn who ran away with 'Cadhla,' I'm me.

Before Brendan can make whatever move he might, Cathal and Aoife amble back to the campsite, their arms around each other's waists. Cathal frowns when she sees us. "Bren, what's going on?"

Brendan doesn't acknowledge her, his dirt brown eyes widening. "You're—"

I ready myself to withdraw my sword, trying to remember the failed lessons from my teen years in the Oige.

"Will there be a fight?" Aoife says, pale eyes gleaming as she clasps her hands over her chest. "Cathal, look. Violence is coming!"

Right. This is why I don't respond to bullies. At least my sword will finally get some use.

Chapter 13

Enna

"And Brendan's fine, but skittish," Oisin says as we begin checking their traps for game. He'd started telling about the trio hoping to convince Callum and me to stay longer. "Was damn near catatonic on that unnatural hybrid lily tea. You heard of it?"

I crouch, inspecting a half-hidden snare under a tree, and nod. "Finn told me about it. Sounds kind of nice."

Oisin snorts. "Sure, once in a while. There're a few memories I wouldn't mind dulling. But they drink it like water here. Suck it down and shove down all the emotions. Terrible."

He meanders out of my eyeline, but I can still hear him. I might need another orgasm if I want my senses to dull again. A smile involuntarily forms on my face at the reminder of Callum as I collect a few partridges. Wiping my face of the emotion, I call out to Oisin, "Why was he drinking all that tea?"

"Got kicked out of the Olthion army," Oisin shouts from somewhere to the south. "Couldn't handle the disgrace."

"Why? He seems skilled enough."

"Got hurt in a battle last year. They left him to die. Can you believe it?" Oisin toddles up beside me, a hare in his hands.

My brows raise. Abandoning the wounded doesn't surprise me after what I'd seen those soldiers do in the clearing. But in my quick inspection of Brendan, I'd seen no lasting injuries or physical maladies that would require leaving him behind at a battle site. "What? He seems *fine*."

I'd remembered a bit more, when I was patching up Callum, about the men and women I'd helped field-heal enough to get them back to the medical tents. Only those we couldn't help were ever left behind. I was glad to have confirmation for what I'd told Callum when we snuck away from those callous soldiers in the woods.

"He was!" Oisin exclaims. "I mean, his ankle snapped, or something. Bone twisted right out, lots of blood. They left him to bleed out instead of healing him. No need to waste the healing magic or herbs, he said. But he dragged himself back to their base, found the healers."

I could guess the rest of the story. "The healer's oath kicked in, they healed him, and punished him for the waste." Not that it even takes much. If a healer can reset the bone and close the wound, you don't even need to use any healing potions. Just a little bit of magic.

"Damn right," Oisin confirms. "Booted him then and there. Brendan was... well, crushed's the best word for it." He shakes his head. "It's their... personality or something, these Netherins. Starts in some brutal school when they're wee. Only way to *belong* is to fight in these damned wars, and drown yourself in tea if you ever want anything else. But command don't take it seriously."

That gives me a deeper understanding of Callum and his need for approval. "How so?"

Together, we check another trap, but it's empty. "Like they get off on it, or something," Oisin explains. "Brendan won't say much about it, too respectful, or scared, of them. Seems like a game to them, and the soldiers are the pieces. Movable and expendable." He rubs his beard. "I gotta tell you, Cadhla, if we'd known about this under the General, might have changed the war. Play the game, beat the player. Cathal keeps talking about going back."

"She likes the General that much?" I ask. I don't remember the woman, but Oisin sounded so disappointed when he'd described why he left. "Even after the General did... what she did?"

Side by side, we crouch beside another trap, working together to clear the brush, grab the half dozen snorlix that fell in, and reset it.

"Cathal didn't think it was all that bad," Oisin says. "And she liked the stability of service. 's why she locked on to Aoife so fast. Aoife grounds her. Gods only know what will happen if Aoife flits back to whatever faery hole she came out of." I huff a laugh, thinking of Callum's nickname, although he's named her the parasite and not the faery itself. Beside me, Oisin chuckles mirthlessly. "If it happens, I'll regret springing her even more."

Curious about my own people, and the memories of battles I have, I ask, "Why did you do it? We may not have many healers, but we could have done something about her limp until one visited."

He plucks a blade of grass and lets it fall to the ground beneath us. "She'd fight until she killed herself."

A deep frown creases my forehead. "We're not like the Netherins," I tell him, although I can't officially confirm that. "Surely the General's command wouldn't have let her."

"No, you're right. Nothing about letting. Cathal's more proud of our people than anyone I ever met. Won't listen to anything against the General, much less Lumadh, even if it's *true*. Feels like she let the General down by leaving." His laughter returns, sounding even more bitter this time. "Feel the same sometimes. Never met the General, not up close at least. Saw her at training, of course. Watched her show some moves. Looked damn good, no one has a stance like hers." He smiles, but it's strained. "I stand by why I left, needed a change, but sometimes I wonder..."

There's nothing I can say, since I don't remember the General, but Oisin doesn't seem to mind. We work for a few more minutes, before he says, sounding shy, "Got a commendation from her once. Could show you my copy, if you'd like."

"That's something to be proud of," I tell him. "No matter what happened later, it means you were worthy."

"Hope she doesn't withdraw it or something. Guess it doesn't matter out here," he says, frowning.

A faint yell sounds from the direction of the campsite. Oisin groans. "That's Cathal. She and Aoife get into screaming spats every now and again."

I hand off the game I've been carrying. "I'll check the rest of the traps. You go handle your house."

"You sure?"

I gesture to the traps we haven't yet inspected, hidden from view except for someone who knows what to look for. "I've got it."

"Gods, 's nice to be around a proper Lumadhan again," he says to himself as he meanders off.

When Oisin finally vanishes, my own expression falls into a thin line. "Come out."

The man from the alley appears between two trees like smoke. "Finally noticed me. Tsk, tsk."

I'd caught him during the conversation about Cathal, but I *should* have noticed him earlier. The consequences of Callum's mouth again. "Fuck off."

"Glad to hear your foul language isn't dependent on your memory," he says dryly.

I don't deign that with a response, instead demanding, "Why are you following me?"

He leans against a tree and crosses his arms around a black tunic that should be dusty but still looks pressed and perfect. "Part curiosity, seeing you with the whelp."

I smother an uncharitable snort. The man's waiflike appearance makes his sharp features more intense, but he can't be much older than my thirty years, and Callum isn't younger than me.

He scowls darkly, as though he hears my thoughts. Which, given the lacking memories about Lumadh is still a possibility. "Partly because Tier would murder me if I didn't watch you."

"She wouldn't hurt a fly. Tell me the real reason."

The scowl transforms into a wide grin, transforming his face into something quite pleasing. "You remember Tier. I wondered if the amnesia was part of the act and this was a very convoluted plan against the Netherins instead of Lumindar. Considering *I'm* supposed to be doing that, you'll pardon my curiosity."

I did remember Tierney, which is when I realized his statement in the alley wasn't about a 'tear' but Tierney, my sister. That and the comment about a glamour and his own glamouring cloak, told me he was from Lumadh and either in *league* with the irritating spellcaster of my memories or *was* the spellcaster himself. If I were betting on it, the latter. "No plan. Simply trying to retrieve my memories and learn a few things."

"With the misbegotten son of Elric?" The man, whose name still wouldn't come to me, laughs, a deep-throated sound. "Intriguing, but I'm the spymaster here. You have all the subtlety of a brick through a window." He cocks his head, looking more like the crow I'd likened him to before. "Unless... he would likely know who you are. Perhaps this is *his* plan against you. But *that* is too subtle for Elric, meaning Callum must be acting on his own. Although Darroch could—"

I won't tell him I don't remember who Elric or Darroch is. "How about you tell me who you think I am and we can go about our day?"

"No thank you, Princess. You put me on these dull spy and retrieve missions. The minimum you can do is allow me to enjoy the situation you're in while I wait for my trap to be sprung."

"*I* put you on these missions, you say? If I did, you're derelict in your duties by bothering me, soldier," I start. But the man vanished again.

At least I know the reason why I hate spellcasters. And have one more hint as to who I am.

Callum

Oisin appears in the small circle of tents, dropping an enormous pile of dead animals to the ground. Enna is nowhere near him. "What the fuck is going on?" he roars.

Brendan doesn't remove the arrow digging into the small of my throat. And I don't withdraw my boot resting on Faewisp's chest, when she'd lunged for me and I'd taken advantage of her accidental fall. Cathal, for all her screeching at us to stop a minute ago, appears bored now, holding Brendan's abandoned knife at her side.

"He's fucking royalty," Brendan spits. "Not just some Netherin, but one of those, up at the castle, sitting high and mighty, wasting away on our skills. Darroch's brother, Can or something."

I release a sneer, his discovery less irritating than being known only as Darroch's brother.

Oisin squints, as though he can see the royal blood within my veins. "That true, lad?"

I don't answer, instead searching for Enna, who is still nowhere in sight.

Oisin frowns and approaches Brendan, fisting his thick hands on his hips. "I see. Let him loose, Bren. Can't blame a man for fallin' for a Valenthian. Left his family for her, after all."

"Did he?" Brendan says, pressing the arrow's tip into my skin until I feel the bite of it. "I haven't been gone for so long that I don't have contacts. They'd certainly tell me if someone in the line of succession had been burned."

The zip of something flying through the air halts further discussion, and Enna's dagger sticks out of Brendan's forearm. The arrow tilts off my throat as he grunts and shoots off into the forest behind us.

Enna stalks forward, her own bow now in her hands and an arrow aimed at Brendan. "Move, Finn!"

I leap out of the way, using Aoife as a stepping stone, who growls under my foot. As Cathal stumbles forward to help her stand, I unsheathe my sword and hold it aloft, positioning it between Brendan and the motionless Oisin.

"The next thing I shoot will land in your throat," Enna says. She widens her stance and cocks a single brow.

Brendan rips the dagger out, a line of dark blood trailing down his forearm, and takes aim at me again. "You don't know who you protect."

"Neither does he," Enna says quietly, her gaze darting between me and Brendan.

Oisin watches them with a calculating gaze, his weathered mouth opening in a gasp.

Enna raises the bow, as if planning on making good on her threat. "But he is mine. Drop your weapon. I won't ask again."

The Protective Princess, my mind supplies. An inappropriate warmth pools in my stomach, distracting me enough for Aoife to lunge at me. Cathal reaches for her, hands clawing at her pale skin but can't stop her. I dodge a wild swing from Aoife's hands, slicing the sword towards her and smacking hard into her chest. Her body feels like stone, the force of the impact sending tremors through my arms. She screeches, a sound born of rage more than pain. As she makes another desperate leap towards me, I tighten my grip on the sword, ready to defend myself. But her body freezes in midair as an arrow strikes with brutal precision, finding its mark in her stomach. She yanks it out, but no blood pools from the wound. My eyes widen, not in fear but in shock at whatever creature she must be.

I sweep my sword again, ducking towards her feet, hoping to knock her to the ground. She tumbles backwards, crashing into the forest floor, the impact of her shockingly heavy body shaking the earth. Cathal and I fall to the ground, my sword skidding from my hands, but Brendan and Enna merely stumble. Cathal lets out a groan as her leg rests awkwardly on the ground at a strange angle. Aoife flips onto her knees and crawls to Cathal, soothing sounds coming from her viper's tongue.

Seizing the distraction Aoife made, Brendan swiftly shoots an arrow towards me. I somehow twist out of the way, narrowly avoiding a collision as Enna slides on her knees toward my sword to snatch it, her hair whipping behind her. With a powerful sweep of the blade, she disarms Brendan, sending his bow flying, the wood clattering in pieces against the earth.

As Brendan reaches for his second bow and Enna grips my sword to aim at Brendan again, Oisin shouts, "Enough!"

Cathal and Aoife hold each other on the ground, their gazes fixed on him. Brendan's fingers clench tightly around his bow, conflict reflected on his angular face. After a tense minute, he abandons the bow and looks at Oisin, who appears weary.

"We'll leave. With no more trouble," Enna says, sweeping her hair from her face. "Thanks for the conversation, Oisin. It was enlightening."

Relief and anxiety etch themselves into my skin. We're safe, but what did Enna learn? I hesitate, my breath stuttering from the exertion, feeling the need to say something. "I'm terribly sorry for the trouble with Brendan, Oisin."

"Fuck off," Brendan says, fists clenching just as Enna hisses, "Don't apologize."

Brendan lunges towards Enna, his fist extending towards her like a striking serpent. The same powerful feeling that motivated me to confront him now propels me to act as her shield. When I throw myself in front of her, Brendan's fist lands squarely on my cheek, the force reverberating through my entire body. I stagger backward, the taste of copper filling my mouth. A rush of heat follows the pain, and my cheek throbs in protest. When my vision clears, Enna has my sword at Brendan's neck, who looks at me smugly.

Oisin chuckles. "We're done, *Cadhla*. Grab your things while I check that your man didn't break nothing."

The shock of the blow ebbs, leaving a pulsating ache, and I watch Oisin smile in a way that looks genuine. Enna hands me the sword silently, her eyes narrowing on Brendan before landing on Oisin. Walking backward, she heads to the tent, not letting me leave her sight. Even when she reaches inside to grab our things, she keeps her neck craned towards us.

Oisin ambles forward and my hackles raise at what he might reveal. With a gentle sweep, he brushes off the dirt from my shoulders, his eyes studying my cheek as he leans in, his voice barely audible. "I'll find you and kill you myself if this is some fuckin' Netherin plot."

I rise to my full height, exuding as much menace as I can muster, channeling Darroch, a realization that will certainly irritate me later. I growl, "I wouldn't—"

"I know that, son. You mightn't have left your family for her, but I know when a man sees he found something special. That there woman is special."

"Should have gutted them in the woods," Brendan mutters under his breath. Aoife laughs, leaned against Cathal's shoulder, both still watching from the ground.

Oisin glares fiercely at them. "May not be part of General's forces now, but I trusted my command for a decade." I tense, knowing Enna is in earshot. Oisin pets my shoulder as he continues, "And that there woman was... part of that command too. Disagreement or otherwise, still have pride for my people."

"You ready?" Enna says, stalking back with our packs in her hands. I take them and maneuver them onto my shoulders. Her golden brown gaze travels over my cheek, lips pursing. As we leave camp back towards the summit of the mountain, she whispers, "And you thought I'd be the one to make trouble."

⚬

Enna

Once we're far enough away that Brendan and Oisin and their group are unlikely to chase after us, I stop and tear a piece from the cloth we'd used as a blanket this morning, withdrawing the same healing concoction of Allanagh's that I'd applied on his leg.

Callum watches me with dark eyes. "Are you going to stab me again?"

"I didn't stab you the first time." I dab the ointment on his cheek. "This is for the numbing. There's no wound to seal."

He smiles down at me, wincing as it tugs on the skin.

I slather a layer of healing ointment there too. "You didn't have to take that hit for me."

"Yes, I did."

Warmth pools, not in my belly, but higher. I replace the cloth and ointment in our knapsack and lean against his chest, smiling as his arms immediately go around me. "Why did Brendan attack you?"

"Why do you think he started it?" he answers.

I tilt my head upward to give him a flat look, and he winces.

"He had a difficulty with... my background that we couldn't overcome."

"That makes sense. Oisin told me he got kicked out of his regiment in Olthion. Did you ever train with him?" Discovering that recruits were little more than expendable arrow fodder until they completed grueling training tests, where their aggression only intensified, gave me a deeper understanding insight into Callum and his struggles with self worth. Particularly since he left so early and could never enlist.

Callum's lips tighten in a frown. "He served with my brother. *He's* the family's soldier, not me, remember?"

I spare a minute to wonder who he is, this son of "Elric" with ties to the castle, a hidden history and even more hidden agenda, but it doesn't matter. His character tells me as much about who he is than his background. Those memories of Olthion, and meeting his former comrades, tell me they'd eat him up and spit him out, killing his spirit. "Good. It's better than being stuck with people like Sid and Garbhan and Grasshopper." I sniff like I smelled something bad, hoping to make him smile. It does, a small one. "You're better off," I finish.

We pick up speed, almost jogging towards the spellcaster, to arrive before sunset. As we scale the summit towards their lair, Callum keeps up well. He underestimates his own strength. Olthion truly doesn't deserve him.

We lunge up the rocky terrain for more than an hour, the air thinning, when Callum asks, in an overly casual voice, "Did you learn anything else from Oisin?"

"Nothing I hadn't already guessed." Something skitters across his face, fear perhaps, and I wonder what he's so afraid of me learning. "Like how my armor isn't the Olthion variety, and I'm likely from a different country myself. I already knew I was a Lumadhan." And highly ranked, since I appeared at war councils with Tierney and managed missions, like sending that irritating wraith of a man off to spy.

His voice tightens. "Anything else about you, or where you came from?"

I cock my head, casting my thoughts back to the conversation with Oisin, since the man in black provided no answers, only more questions. Oisin and I worked well together, in tune with each other even, as if we had actually served together. Or at the very least, were trained by the same commander. But working in tandem with him was all muscle memory, with no new memories resurfacing. Callum still seems to be the catalyst for that.

"Before we got to the hunting grounds," I tell Callum, "he'd already told me all about the regiment he served with. I couldn't tell him about mine since I still don't remember it. We spent more time talking about Brendan than anything else. Oh, but he was going to show me his prized possession, a commendation from the 'General. What a name. The 'General.' Seems silly."

Callum stumbles, and I grab his elbow, saying, "If you want me to remove your pants again, you don't need to get hurt as an excuse." He huffs a strained laugh as I add, "Oisin had little specifics to provide about this *General*. He respected her though, no matter that he deserted."

"The mark of a good leader," Callum says, sounding slightly tense. "Do you... remember her?"

With the few memories I have and the wraith's hints, I probably served with her, perhaps directly under her. *What if she did this to you as punishment?* I quickly disregard the thought. A respected General, pompous title or no, wouldn't play those games. No matter what the Netherins apparently believe, war isn't for games. If she wanted to kill me, she'd kill me, not have someone kidnap me, remove my memory, and leave me as unarmed prey. From what Oisin revealed, it was this *Mouric* that would do something like that. I slide my gaze to Callum. *Or a Netherin himself.* Whoever this Elric is. *It's more likely an enemy did this to me.* Someone from Olthion.

"Enna?"

I blink away the conspiracies. It certainly wasn't Callum, he's not that good of an actor. And if it was his family, he's going a long way to prove he isn't them. All this tells me is that I need to return to Lumadh as soon as possible. There must have been some sinister reason for taking my memories and the longer I delay, the worse things could become. I finally answer, "Do I remember the General? No, but I must know her."

Callum swallows, the movement following the long line of his neck, his Adam's apple bobbing. I don't recall being attracted to Adam's apples before. I doubt it's the amnesia.

A sudden fog curls around our feet, stopping the conversation as we both snap to attention. I bury a sliver of pride at Callum's immediate reaction. After this and his fight with Brendan, a few more orgasms and he might be confident enough to take on an entire army. *Together, perhaps, if his family did this to me.*

"WHO GOES THERE?" A voice booms out from somewhere ahead of us as the fog thickens and forms a curtain covering the path forward. Callum drops the bags and withdraws his sword. I rest my hands on my daggers.

"Enna of Lumadh and Callum of Olthion," Callum says, his voice firm.

"AND WHAT DO YOU SEEK?" the voice shouts, the sound making my teeth rattle.

"Are you Eodez?" I ask.

"THAT DEPENDS ENTIRELY ON YOUR ANSWER TO MY QUESTION. WHAT DO YOU SEEK, INTERLOPERS?"

"We seek information," Callum answers, his fingers tightening on the sword.

"You're not, like, looking for a spell?" The voice rises in pitch, softening.

"No. Only information," Callum confirms.

As quickly as the fog came, it disappears, like the snuffing out of a candle. Callum and I both blink in shock as a young girl appears where the fog was densest.

"Hey there, hi, how's it going?" the girl says, wiggling her golden brown fingers at us. She's slight, wearing a long dress with a swirling pattern in hues of indigo and violet. Ebony hair cascades down her back, streaked in turquoise and magenta. Her fingers and toenails are colored orange, and silver bracelets run from her wrists to her elbows.

Callum and I exchange glances. "Are you Eodez?" I ask again.

"Duh. Who else would I be?" She turns, skipping into a crevice that's appeared between two rocks and vanishing. A moment later, she reappears, frowning at us. "Coming?"

Callum shrugs and starts to follow, but I hold him back. "If anything happens, I want you to run."

"I'm staying with you," he says firmly. "We're in this together."

Unable to help myself, I give him a fierce kiss. He parts his lips for mine and I have to forcibly pull myself away from him. I lick the taste of him from my lips, looking over how I've affected him. His hair is tousled, his cheeks and mouth are pink, and somehow I dragged his shirt up enough to reveal the edge of the hair trailing towards his pelvis. I have to physically force myself back towards Eodez rather than take advantage of him right then and there.

As we start through the mysterious looking crevice, Eodez calls back to us, "I know you said you wanted information. But could I also interest you in some jewelry? I make my own."

"We'll certainly take a look," Callum says, cheeks stained with a blush from my kiss. That pink is quickly becoming my second favorite color.

Chapter 14

Callum

"And this one is made with faewisp bones," Eodez is saying, as she points to her wares. The one in question is a necklace fashioned from twisted vines with tiny finger bones hanging from twine. "You'd like that one, Callum."

I hum politely. My arm muscles are still tense from hitting Aoife, meaning she's not wrong. But her knowledge is unnerving regardless.

"I'm just, like, tired of using all my stuff for spells, you know? Crack this bone to curse your neighbor, stick this feather in your shoe to remain dry in rain, bury this vine to yield a better harvest this season." She gestures to the table. "These are my creative materials, not spell fodder. That's why I was *so* glad you weren't wanting a spell. The last guy only convinced me because I was hard up for more supplies." She withdraws another bracelet that looks to be made of braided animal hide and interwoven with river rocks and crystallized butterfly wings, holding it out to my wrist. "How about this one?"

I clasp my hands behind my back, hiding them. "We don't have any money at the moment, but we could return to purchase at a later date? After we get our information."

Eodez tries on a bone ring and displays her hand to the air. "I'd *never* ask for anything as boring as money. Magic is all about tangible things. I want something intangible, something this plane's magic can't touch. What about a memory?" She giggles. "No, Enna's got too few for that."

Enna's neck snaps to look at her, dropping a necklace made of stained feathers. "How do you know that?"

"Magic, duh. It's why you're here, after all. You can't access your memories. Which is a real bummer, since you have some interesting ones."

Enna's expression shifts to one of disgust as she stares at the gruesome object in my hand. "You just said magic can't touch intangible things. Like memories. Then—"

Eodez rustles through her piles, withdrawing something made of (what I hope isn't) human teeth. "You can't... change your personality with magic. Like, magic won't make anyone less fearful or more confident. Sorry about all that wasted time, Callum." She holds the tooth necklace up to Enna's neck, who stares at me questioningly even as my stomach starts to hurt.

Eodez frowns and grabs another necklace to display, still chattering about magic. "You can't remove memories or take them, but you can alter someone's brain so they can't access them, like hiding information. Like I did with you."

Enna's fists clench and I move to stand closer to her. I force down my own questions about what Eodez has revealed, how *knowledge* can be tangible but confidence isn't, or that failing to change after being spelled wasn't *my* fault but because the magic literally couldn't work. *Gods, what would*

Father say if I told him? Would he still blame me if he knew the truth?

I swallow hard and address Eodez. "Eodez, can you give us the information on how to... access her memories?"

"And who did it?" Enna adds, her lips pursing.

"We're still negotiating terms! Information and jewelry for something of yours." She looks at me slyly. "I'd say you could give me your first love, but I think we're all still in the middle of that. What about a whispered secret?"

Desperate to stop before she reveals something else, I grab two necklaces at random. "Fine. These necklaces and the information we ask for in exchange for a secret. Something that stays a secret."

"I was talking to Enna," Eodez says, more to herself than aloud. "Deal. I'll take one of your secrets, Callum of Olthion, son of... oops! *That's* not the secret I'm after."

Enna crosses her arms. "Do you know who sought to spell me and take my memory?"

"Sorry, En. I can't talk about that. We were under the shroud of silence." Eodez dances over to Enna, grabbing her hands and squeezing them. "I know. I *know*. It's super annoying. But the sanctity of the shroud of silence means that anything said under the shroud of silence can't be repeated outside the shroud of silence. Or else the shroud of silence wouldn't be silent."

"Is there *anything* you can tell me?" Enna hisses out an irritated breath. "Even a hint? Or will it all be games?"

Eodez cocks her head, her black hair gliding down to her hip. "I mean, if we get under the shroud of silence, I can tell you." She points to a dingy silk scarf draped over a small table. "Don't you know how shrouds of silence work?"

"The what?" Enna's voice is flat.

"I *just* explained it. Whatever you say under the shroud of silence cannot be repeated outside the shroud of silence, so... we go under the shroud of silence and I can share what I know."

Minutes later, the three of us are crowded under a gauzy silk scarf riddled with stains and smelling, oddly, of lemons. My nose twitches as I suck in a sneeze. Eodez snuggles up to my chest, rubbing her forehead against my sternum before doing the same to Enna's collarbones, like a cat marking her territory.

"This is so cozy," she says, oblivious. "Isn't this cozy?"

Enna tenses at each pass Eodez makes over her neck. "What about the information I asked for?"

"Fine," Eodez says, drawing out the word and stamping her feet. "But don't be mad. I don't actually know his name."

Enna's eyes light like a flint, ready to immolate Eodez, the shroud, and anything else standing in her way.

"Don't irritate the practitioner," I whisper.

Eodez turns back to me and offers a toothy grin. One of her teeth has been replaced with an acorn. Absently, I remember she had all her teeth when we shuffled under this shroud. A shiver threatens to overtake me but, like the sneeze, I restrain it.

Eodez pats me on the chest. The orange on her fingernails isn't a disease, like I'd feared, but some kind of lacquer. "Don't worry, folks. I'm not as irritating as the 'truthteller.' Their name is Tait, by the way. I bet they didn't tell you *that* when they were offering all their fickle truths."

"Eodez, you brought us under the shroud because you could tell us something that you weren't otherwise able to," I say, attempting to sound reasonable to the spellcaster that I've realized isn't entirely sane.

"Right, right, right." She spins back around to face Enna. "I don't know his name, but he is someone very close to you. Not physically of course, but wouldn't it be hilarious if Callum did it?" She digs her elbow into my gut.

Enna's caramel eyes narrow. "Do you know anything *else* about him? A description, maybe?"

"He has black hair. Not overly brawny, but a decent physique. Someone who could still throw a lover around, but doesn't. Poor relationship with his family, too. He had a lot of complaints about them, and it started super young, too. It's honestly sad. If he'd just talk to someone about it, I bet he'd be happier." She spins again, eyeing me. "Still not Callum but, wow, you'd be a good suspect. You fit like every descriptor. Especially with the secret I took from you."

A beat of sweat forms at my low back, from nerves at what Eodez might accidentally reveal, or because I've got a dirty cloth on my head.

"Focus, Eodez," Enna says, gripping Eodez's arms firmly. Eodez's bracelets clang together, sounding like bells. "How do I get access to my memory?"

"That is the easiest part," Eodez says, beaming. The acorn tooth is now a blue jewel.

More sweat pools on my forehead and I wipe it with the back of my hand, knocking part of the shroud off me. "If you've told us everything about the man, must we remain under this thing?"

"I thought we were bonding under it," she whines. Then she scowls and whips the shroud off our heads, tossing it to the ground. She snaps her fingers, and it dutifully rises and floats to cover the back of a chair. It's the first bit of real magic we've seen so far, aside from the harrowing teeth swap. "Come, come," she says, directing us to the table and plopping down on the seat with the shroud. Another snap of her fingers lights a candelabra over our heads, with candles down to their nubs.

Once we settle into the other mismatched chairs, she pulls out an ornate tea set. The pot appears to be made of molded silver with intricate engravings in a pattern that looks familiar, and the spout shaped like a dragon's sinuous neck. The teacups, resembling miniature chalices, are made of some kind of white bone and hand painted in a rainbow of colors, depicting scenes I don't recognize from any stories.

"Beautiful, isn't it?" Eodez hands me a teacup with two painted figures, a man kneeling before a wild-looking woman.

I swallow a cough, peering at the cup she gave Enna, which portrays an amorphous blob. A tight knot clenches inside me. As Eodez lifts the teapot to fill our cups, I still tell her, "It *is* stunning. I feel like I've seen the pattern on the teapot before but can't remember where."

Eodez leaves the pot aloft, twirling her finger until it spins slowly, exposing the entire pattern. "Of course you've seen it before. It's the pattern of our part of the universe, of Lochmorae. You've just never seen it like this." She points to images that fade in and out on the silver. "There's the Valenthian and the Netherins. There's Lochmorae without borders. The four gifts that broke the world. You know, the sword, the spear, *et cetera*."

I squint, straining my eyes to glimpse the unknown images she's describing, but they evaporate the moment I fixate on them. Then she points to each creature that spins past. "There's the Oros, dragons, faewisps, snorlix, kelpies, bogle, and shellycoats. And there's me!" She finishes, pointing to a feline-dragon-bovine hybrid I've never seen before. Either way, it isn't human. Enna and I exchange another wary glance.

"You were going to tell us how I could regain my *memory*," Enna says through clenched teeth.

Eodez tips the spinning teapot to pour tea in our cups, but nothing comes out. Like a child playing pretend, the cups and pot are empty, waiting to be filled. She gestures for us to drink from our cups. Enna clenches her fists before shoving them under the table, leaving me to lift the cup and tilt it toward my mouth. There's a hazy sheen on the edge, so I hold the cup away from my lips, feigning sips.

Eodez scowls at me, her gaze trailing from my face to the table. "Don't spill, Callum. You're better than that." She shifts, resting her elbow on the table and leaning against her bent wrist. "So impatient, Enna. Here I thought you liked not having your memory. Callum surely does." My own fists clench against the teacup. "But fine, that is why you're here. If you confront the one that marked you, you'll get your memory back."

Enna straightens. "I assumed you could do it, as the spell-caster who did it. That you needed to do whatever you did to hide it and then reverse it."

Eodez giggles as a dull flush crawls up my cheek. "Nope. Most spells, anyone can remove, unless they put in a safeguard. Which I did." She winks at me. "Good thing *that* worked out, right, Callum?"

Ennas' lips tighten. "You marked me with magic," she says, glancing at me briefly. "So I confront-"

"Not me." Eodez leans back. "I didn't physically mark you."

Enna growls. "Okay. So if I find the person who *came* to you, the black haired—"

"Not outside the shroud!" Eodez shrieks, her hand clutching a newly revealed pebble necklace at her chest.

"If I find *that* person who will remain undescribed, and confront them, then I'll get my memory back." Enna clarifies.

Eodez hums, all irritation at us speaking outside the shroud gone. "That's not what I said. Do we need to get under the shroud again?"

I clear my throat. "No, we remember the description. You said she needs to confront whoever physically marked her." Enna tilts her head, her brows furrowed as she tries to decipher my words. Grateful I can help, I continue, "It's like with the truthteller, a bit of a puzzle. We asked who overpowered you. They directed us to Eodez. Someone veiling your memory is certainly overpowering you, or the mental part of you."

Eodez bats her eyelashes at me. "Go on..."

I ignore her, continuing to work through the puzzle. "And you were marked by bruises, and that head wound. They used a sword or their hands. That's the tangible item. To regain your memory, we must find the person who is responsible for that and confront them. Which could be the man that asked Eodez for the spell, or someone else, if he used another person to attack you."

"He really *is* clever, isn't he?" Eodez says, elbowing Enna. Gratifyingly, my body *doesn't* react to her praise. She isn't looking for an answer though, as a feather falls from somewhere above us and she tries to catch it.

Enna collapses back in her chair. "That makes as much sense as anything. Is there anything else you can tell us, Eodez?"

Eodez's head snaps up, her fingers wrapped in twine that materialized out of nowhere. "What was that?" She holds out the twine and the captured feather. "I'm making a new necklace.

Enna's lips twist. "I'd like to look at more of your jewelry. Do you have anything in the back we haven't seen yet?"

Eodez leaps from the table, the twine vanishing. "I do! In the back, just like you said!" She quickly frowns. "But they don't, let's say, fiscally resonate with the market like my other pieces, you know? *Avant garde* is the way to describe it."

Enna mouths the terms—*fiscally resonate* and *avant garde*—to me, but I shrug. I don't understand the phrases either; I don't even know what language they're in, something that seems to be a common with Eodez. "We'd still love to see them," Enna says, offering a forced smile.

When Eodez skips out of the room, Enna turns to me, her shoulders slumping. "I'm thinking I should just move on. Return to Lumadh as an amnesiac and deal with it there."

Something in my stomach sours, but I swallow it down. "You would go back now?"

She smiles ruefully. "You'd have to come along, though. Since you've been the key to recovering the few memories I have now."

Hope rises within me. "Truly?"

"Sure. We could use you as an advisor. Someone with your talents, and know how of Olthion would probably do wonders." She laughs, but it sounds hollow to my ears. "But who knows? I certainly don't. Don't mind me, Callum. I'm just teasing. Some levity for this chase without end."

The hope drops as though one of her arrows shot it out of the sky. "It's fine. We'll go to wherever you woke up and look for clues as to who abandoned you there. You're a talented swordsman and soldier. We know you likely injured them."

"Damn right." She smirks before frowning. "Did you know any spellcaster could release the enchantment? If Eodez hadn't used that 'safeguard' she mentioned."

"I..." My eyes fall shut. "Yes."

Her hands around my neck force my eyes back open, and she peers at me with pursed lips. "I get it. It's alright. I can imagine what you were thinking when you did it."

I want to ask her more, but fear, back again, keeps me silent. Instead, I wrap my arms around her back. "There's a chance the person to confront left something else in the forest that could help us find them. We could do a locator spell with another spellcaster."

"It's exhausting, having to rely on others when I should be able to end this on my own. The truthteller, Eodez, another spellcaster." She tips her head back to look me in the eyes again and I give in to my impulse to stroke her hair.

"And me?" I ask quietly.

Her lips ignite with a radiant smile. "I don't mind your inclusion."

Even the tepid praise tightens my stomach. "I'll stay until you send me away."

"At this point, I can't imagine myself doing that," she says slyly. "We still need that bed."

I frown as I imagine the exact scenario where she would, when she realizes who I am and the orgasms fade. When I become yet another in the long line of her conquests, and she leaves for Lumadh.

Eodez emerges from the door behind us, halting further conversation. She carries several boxes in her hands and lays them out on the table. "Now I know I'm biased about my 'unique' pieces, but I know I'll find a home for them some day."

No longer able to continue our clandestine conversation, Enna and I halfheartedly open the boxes and peruse the offerings. Immediately catching my eye is a delicate silver chain, intricately woven to resemble a vine, cradling a fox pendant at its core. The pendant itself is molded with remarkable detail, complete with topaz gems that gleam like vivid eyes.

"Can I add that one to our bill?" I ask, unable to take my eyes from the lovely piece that will look perfect on Enna's slender throat.

Eodez's yellow eyes widen with glee. "Really? I've been holding on to that one since the mountain formed. You can have it for a song."

I take the necklace and twirl my finger for Enna to turn so I can clasp it around her neck. When she turns back, her fingers caress the fox as she gives me a soft smile.

"Hey, no, I wasn't kidding," Eodez says. "I want a song. Start singing, Callum."

Chapter 15

We leave the next morning, the two necklaces Callum 'bought' shoved at the bottom of our knapsack, while the third hangs proudly around my neck.

Eodez let us sleep by her hearth rather than find a spot in the outdoors. Callum looked more excited than I'd seen him, except for those moments when one of us has our pants off. I playfully teased him about the hearth as a substitute bed, but Eodez overheard and eagerly joined as our audience, expecting a show. Callum wasn't interested in performing then. Me either, as I'm finding myself more possessive of him as the days go on, something that feels new, missing memories or no.

"Make sure to eat your vegetables and only kick someone if they try to kick you first," Eodez says as we stand at the opening in the rocks that leads to her home.

"I'll just not kick anyone," Callum says, a slightly indulgent look on his face. He likes Eodez, no matter how he might try to deny it. I'd say he must have had better encounters with spellcasters than I did, but I heard Eodez's remark about Callum's fear and confidence. What kind of doomed spells did someone try on him to change that? All the ideas I come up with paint an even grimmer picture of his home life.

"That's how your shins get bruised, but fine." Eodez brandishes a waterskin. "Now take the tea you didn't finish last night. You need it. Don't think I didn't notice."

I wrap my arm around Callum's waist. "We've got a lot to carry. How about we return for the tea?"

"You'll come back?" Eodez clasps her hands under her chin. "You swear it?"

"Yes," I promise between clenched teeth. My capacity for Eodez reached its limit yesterday.

"That's awesome! I mean, I *know* Callum will visit alone soon. He's always alone, that's inevitable. But you're unpredictable. Now, Callum, take a drink to tide you over. You've got a long day ahead of you. Emotionally, that is. Come on." She opens the thermos, empty just like the teapot from the night before, and grabs Callum's chin with bony fingers.

Callum turns green eyes to me, mouthing "help" and looking suddenly mournful. But Eodez takes advantage of his open mouth and tips the edge of the thermos up against his lips. He sputters, hacking as though he's been drowned, but no liquid spills to the ground.

"What happened?" I rub my hand over his back, trying to settle his coughing.

"The tea," he and Eodez say in unison, although Eodez's tone sounds like she wants to add 'idiots' to the end of her explanation.

"It's real," he says, mouth aghast. He grabs the container and takes another small sip. "It tastes like... the sea. Or brine mixed with..." He trails off, looking at me as his cheeks flush. My brows furrow at why he'd be embarrassed.

"Of course it's real," Eodez says, hands fisted on her hips. "It's invisible *magic* tea. And it tastes like whatever you might miss the most." She grins. "When you come back, we'll find out if the taste changed, Callum."

"Next time," he says, his expression grim.

Before she can give us anything else, I yank him through the crevice. As soon as we breach the barrier, the opening vanishes, leaving us back on the path.

"That was an experience," I say, shaking my head. I'm certainly finished with spellcasters, if I can manage it. "At least she gave us a description of the person. Do they sound familiar to you?"

I'd forgiven him for his lie from yesterday, not only because it worked out. Had we gone to another spellcaster, I'd still lack my memories and not know how to retrieve them. But with what I'd discovered about myself, being cautious with me—a member of an opposing force when he's someone important in the Olthion dynasty—showed excellent skills. I'm proud of him, though I haven't gotten the chance to tell him, with Eodez around. Given how he physically responds to a few compliments, I don't think he would have enjoyed it in her presence.

"No," he says, sounding glum.

"We'll figure it out," I tell him. Callum just looks at me, his eyes downcast. "Do you want to carry the map?" I offer, hoping to cheer him.

"No."

With no other ideas—not without that bed—I leave him to his thoughts as we amble onward. As we make our way towards where I woke up, the crisp morning air fills our lungs. We take a different route down the mountain than we took up, better for Callum not to meet Oisin's crew again. Although I didn't mind seeing him wielding his sword. It was a good look for him. By the time I regain my memory, he really *might* have the confidence to meet those high expectations Allanagh mentioned.

After walking in silence for too long, I finally break it, asking, "Do you think we'll need to find a resting place today?"

When he answers, his tone is filled with gloom. "Not likely. With your help in keeping us on course, we circled back, so we should only have a few hours until we descend the mountain and reach the nearby border forest where you said you were found. You could have your answer this evening."

I'm cheered by the prospect, but Callum isn't. He refocuses on the walk, his eyes not straying to me. The path is rockier than the other, and the descent proves challenging. Watching him tiptoe over the uneven terrain, I purse my lips in memory of what happened after he'd fallen days ago.

"Are you laughing at me?" His voice comes out in a huff and I miss the gleam in his smile.

"No, just... admiring the view." He turns and scowls at me, and the laugh pulls from me without my will. "I mean it. I keep hoping we'll turn a corner and find an inn."

Now it's his turn to hold in a smile. "It's a mountain. There are no inns."

"Pity. We *could* have borrowed Eodez's sleeping pallet."

He snorts. "It would likely be spelled to spy on us." He tiptoes another few steps forward, before asking hesitantly, "You really want to... *engage* with me physically?"

Again, his eyes appear distrustful and sad and I try to fluster the emotions away. "I haven't exactly been subtle about wanting you, Callum." My second favorite color emerges:

the blush on his cheeks, and I continue, "I mean, have you seen you?"

"The near-death experience part was my guess," he mutters, concealing his face as he rakes his hand through his hair.

I tilt my head in thought. "Would we consider being with Eodez as a near-death experience? I guess we could have died of irritation. Although you seemed to enjoy that shroud-"

"Not her," Callum says. "With Oisin's gang."

I look at him slyly. "Are you telling me you got all riled up after that?" The blush returns to his cheeks and I stop, fisting my hands on my hips. "And we went straight to Eodez instead of taking a detour?"

He doesn't stop, straying forward as he asks wryly, "Would you have wanted to wait to get your answers?"

"Knowing what they are now? Yes. And the sleeping pallet was a big reason why I stopped with Oisin." He stumbles, turning back to look at me in wonder. "But you're right," I continue. "I wanted to finish this."

The fleeting look of confidence and happiness that I had drawn out of him vanishes, plunging us back into silence. I can only guess *he's* unhappy about returning home so soon, knowing the little I know about his family and background. Once my memory returns, he will achieve his goal and retreat into hiding, unless I've helped him after all.

As I glance sideways, my eyes lock onto him, unable to look away. *Must he remain in Olthion when my memory returns?* I'd been teasing him earlier, but why not? Lumadh could always use another advisor. Maybe Tierney could do with another friend, better than the snarky spy. Assuming the 'General' or another of her ilk didn't betray and attack me. And in that case, I'd have two advisors helping me plan revenge.

We continue downward, the silence only broken by the distant echoes of wind and the crunch of our boots on the loose packed dirt. As the path curves around a blind corner, I feel eyes on my neck, an instinct I know kept me alive through countless battles. My hands go to my daggers as I scan the shadows that cling to the landscape. I strain my hearing for some interloper, but there's nothing.

The feeling intensifies, and a guttural growl echoes through the still air. I halt; Callum stumbles to a stop beside me. He clumsily withdraws his sword and holds it aloft while I slip the daggers from their holsters.

From a copse of trees emerges a massive figure, a predator of mystical proportions: the Oros.

It stands on two legs, towering over us at twice our size. Its fur is a mesmerizing blend of deep blues and purples, reminiscent of the twilight sky just after sunset. The creature has two sets of eyes - one perched atop its head-like protrusion from its neck, with irises matching its fur, and another near the top of its chest - narrow and white, focused intently on us. With teeth bared and muscles tensed, it sniffs the air and creeps forward on its three-toed feet, leaving deep imprints in the ground.

"Good Gods," Callum whispers, pressing me closer to him. "We aren't their usual prey. Perhaps it will wander away and leave us alone."

"It likely depends on how bountiful its food is this winter," I whisper back. My eyes narrow on the creature, which seems agitated, its gaze fixed on me. I lift the daggers. "Brace yourself."

Callum angles the sword closer to the beast as we stand our ground. At our movement, the Oros charges, lumbering forward. Its body is too large for it to move quickly, and we both easily sidestep the attack. I slash at its flank, but the fur seems impervious to the blades. Callum thrusts his sword too, but it bounces harmlessly off its hide. It becomes a chaotic dance, the Oros stalks forward, we leap from its path and try to halt its advance. Each strike is ineffective against its enchanted hide.

"We should run," Callum says, breath heaving from exertion as the Oros spins to pursue us again. "There's no reason to keep defending when we can outpace it easily."

We *could* outrun it, but it might follow and we lead it to an innocent. Callum's eyes flutter in surprise when I explain that and he says, "Well, we can't harm it enough to kill it."

My mind works furiously to understand its motivation. *Why had it pursued us?* Callum was right, we're not its normal prey. Even in a *dreadful* winter, there are nearby bogles available. As Callum slices to the left while I defend from the right, realization strikes me. It isn't attacking indiscriminately, but is solely focused on me.

Callum must come to the same conclusion because he drops to his knees and frantically searches through our bags, searching for our stash of healing potions. The Oros continues its slow advance towards me, snarling and growling with each step.

"It's your scent," he shouts over the growls of the Oros. "Remember what Grasshopper said?"

I do, and I know what he'll suggest. But all that waste isn't worth it. "Those are precious," I shout back. "We can't lose potions that way."

"Allanagh can make more!" Callum sounds near hysterical as the Oros takes a slow swipe at me. "You're more precious than potions, Enna!"

Inappropriately timed attraction bubbles in my stomach, but I force it down, sheathing my sword and racing towards Callum. The Oros follows, but not fast enough. We pour our stash of healing potions over my head, the scent of herbs and magic filling the air. The Oros falters, its misshapen head cocking before shaking it vigorously and charging forward with a snarl. My nose is assaulted with the scents of lavender, lanolin, rosemary, mint, sage, and cinnamon, but it's not enough. There must still be some essence of Oros on me. I stifle a sneeze as it continues its relentless pursuit. *Running may be our best bet after all.* As I turn to shout directions to Callum, his gaze darts frantically over me. With an inhaled gasp, he rips my leather armor from my chest, tossing it to the side. In the same motion, he tears his shirt over his head and wraps it around my naked torso.

Like a wind-up toy losing its momentum, the Oros abruptly comes to a stop. One set of eyes watches me while the other seeks my discarded tunic. It drifts to the tunic, sniffing it and growling low in its throat. It turns back to me, its gaze a mixture of curiosity and recognition. Quickly, I unlace the pants and toss them toward the shirt. One leg lands on the Oros' enormous foot and all four eyes blink in surprise.

As if we planned it, as soon as the Oros returns to sniffing my abandoned leathers, we both start walking backward, making a careful retreat. The Oros grabs my leathers with its three fingered claws and drags them towards its face. We disappear into the trees just as it releases a desolate crooning cry.

Chapter 16

When we've thoroughly lost the Oros in the forest, and would likely be lost ourselves if not for Enna's talents, I drop the bags and search for something to clean her off. The healing potions cling to her skin, some oily and greasy, others thick and lumpy. My shirt sticks to her body where it touched the tacky potions.

"It shouldn't chase us," she says, rubbing at her skin. "Not with its focus shifted to the scent on my clothes. And there's little danger it will search for another person in our place."

I gather what I need while thinking about what her behavior has revealed. She could have died, rather than lead the Oros to another potential victim or squander potions. *Where is that barbarism her people are known for?* As I pass her one of Allanagh's dresses and withdraw a fresh shirt for myself, a frown forms on my face.

Without warning, she sinks to her knees, her hands gripping her head in distress. I fall to kneel beside her. "What's wrong?" My mind catalogs all the potions I dumped on her. None of them should counteract with each other. With a cloth retrieved from the knapsack, I gently wipe away the potions from her face. She blinks rapidly, eyes bloodshot.

"I'm fine, I'm fine," she says, shaking her head, letting flecks of wet ointment speckle my skin. She lolls her head back to look at me, pursing her lips.

"Are you sure?" I run my hands over her tacky hair. "Did the Oros get you?" If she hurt herself with that self-sacrificing behavior, when my time with her will already be limited, after I forced off her shirt—

"No. Never even touched me."

I clutch her close. "Thank the Gods. My nerves were on edge. I'd hoped removing your clothes would help when the potions didn't. There'd have been no forgiving myself if all I'd done was make you more vulnerable."

"It was clever," she says. There's that word again and I fight down the reaction hearing it in her voice has on my body. "It must have been its own dye that mar—that covered me."

"Or of a potential mate. The scent of a compatible beast," I suggest.

She peers down at her sticky hands. "There's a lake just around those trees. I should clean off."

"Is that the one *Brendan* mentioned?" I can't keep the irritation from my voice at his name. "Cathal and her pixy-monster partner spent a few hours wading there yesterday. I would rather not run into them again."

"They aren't there," Enna confirms. "It's empty for now."

"I'm not sure..." I believe she's right, but, "What if the Oros returns?"

She furrows her brow, her eyes locked onto mine, as if I am a riddle she must solve. Odd, since she's the surprising one. One hand clutches the necklace I gave her, fingers trailing over the fox's jeweled eyes. I suppress the surge of pride and desire that bubbles up within me, knowing that I gave her something she likes.

Her lips break into a tender smile, and I hope I've put it there. "Then we'd better make sure I'm extra clean."

With a hop, she springs to her feet and dashes into the forest, her nimble movement evidence that she is as fine as she claimed. I stumble after her, the branches scratching against my skin, until we find a small crystalline lake shimmering in the sunlight. Pine trees hug the shore and a rocky outcrop decorates the edge, trailing into the mountain range we're soon leaving behind.

Enna drags my shirt from her shoulders, the dappled sunlight making patterns on her body. Her amber eyes gleam as she tosses her hair over her shoulders. She looks like a nymph from the old stories, one that will enchant me into the water. *Temptress*, my mind supplies. One I can't resist. I almost expect to see a dark-furred kelpie at her side, her wild accomplice to lure men to their tragic watery deaths.

She looks back at me, her eyes crinkling with a smile. "No complaints about *me* being naked anymore, right?"

"No," I whisper. I feel like if I speak too loud, the illusion before me will shatter, and she'll disappear like a mythical thing, leaving me alone with only my imagination.

"Because it's my body and I can share it with whomever I please, no matter who they are," she says, brows high on her forehead.

"Of course," I respond quietly. *And I am blessed you're sharing it with me now.*

She lets the shirt fall and walks into the lake, her feet dragging through the low water. "Come with me," she says, holding out her hand when her body is half submerged. Her skin, like smooth caramel, beckons me towards her, and I can do nothing but obey.

I unlace my pants, kicking them and my boots off. My skin flushes at the realization that this is the first time she's seeing my nude form. Enna's eyes widen and her gaze follows the length of my body, starting from my hair and ending at my toes. My cock hardens at her perusal and I shuffle into the water myself, hissing at the cool temperature.

She meets me in the water, pressing up against my chest and wrapping her wet arms around my neck. Her head reaches to my chin, and she leans back to look up at me. "So *accommodating*. No problem getting naked *with* me?"

I rest my hands on her hips. "No." Although this is my first time baring myself to another, it feels right.

"You know I don't give a damn who you are," she says, leaning into my collarbones. My heart stutters as her breasts press into my chest. I hope she thinks the erratic pace is because of her body and not the truth. "And there's no reason I *should* care who you are, right?"

"No..." The word is more hesitant than I'd wish.

"And you know me," she says, rubbing her slightly sticky cheeks against my bare chest. I tense and attempt to move her away, but she keeps a firm grip on me. "I'm not an idiot. You reaction was odd when I arrived, when you figured out who I was. Finding a stranger in your home wouldn't have you behave that way. *Unless* you knew me."

I tiptoe around the truth without outright lying; no need to add to my sins when she regains her memory and I must account for them. "I didn't know you... personally."

She stares into my eyes, her caramel ones guileless. "But you knew... of me?"

"Something like that." How can I explain who we are to each other and who we aren't? Eodez's words when we left were branded on me: that I'll return to her alone, that I'm always alone. Which means when Enna discovers who she is, and who I am, something will force us apart. Likely my lies of omission. Or Enna's feelings, that I'm one in a long number of her near-death conquests. Nothing special, just a lark while we recover her memories.

She hums and rests against me. Never more than now have I wished for Allanagh's mind reading powers. To know what she's thinking and what it will mean for me.

"Is that why you were sad today?" Her mouth brushes against my skin with each word spoken. "Because you're afraid our identities are incompatible?"

My eyes fall shut, blocking out the idyllic setting. "Something like that."

"Will you tell me who *you* are?"

"No, not... yet." *Not until I must.*

"I see."

My eyes pop open to find her gazing up at me, a frown etched on her face before her arms reach for my neck. Wrapping her arms around me, she pulls my face towards hers. But instead of my anticipated kiss, she dunks me under the water.

I come up sputtering, and she's danced another few feet away, edging towards the shore.

"You needed to get clean," she says, a teasing grin pulling at her lips. In the shallower water, her body is partially submerged, exposed up to her mid thighs.

Swallowing hard, I inch closer to the shore, unable to tear my eyes from her. "I'm not the sticky one."

She raises her brow and looks pointedly at my pelvis, my cock bobbing in the air. "Really?"

A flush of warmth spreads across my cheeks as her lips curve into a wicked grin. Her hips sway as she glides through the water until we're chest to chest again. Without warning, she leaps upward, her legs wrapping around my hips and arms winding around my back. My hands cup her thighs to keep her aloft.

"You're so strong," she says, her voice a soft coo. My cock throbs against her and her hooded gaze drags over my face. "It doesn't matter who I am, does it?"

My mouth dry, I can only shake my head.

She hesitates, a flicker of something crossing her features. "Let me relax here for a bit, while you dry off on that flat area over there," she says finally, curling one hand around the nape of my neck, and gesturing to a hidden spot near a group of trees with the other. "I want to get clean and then I want you to take me home."

"To—"

"To your home, Callum. To your bed."

I lick my lips, struggling to find my voice against what she's just implied. It takes two failed attempts before the words finally break free. "What about recovering your memory?"

Her focus strays towards the trees behind us and I want to kick myself for not taking the chance while I had it. But then, she says quietly, "It can wait."

Enna

After Callum disappears from view, I silently stalk to the shore and into the trees, in search of the black blur I glimpsed from the lake. The black blur that could only be the aggravating stalker, the wraith clad in black armor, and my Lumadhan spy.

Niall emerges from behind a tree before squawking and spinning away from me. "Godsdamn it, put some clothes on."

I strike his shoulder until he is forced to turn around to stop me. He tilts his head to the sky to avoid looking at me, two red spots appearing on his pale cheeks. Rolling my eyes, I say, "Don't ignore me, Niall. You've seen worse at the training camps."

His eyes remain on the sky. "Doesn't mean I *want* to see it."

Remembering what I'd told Callum in the cave, I stomp back to the shore with a scowl on my face. He's still hidden around the grove of trees, but I can't waste time with Niall's attitude. With my memory returned after the confrontation with the Oros, I know now that I return to Lumadh immediately and can't delay much longer. I've run out of time, but can't leave Callum yet. *Tonight, I'll return tonight.*

Grumbling, I tug on Allanagh's dress, frustration growing with each step. Niall is leaning against a tree when I return. "Can Callum hear us?" I ask.

Niall's jaw tightens, a flicker of annoyance crossing his sharp features. "Likely. So mind you don't shout at me."

"Cast something," I demand, crossing my arms over my chest, the fabric of Allanagh's dress tight against it.

He glares at me, but complies, dropping to his knees to withdraw two handkerchiefs from his boots. "I can't stop him from hearing us, but I can keep us from being heard." He places it over his head, the cloth falling over his face, and holds out the other.

"No, something else." I suppress a shiver at the memory of being shoved under Eodez's 'shroud of silence.' "I refuse to put that on my head."

He yanks the cloth from his head, his teeth clenched, and rips two pieces from it. After shoving one piece under his tongue, he hands me the other with raised brows, as if he's daring me to protest again. Wincing, I shove it in my mouth, the cloth tasting like sweat and spice. *Fucking spellcasters.*

My voice is only slightly garbled when I ask, "Did you do this to me?"

"Give you amnesia?" He wrinkles his hawk-like nose. "No. Tier wouldn't forgive me."

I hadn't truly suspected him, no matter he could fit Eodez's description too. But better to check him off my list. Now there's only Mouric left, and another reason I must return to Lumadh immediately. I silently curse and envision all the sucking up I'll be forced to do for Cat and Tier. I should never have promised them I'd do it Cat's way. My irritation narrows to Niall, the only person available for my ire.

"You could have told me who I was days ago," I spit. Not that I'd minded the time with Callum, but Niall doesn't need to know that. "Instead of letting me run around trying to regain my memory."

He takes a step closer, his voice low but unwavering. "Let you? No one *lets* you do anything. You decide, and then you do it. Damn the consequences." His dark eyes trail down my body. "And look at the consequences."

A tense silence settles between us, broken only by the gentle lapping of water against the lake shore, before I finally release a weary sigh. He's not truly the focus of my annoyance. That should remain where it belongs: on Mouric, on Elric, on the damned war. "Fuck off, Niall."

"Isn't Callum supposed to be doing that?"

I bare my teeth at him. "As soon as I can get you from my sight. Have you learned anything during your time here or were you having too much fun following me and Callum?" I'd sent him on an intelligence gathering mission a week before my meeting with Mouric. Although we didn't know if there were mind readers in Olthion, his mind is immune. That and his status as a spellcaster *should* make him the perfect spy, but sometimes I remain unconvinced. Like his decision to abandon his mission to watch me.

His jaw clenches. "I learned both brothers are equally dimwitted and eager to please. You'll have to do a comparison when you inevitably fuck this one."

And still an asshole. I tease at the cloth in my mouth with my tongue to avoid shouting at him. "Did you discover anything *useful*? Like about the sword?"

He makes a show of inspecting his fingernails, displaying his long-fingered hands. "Let's see. You'll find it unimportant but Callum tried to get Rian and Elric aligned against Lumindar, in hopes Mouric couldn't handle an attack from two angles. Rian agreed to a temporary ceasefire to refocus on us, but he's been sending in spies to disrupt Elric's army. Betrayal truly is all they know."

The man who started the brawl at the pub, a Naithair to expel Olthion soldiers, crosses my mind. "It's a game," I say, echoing Oisin.

Niall blinks. "That's all war is. The players moving their pieces."

And it isn't working. I furrow my brows, my mind latching onto something he said. "Why did you say I'd find it unimportant?"

"Because it's a game to you too, just a different kind," he says mildly, as though he hasn't just punched me in the gut. "There are countless ways to use that information, but you won't, not unless you're there to single-handedly guide the process."

"What are you suggesting? Of course I need to guide it, I'm the General."

He frowns down at me. "But you don't have to do everything yourself. You have no confidence in any of us to act without your permission. You refused to allow anyone to accompany you to meet with Mouric. You completely disregarded Catriona's ideas before the summer meeting with Elric. Gods, you only agreed to let me spy because Tier convinced you. Even then, I assumed you were in Olthion to monitor me. Again."

Although I know he speaks out of genuine concern for our cause, his audacity grates. I ignore his complaint about my following him before. It wasn't a lack of trust in his abilities, but a need for oversight. *Clearly still necessary given where he is now.*

"Tierney's my advisor," I protest. "I didn't select you as a spy until she proposed it, because that's what I'm supposed to do. Listen to my advisors."

"You did it out of *love* for your sister because she… cares for me." He stumbles over the words before rallying and continuing. "Not out of trust for your advisor. Or me as your spy. Even now, without true authority over anyone, you've assumed control and made all decisions. You decided where to stop, you decided to join those deserters."

"Callum has no survival skills. I took charge for our safety," I snap, although I don't know why I'm arguing with Niall. A good spy he may be, but we've never gotten along. I should have dismissed him and gone back to Callum for the few hours I have left.

He sneers, a heat in his eyes. "Can you really say you'd have done anything differently if I'd been out here instead?"

I wouldn't have made out with you, I think mutinously.

He shakes his head. "You and Elric truly are similar. At least he doesn't pretend to offer a choice."

"You forget yourself, Niall." I poke him hard in the chest. "I am your commanding officer. I may play friends, but you would do well to remember my status."

As Niall washes his face of expression, his eyes meet mine in a tight nod, and I feel the anger in me fade away.

"I have great respect for you, Niall. You've been a good spellcaster these five years, ever since Tierney suggested you. My love for my sister does not override my duties to the kingdom: I wouldn't have selected you had I not believed you were right for the job. I wouldn't allow you to go into enemy territory unless I trusted you would do well for Lumadh. And my love for my sister does not override your duties to me, and insubordination is not acceptable."

"I… understand," he breathes.

"We're on the same side, Niall. We all want the war to end. My plans to do so haven't changed with the loss of my memories." I crane my neck towards the group of trees hiding Callum from sight before turning back to him. "But back to why I sent you here, what did you find out about the sword?"

Niall regains a little of his confidence, smirking. From behind his back, he pulls out a small burlap sack and tosses it to me.

I catch it easily, but it feels... off, like it holds something too large for the sack's size. Sticking my hand inside the small opening, I touch cool metal and withdraw a silver-etched sword, the length of my wingspan, with a gleaming blade. "This is...*the* sword?"

Niall's smirk widens. And damn him, but the smugness in his expression is deserved as he says, "This is the sword."

Elric's supposedly unbeatable sword. One that if he personally draws in battle means his army won't lose. It's only been luck that he hasn't entered battle himself for the last few years. Our intel said he too feared that his sword might be taken from him. Instead, he let his men fight, leaving the outcome of the battle up to fate. Fate, thus far, was on our side. But things can change in a heartbeat, my own fate is evidence of that.

"Now, I just need to draw *him* into battle and take him down," I say, thinking aloud. I quickly shove the sword into the sack and hand it back to Niall. "We'll be leaving tonight. You will meet us in the woods to the north of Callum's cabin."

"Us?"

I remove the sodden cloth from my mouth and let it fall to the forest floor with a wet plop and smile tightly. "I'm bringing Callum with me. Find something to occupy yourself with until then."

Chapter 17

I let out a frustrated sigh as I watch Niall's retreating figure. Niall wasn't the first to take issue with my leadership style. Cat had done so right before I left, too. But returning with Callum will prove that the negatives of my meeting with Mouric are outweighed by the positives. We'll have two new weapons in our arsenal, the sword and one who intimately understands the Netherin mindset.

The sound of low splashing draws my attention, and I turn to see Callum trudging through the low water, still nude.

"Ready to go?" he asks, somewhat shy. Water speckles over his chest, and his long black hair clings to his shoulders. His cock twitches at my perusal and I release a smirk.

"Absolutely."

We go straight to his cabin from the lake, something that should take a full day but we both nearly sprint there. As we travel back, a palpable sense of anticipation hangs in the air. He keeps looking at me with bitten lips. I want to bite them myself.

Sooner than I expect, we're back at the clearing that opened into his house. In the fading afternoon light, a fire's glow can be seen through the windows.

Callum answers my unasked question. "No one is here. A spellcaster spelled the fire to remain lit for me during winters."

He jogs ahead, boots crunching on the packed gravel leading to the cabin, and opens the door for me.

I pass him in the threshold, letting one hand drag over his taut clothed stomach. "I thought you kept it unlocked because of the wards?"

He grins down at me, boyish charm on display. "I thought opening the door might be gentlemanly of me."

"You've got it all," I tell him once he's closed the door behind us. The sadness that branded him after we left Eodez's is gone and I want to keep it that way. "You're handsome, clever, kindhearted, brave, *accommodating*."

He marches towards the fire room. "Only to you."

"I'm sure that's not true." But I'm not in the mood to talk about his background. I follow him down the hall. "I like that word. *Accommodating*. Do you?"

Adding another log to the fire, he turns to me, appearing as a dark silhouette against the flames. "I... I... yes."

"You are a *clever* one, so you can tell me." As he shivers at the compliment, I stalk forward and untuck his shirt so I can run my hands over the stomach I'd been admiring earlier in the lake. "Doesn't accommodating also mean generous?"

He swallows and helps me pull off his shirt, the fabric slipping through our conjoined fingers to fall on the floor. When he's bared to the room, he wets his lips. "Yes."

"Which you've been. Generous, that is." I run my fingers over his bare shoulders, feeling the wiry power there. The memory of his strength at the lake lingers. "And helpful. That's also part of it, yes?"

"Yes." His voice is a sibilant hiss.

"And you've been *so* helpful." His cheeks flush and I drag my fingers up to his face, cupping it in my cool hands. "What about *obliging*? That's part of accommodating. And I like that word *much* more."

He nuzzles into my hand, like he can't help it. "Oh?"

My fingers gently trace back over his shoulders, exerting soft pressure as I guide him down onto his knees. "Will you oblige me, Callum?"

Kneeling there, he looks like a supplicant for the Gods of old. He nods, his mouth open. "Whatever you want."

"I want to fuck you, Callum of Olthion." With a firm grip on his hair, I delicately tilt his head back, exposing his vulnerable throat. "Will you finally let me?"

"Yes," he says hoarsely.

I push him onto his back and falls willingly. "Pants off," I demand.

He complies quickly, flinging them towards his discarded shirt. I straddle his waist, Allanagh's dress sliding upward until it catches on my bent thighs, and his cock presses against my still-covered core. He groans, his hands grasping onto my hips. I rake my fingernails over his chest and he throws his head back. As his fingers drop to my thighs, I marvel at how much these simple touches affect him.

I brush over his lips in a series of feather-light kisses, threading my hands through his hair. A deep, primal moan escapes his throat as he thrusts upward, and I echo him. Emboldened, he plants kisses down my throat and trails them over my collarbones until the barrier of my dress halts his lips.

I undo the buttons on my borrowed dress, and it pools around my waist. With a raised brow, his darkened eyes search mine. I guide his hands to my breasts, a mirror to our time in the cave. But this time, he's not idle. His hands trace my curves, fingers pinching at my nipples, nails dragging over my back. I writhe atop him and he thrusts again, his cock slipping against the wetness dripping onto my borrowed dress. Groaning in frustration, I hike my leg off him.

The hand that had cupped my ass squeezes tight. "No," he whines.

I lean down to kiss him again. "I need to take off the dress."

"I don't mind it." He sits up, hooking his large hands around my back and forcing me to remain on his lap. "If it keeps you on top of me."

"It's Allanagh's, remember?"

He mock gags, and immediately releases me. "Good Gods, yes, take it off then."

Loose now, I jerk away from him, yanking the dress past my hips and down towards my feet with frustrated hands, kicking it off somewhere. When I'm finally just as bare as he is, wearing only the necklace he gave me, I swing back over his hap, straddling him. His cock nestles up against my slick cunt. We moan in unison at the pleasurable heat.

"Are you ready?" My voice wavers. I think I want this as much, or more, than he does, sex with this complicated and overlooked man. The second son to a monstrous father, the forgotten shadow to his militaristic brother, talked about in hushed whispers on the field as the disgrace of Olthion. The man who just wants to prove himself, even if it means proving he's valuable to the woman who plans on overthrowing his father.

He shudders against me. "For you? For anything," he says, his eyes shining. I can only hope he still feels that way when I demand he betray his country.

———◆———

Callum

She slides her hand between us, grasping my cock, and I hiss a breath as she lifts and angles it towards her. She sinks down and we groan as I finally fill her.

I press my face against her collarbone, kissing the heated skin as I draw my hands over her ribcage and around to her back. We breathe in together as she rests against me, letting me be within her. Her touch is gentle as her fingers trace a path across my shoulders, while her lips meet mine in a tender kiss. My fingers glide along her back, feeling the ridge of each vertebrae before finally reaching the nape of her neck and tangling in her soft hair. The contours of her body mold perfectly with mine. Our bodies remain connected, softly and delicately entwined.

And then it changes, like a slow-burning fire that finally lights and sets the forest ablaze.

She rises, teasingly slow, until she has taken only the tip of my cock, and then she slams down. My hands fall to her hips, not controlling her movements, just wanting to feel them. She makes little noises that sear into my mind, ones I know I'll return to when she leaves, the gasps and moans drawn from her body. Gasps and moans I'm drawing from her body.

"You feel so good," she says. *You too*, I think, almost deliriously.

"So good at helping me...obliging me...fucking me."

My skin feels feverishly hot as she gains friction, and that pulsating hunger, that demand for power, for submission, gets needier, gets stronger. With each thrust, she rises just enough to taunt me before crashing back down. The swing of the fox pendant when it hits my chest is the only place on my body not an inferno of her heat, her touch. My breath turns shaky; I feel like I could burst from my body. I bury my face into her neck, pressing my lips against the sharp edge of her collarbone. Her lips gently brush against my hair, a tender contrast to the harsh motion of her hips.

Then she claws at my back, dragging her fingernails up over my shoulders until she can pull my face up to her. The look in her eyes should scorch me and I wonder if she will, if she'll take those hands and claw me open and let the fire consume me.

But she doesn't. She brushes her lips against mine, slipping her tongue into my mouth. And that's even better. There's no pain, only pleasure. Only Enna. It's the only thing I'll ever need.

One hand snakes between us as she begins touching herself. Her *clit* and suddenly I'm remembering my face between her legs, the heat and chaos I'd felt as her scent almost suffocated me. I rise to meet her, arching into her writhing hips.

"Will...you...come?" she asks between thrusts. "Will...you...come...for me?"

The idea of doing it at her command fills me with an unhinged arousal I've never felt before. It's too much. Her scent clings to my every breath, the feel of her body will be imprinted on my skin.

She moans my name.

And it ends me.

Light bursts around me as she thrashes atop my cock. My teeth sink into her shoulder as I come, filling her and shuddering at the thought of my seed within her body. She moans, low and loud, a symphony of sound I will never forget.

My cock softens within her cunt and she slumps atop me. I look at her above me, face flush and smiling as though nothing else in the world matters.

Even though I know it can't last.

***

Enna

The fire is warm against my back, and Callum a furnace by my side as I curl into him, tracing shapes over his stomach. I inhale deeply, savoring the musky smell of him, and close my eyes. Now that we've both gotten what we wanted, I need to reveal that I remember everything now and ask him to join me. I owe him that.

Since he already knew who I was, confirming my identity *shouldn't* make any difference. But he doesn't know my plans for his people, the plans I put on hold when Mouric drew blood against Lumadh, the plans to put in place now that I have the sword. I trail my gaze over the sharp planes of Callum's face, illuminated by the fire. I wonder absently if he'll deny me. If he'll decide who he is and who I am are incompatible.

"We should get to that spot, the one where you woke up," he says, unwrapping me and crossing his arms around his chest protectively. I crane my neck to see him gazing upward, a blank expression on his face.

"We don't need to." I snuggle back into him, but he's like iron beside me, hard and unbreakable. He doesn't move towards me, doesn't shift to take me into his arms; he just stares at the ceiling, impassive.

"We might as well. There's no point in waiting." He crouches to stand, gathering his clothing and slipping on his pants.

"Why the rush?" I sit up. I'm gratified that his eyes stray towards my breasts, no matter how surly he seems.

He crushes his shirt in his hands, wrinkling it. "It's inevitable. You need to discover who you are and get back to your life."

"It's not inevitable."

He drags the shirt over his back. His hair is wild from my pulling on it, his throat marked by my lips and his clothes wrinkled. "Yes, it is. I know it, Eodez knows it. You're not an idiot, meaning you must know it too."

"Eodez? How is she connected to this?" She was irritating, but nothing she said should have pushed him away from me. "Is this about the spellcaster lie? I told you it was fine, and that I understood. It was actually smart to—"

"She knew I'd be alone, that I'm always alone." He claws his fingers through his hair, the strands looking wilder, and starts pacing the room. "You'll get your memory back and then leave, go back to Lumadh and find some other person to warm your bed while you live your life, and I remain here."

I frown. "A fantastical tale, Callum. What's next? I die heroically in battle, the general fighting your bloodthirsty people, while you suffer in silence in the shadow of your brother?"

"Yes!" He stares down at the floor, not catching my hints about my memory's return. "I'm not... worthy, Enna. Everyone knows it," he says miserably. "Everyone we've met since you arrived has done a great job of bringing it up." I remember the taunts from Oisin's friends, the insults from Sid and Garbhan, even Eodez's teasing him about his family and fear. But Callum isn't finished, saying, "You'll regain your memory and figure it out and find someone better. A warrior that can keep up with you."

I heave a breath. "Well, joke's on you," I say, trying and failing to hide the irritation in my voice. "I already got my memory back. And you're still the person I want to spend time with."

He halts, his body freezing. "What?"

The tension between us eases enough that I offer him a small smile. "It returned after the Oros, before we went to the lake." I laugh. "It was a puzzle, like you said. His dye was the dye that marked me and when I confronted him... hello, memories."

"And you didn't tell me before we... did that?"

I toss myself back on the floor. "You didn't tell *me* who you were when I asked at the lake. I figured it didn't matter."

"That's not f—"

"And you knew my identity. And apparently didn't care." I scowl up at him before letting out a gusty breath. "Why are we fighting? You knew who I was and who you were, and chose to fuck me. I know who you are and who I am, and I chose you, too."

"For now," he says in a small voice.

"Not for now. You'll come with me, Callum. To Lumadh. We could use another advisor. Be clever on our behalf, where you'll be… appreciated."

A faint grin unfurls and his green eyes brighten, as if he's imagining what I've proposed, before he stares skeptically at me. "What about whoever did this to you? Don't we still need to address that? Did your memories reveal their identity?"

"No, I know who it was," I admit. Eodez's description, while matching Niall, could only describe Mouric. He was the last person I saw, after all. "And I have plans for him, but would love your—"

"Cally! That delectable healer friend of yours said you'd be here," a deep voice calls from the front door.

Callum's face blanches, and he tosses me Allanagh's dress to cover myself. Restraining an eye roll, I lay it over my reclined body.

"Try to disguise yourself," he hisses. I look around the room and raise my hands in question. Unless he wants me to pretend to be a piece of furniture, there's no camouflaging me here.

The body belonging to the voice stomps towards the fire room from the hall. "Cally? What the fuck, you never do anything. Where are—" The figure stops at the threshold and gawks at the scene.

I inwardly groan as the man is revealed and better tuck the dress around myself. Callum stands in front of me, as if to block the newcomer's view.

"Hello, Darroch," I say from between Callum's legs.

"Enna?" Darroch's mouth drops open unattractively. It's the only part of him that *isn't* attractive right now. His hair, as long as Callum's, is lighter and peppered with the highlights that come from spending time outdoors, the wavy locks wild as though he's been running. He's wearing his traditional armor, the leathers tight against his muscular form. He withdraws his sword before thinking better of it, which is probably one of the few times Darroch has thought before attacking. He gazes at Callum with stormy blue eyes, then leans around him to catch a glimpse of me on the floor.

For all Callum is the 'smart' brother, Darroch isn't a complete idiot either. A bright grin splits his lips and the tip of the sword dips to point at the floor.

"You two know each other?" Callum can't seem to decide where to look: at me, Darroch, or the spot on the ceiling he was memorizing earlier.

While I hold my arms against my chest, the dress slips off slightly, and Darroch's inspection turns into a leer. Callum draws nearer, blocking Darroch's view, prompting me to swiftly don Allanagh's dress.

"We meet on the battlefield every now and again," I explain. Olthion's reliance on pitched battles means we know who we're facing and when. *Usually*, and even then, when Elric betrayed us this summer, my army stayed nearby and we thrashed Olthion's forces due to sheer rage. But I'm tired of battles; it's time for genuine change. *It's why advisors are important*, I remind myself. *Who I listen to, thank you very much, Niall, hence the sword. And it's why Callum would do better there.*

"Oh," Callum says, his brows furrowing.

Darroch leans against his sword, digging the tip into the wood floor. I don't bother restraining the eye roll now. Just like Darroch, to act so idly, damaging the point of his blade and Callum's floor.

"Not just then, Princess," Darroch says, his voice deepening.

Callum hisses, and I know what Darroch will say before the next words spew from his pouty lips.

"Cal, do you remember when I came back from that fact finding mission to the Beinn Ridge in the Foirge Range?" His blue eyes darken mischievously. "and was all scratched up after getting caught in the landslide?"

Dread fills Callum's expression. "I do..."

"Darroch, don't—" I start, but it's too late.

Darroch smirks. "Let's just say not all those scratches were from the fall. They were female made." Callum turns to me, betrayal in his gaze. But Darroch isn't finished. "Made by Enna," he adds smugly.

"We got that, Darroch." My teeth clench as I attempt to explain. "We had to kill time while we were dug out."

Callum rubs a hand over his face. "You knew who I was. You knew it before we... slept together."

My head tilts. I only learned his identity hours earlier, not when we shared a pallet.

I try to tell him that but he interrupts, growling, "When we had sex. Gods, Enna. I thought you said you weren't an idiot. That's a euphemism anyone should get."

I stand then, drawing myself to my full height. Callum still has a full hand span on me, and Darroch taller still. Side by side, the two look more similar than I'd remembered. It must have been Darroch I'd thought was familiar when I'd first seen Callum's painting. "Don't speak to me that way, Callum. I understand you're upset, but you shouldn't be rude about it. It was meaningless, like all the rest of them."

Darroch nods. "Just a full day of mindless, passionate, sex."

"You're not helping, Darroch," I hiss.

"I can't believe you," Callum says softly. He tugs at his hair, grimacing. "I thought..." He trails off, glancing at Darroch before lowering his voice. "But this is just what you do. You meet people, you decide you want them, and you fuck them. The Promiscuous Princess."

The sympathy I'd felt at his self-consciousness rises and falls with his words. I want to reassure him, to abscond with him away from unappreciative Olthion, but the viperlike sting of his insult stays my tongue. "You're right, I do. And I'm not ashamed of it. I've dedicated over ten years to fighting for my people in a war we desperately want to end. Every fucking time I go out there and wonder if I'll live, if my companions will. We have only this life, and with Olthion hoarding the healers out of fucking spite, mine likely won't last very long. So why wouldn't I enjoy myself anytime I get the chance?"

Callum finds his anger. "So you'd do it with Darroch?" Sarcasm drips from his words as he said, "You'll fuck the people who are supposedly at *fault* for your short lifespan? Woe, what a chore, what a sacrifice, to find pleasure with your enemies!"

"In our parents' stupid war. You can't tell me you don't long for its end too, Callum. It's meaningless. We don't even remember what we're fighting about." He bites his lip and I press my point harder, turning to Darroch who watches us with rapt attention. "We're on opposite sides of this, Darroch. We have been since Liam died and I took up his helm. Do you want to murder me right now? Since I'm your enemy?"

He taps his chin in thought, flexing his biceps as he moves them. "You did personally take down eight of my best archers this summer."

"Because you carelessly brought *archers* against my close combat battalion. Poorly trained archers, I might add. After we arrived at what was supposed to be a peace summit but your *father* unilaterally turned it into an unsanctioned pitched battle and then hid back in Liaf!" Mouric and Elric were similar in that way, neither honored the rules. It's why they *both* needed to be dethroned.

"Oh, yeah," Darroch says. He addresses Callum, saying, "It's just war," the same way some people might say 'it's just business' or 'it's just spilled milk.'

"And you willingly spent a week with your so-called enemy," I remind Callum, whose face is steadily flushing. "Hoping to gain information, no doubt. Trying to prove yourself, I'm guessing? Not so pristine there, Callum."

Callum tips his chin up. "But I abandoned that days ago, before we—No. You're not wrong about my wants, and if you'd asked me to go with you to Lumadh this morning, we'd already be across the border."

"Wait, what?" Darroch asks.

A flash of pain skitters across Callum's face. "If you'd told me about Darroch before, if you hadn't decided it wasn't a problem *for* me, damn the consequences."

The argument with Niall flashes through my mind. *No one lets you do anything. You decide, and then you do it. Damn the consequences.*

Callum's eyes shutter. "I can forgive a lot of things, but Darroch?"

Darroch makes an affronted sound that we both ignore.

"Gods, Callum. I can't change the past," I snap. "All I have is the future and I've told you I wanted you. This shouldn't matter. I know you have a validation problem centered around your brother, but *fuck*."

I know the words will hurt as soon as they burst from my lips. But I can't, and won't, take them back.

"Eodez was right. I told you this was inevitable," he says softly. "That something would come between us. I simply didn't expect it to be Darroch. You and Darroch can try to kill each other in the clearing, or fuck each other again. I don't care." And he stalks from the room.

My eyes fall shut. *How did that go so wrong?* He was about to join me in Lumadh, at least I think. *Perhaps I should have told him about having sex with Darroch earlier.* I shake my head. *No, that's not on me. His relationship with his brother is his own... But I* did *make the decision for him.*

"You still in there, En?" Darroch's troubled voice interrupts my internal argument.

I stalk to the hall, scooping up Allanagh's knapsack. The nearly empty bottles of healing potion are still valuable. "Why are you here, Darroch?"

He scratches his head and shrugs. "Actually, Rian and I were going to look for you. See if we could join forces and ransom you back. Our intelligence says Mouric is trying to rally all the Valenthians to him, with some sympathy play. We figured finding you would stop his momentum and then we could exploit the surprise, since you Lumadhans stopped agreeing to pitched battles."

"That's probably one of your smarter ideas." I admit. "Elric approved it?"

"No," he says, rubbing his hand on the back of his neck. "He's still waiting for Lumindar's response to the battle invitation. But Father's all riled up about another skirmish after the autumn lull, so I thought he'd be happy if we succeeded."

Another of Elric's sons who just wants his approval. "Aren't you tired of this? Fight, recover, fight, recover, with no hope of an end?"

Darroch frowns. "I dunno. Father says war is all we have."

"What would you do if you weren't obligated to follow his violent whims?"

He purses his lips and appears to actually be thinking about it. A small sprig of hope takes root. I will still need to deal with Callum at some point, but any ally on the inside can help me stop the bloodshed and still allow me to use the week lost to amnesia for good.

"I've never thought about it. Maybe be a bodyguard." He smiles. "Might be nice to stop someone from hurting a person rather than being in charge of doing it. Now, stay still, En. There must be a rope around here somewhere to tie you up."

I laugh mirthlessly, thinking about the fun Callum and I could have had with that. "That will never happen." Not again. *Fucking Mouric.* "Think about what I asked, and whether there's more you want out of life. See you on the field, Darroch." I slam the front door open and make a break for the trees.

Once I breach the forest, Niall steps out, his signature scowl in place. He raises his brows and makes a show of looking around us.

"Don't start," I tell him. "Let's go home."

Chapter 18

Callum

My face feels cool against the wooden table. Although the shroud of silence over my face isn't comfortable.

"You'll love the tea," Eodez is saying, pouring more into Allanagh's cup.

With a loud sniff, Allanagh takes a long sip from her glass. "It reminds me of... being at my mother's house as a child," she says. "Is that possible?"

"That's what you'll miss the most! That's so sweet," Eodez coos. I stretch my arm forward, trying to snag a cup, but Eodez slaps my hand. "No tea for you. It's embarrassing, Callum. You'll drown yourself in it." Her voice becomes background noise as she delves into the magical properties of the tea, and I cover my ears to escape it.

Enna left a week ago, after I'd thrown her out. Darroch had vanished around the same time, searching for her, no doubt, to fulfill whatever godsforsaken plan Father has in mind now. After wallowing alone, denying Allanagh entry, I'd returned to Eodez. Eodez had taken one look at me and tossed the shroud of silence over my head, saying she hadn't 'wanted to hear about it.' Allanagh arrived not long after, and the two of us have been bunking with Eodez for the past few days.

"This could be as addicting as that hybrid lily tea too," Allanagh says when I refocus on the two. "Callum's been begging me to distill some with my leftover petals, what with the greenhouses somehow incinerated, but I refused."

Yes, she had. The stockpiled tea is all but gone, and only a few healers have a handful of petals left, none of whom would give me any. I'd gone to my best friend to help me, to soothe my wounds, and gotten down on my knees—

"You weren't on your knees. *That's* only for Enna," she says. "And it's unhealthy not to deal with your feelings."

I was *begging* for relief. And she'd denied me, laughing at my pain.

"I didn't laugh at you," she says. I lift my head to stare at her through the gauzy cloth of the shroud until she huffs. "I *maybe* giggled, inappropriately mind, that you finally have the confidence to stand up for yourself and you chose the worst possible time and the worst possible reason. Bad luck, really."

"It wasn't luck," Eodez says, her fingers twisted in a pile of ribbons. "It was sabotage."

I sit up, dislodging the shroud of silence from my head. "What do you mean sabotage?"

Eodez stares at me, craning her neck as if to confirm I'm uncovered, before answering, "Self sabotage, of course. That was the secret I took from you, after all, your fear. You finally found someone who saw you as worthy and you removed her from your life before she could change her mind about you and you feel as though you lose that value. It's the fear in you, just... changed. And here we are, you alone. As I thought."

"You told me I was *going* to be alone," I spit. "You predicted it!" It was her damned words that got my head all flustered at the lake. And then Enna had invited me to Lumadh, and I'd spoiled it by letting vivid images of her and Darroch's entangled bodies overtake my mind.

Eodez blinks at me. "I don't have seer-sight. I'm just good at people. Silly Callum." She turns to Allanagh as my heart pounds. "These Netherins. So hot headed! Did you know they used to be one people with the Valenthians?"

Allanagh takes another sip of tea and holds out her empty hand. Without my usual hesitation, I take it, the contact grounding me.

"Yes," she says, squeezing my fingers. "We learned in school that they were once all united, but then the Valenthians attacked and started this war. I never thought it was the complete story."

"It isn't. The Gods were involved back then. Absolute jerks, if you ask me, and four of them gave a family in each corner of the land a gift that—"

"Eodez!" I snap, crushing Allanagh's hand to keep from reaching out and shaking the spellcaster. "I trusted you, that you knew what you were talking about, that it was inevitable. Don't you have anything else to say?"

"I have lots to say," she says, smiling brightly. "But about what?"

"The... with... about Enna!" For all I know, Darroch found her and the two are kissing or killing each other. Both thoughts make my stomach hurt. No matter the fight, my affection for her still lives. If time travel *was* an option, I'd ignore Eodez and—

"She's a real firecracker," Eodez says. My irritation falters long enough to exchange a confused glance with Allanagh. "Oh, those haven't been invented yet."

"You just said you don't have seer-sig—no. I don't care." I shake my head to dislodge the spinning thoughts that being around Eodez seems to produce.

"He cares too much about what other people think," Allanagh says, ignoring me. "Enna was supposed to be the perfect chance to overcome that, but you saw how *that* went."

"That's not what happened," I mumble. "It was about Darroch." Allanagh stares at me silently until I wilt. "Fine, it was about what Enna thought about me *compared* to Darroch."

"You should work on your self-esteem," Eodez says, nothing I hadn't been told by Allanagh before. "You're an incredibly attractive man, Callum. I mean, if you were eight thousand years older... yes, please."

Even thinking about it makes my stomach uneasy. Allanagh pokes me sharply in the side and I amend my thoughts. It isn't *Eodez*, but the thought of anyone.

"Although I'll deny it if asked again, he really is pretty," Allanagh says, eyeing me up and down. I scowl at her and she continues with a hint of amusement, "Although *this* self-pity panic thing isn't a great look."

"Swordsmanship and battle lust isn't everything," says Eodez.

"If not for the tea, I'm betting more people would agree," Allanagh says. "But its all 'fight, death, glory.' That's why Enna seemed perfect," Allanagh says, nodding. "Someone with no preconceived notions of him and a giving heart."

"Did you know her before her arrival here?" Eodez asks.

"No, but I delved deeper into her mind than she realized. In fact, I overheard her original pla—"

I take two deep breaths to release the rising irritation. "Eodez, please. Can you tell me anything about Enna? Where she went? If... if she's safe?"

"I assume she went home after you threw her out." She cocks her head. "Or Darroch has her."

Dread drains the blood from my face, and I feel ill. I can't even follow her now.

Allanagh pats my hand. "How about we try to find her, just in case?"

"How?" I ask glumly.

"The truthteller."

Behind her, Eodez rolls her eyes. "Fine, but I'm coming too. I want to see if Tait's still as irritating as they were a millennia ago."

⎯⎯◆⎯⎯

Enna

For a long week, Niall and I journey across the countryside, making our way to the Lumadh stronghold. As soon as we breach the town surrounding it, Niall disappears into the crowd, likely looking for Tierney. I was exhausted by his personality, so that was fine by me. He took the sword with him, to hide it from anyone who might be ambitious enough to use it. Also fine by me.

I immediately make my way to my quarters, ready to change out of Allanagh's borrowed clothes, all that I had left after the journey. A half dozen servants greet me as I arrive, all thankful I made it back alive. I hadn't considered how similar my disappearance was to how Liam died. He'd left for a pitched battle in Olthion and never returned. I left for a meeting with Mouric, who they knew murdered a number of our men. The similarities were bound to be made.

As I enter my room, I'm met by the sight of my mother sitting on my bed. She stands, her hands trembling, sweeping me into a tight embrace.

"Gods, Enna," she breathes. "When the servants told me you had been spotted in town, I could scarcely believe it."

I wince at the unconsidered ramifications of my weeks gone, and how worried she must have been. "I'm fine, Mama. I promise. More irritated than anything at the whole ordeal."

She releases me but keeps her hands on my shoulders, holding me at arms length and studying me with an intensity that only mothers possess. Her fingers brush away a loose strand of hair from my forehead. "Now, tell me what happened."

The words pour out of me in a rush as I recount my journey from leaving to meet Mouric to returning with Niall by my side. The only thing I leave out is the physical... and emotional... aspect of my relationship with Callum. He was a side character in the tale, a helpful comrade and not... not who he was.

Mother's face darkens with each detail I share, her grip on my arms tightening. I see the storm brewing behind her eyes, a fierce mix of fury and concern that would send shivers down my spine if she weren't the leader of *my* people. When I finish, there is a moment of heavy silence between us, broken only by the soft crackling of the fireplace.

"Mouric must be dealt with," she finally says, her voice laced with steel. "Too long have I let my brother's son wreak havoc upon our kin. But your discoveries from Olthion are equally troubling. I am not one to condemn another ruler's ways, no matter how much I disagree with Elric's decisions, but the fact that his people feel the need to drug themselves in order to endure their lives, in and out of battle... it cannot be ignored."

I stand and pace in front of the hearth, my racing with plans and strategies I hadn't let myself think of until we were safe in my territory. "I agree. I need to handle both issues swiftly. My... incident could actually work in our favor if I play my cards right, I'm sure of it. We'll overcome Olthion and Lumindar and only have the aggressors from Naithair left." I glance at Mama, knowing she has likely already been informed of Mouric's current state. "Niall's network tells me that Mouric has been subdued for now, that you and Father have prevented him from causing further rebellion so far. And that he is yet unaware of my survival.." A small smirk tugs at the corner of my mouth. "We can use that to our advantage an—"

"Enna," Mama says, her voice cutting through the air like a sharp blade. "Tierney would despise me if I failed to remind you of the promise you made before your disappearance."

I halt mid-stride to stare at her, feeling a mix of guilt and frustration flood through me. "She told you about that?"

"Major Catriona, in fact."

My shoulders slump. "I promised I wouldn't rush off and do the next plan alone. I'm not, Mama, truly. But I still must hold the reins—"

"No, Enna," Mama says, her gaze softening. "There are times when the greatest strength lies in sharing the burden."

My brow furrows. "Certainly. I am not a one-woman army, but without my leadership, we can't stay the course."

"Even the most steadfast of rulers must learn to trust those they lead." She rises from her seat, her movements graceful as she approaches me. "In Lumadh, no monarch stands alone. We have councils, advisors... Generals have lieutenants. It is our way—and it is not weakness to rely on it. Unlike Mouric, whose solitary rule breeds tyranny and unrest. And, as we know better now, Elric and that misbegotten sword."

The words land heavily in my chest and I swallow the lump forming in my throat at the comparison. That damned conversation with Niall runs through my mind. And my last argument with Callum, how I'd told him only what I thought necessary, how he wasn't part of the 'team,' but a piece to move. I thought he'd enjoyed that, but I'd been wrong.

"But," I start, frustrated, "how can we be sure all won't be lost? That without my hand to guide every decision, all that we've built will crumble."

As if sensing my internal struggle, she places her hand on my shoulder. "True leadership is knowing when to take charge and when to let others shine," she says, her voice gentle, but firm. "Your brother Liam... he trusted his comrades, even unto the end."

"Yes, he did. Tierney's got the scar to show for it. And I—"

"Must learn to do the same," Mama finishes.

My fingers brush against the cool metal of the fox necklace concealed beneath my tunic, an involuntary gesture that doesn't escape Mama's notice. Her eyes narrow slightly, a hint of curiosity lighting up her features.

"Enna, what's that you're wearing?" Her tone was casual, but there was an edge of surprise to it.

"It's nothing," I say quickly, trying to hide the pendant with my hand.

Her eyes narrow in suspicion, mirroring my own stubbornness.

"It's... a necklace," I admit reluctantly, my hand stilling over the spot where the necklace lay hidden. "A gift."

"From whom?" The question hangs in the air, expectant and a little intrusive. With the 'free love' mentality of our armed forces, such gifts are uncommon, as there is no favoritism, only bodies for release. Callum's gift has meaning. *Callum* has meaning.

"Callum," I say hesitantly, his name tasting both bitter and sweet on my tongue. "He... he liked my being in charge."

"Is that so?" Mother's tone holds unspoken questions. "Perhaps your desire for control can find a more appropriate outlet now. Your father and I like to play a lovely little game where I tie—"

"Mother!"

She arches a brow. "You and your soldiers flaunt your sexual escapades all throughout the kingdom, but I cannot discuss my loving relationship with—"

"No," I interrupt. "That's different."

Before Mother can say more, Tierney sidles into the room.

"I couldn't help but overhear that you were home," Tierney confesses, her grin infectious.

"Thank the Gods you didn't overhear more," I say under my breath.

Ignoring my quip, she reveals a knitted creation she'd been hiding behind her back. "And I brought you something."

It's an unruly mass of yarn, with colors clashing in ways that nature never intended. The reds and greens seem to fight with the purples and yellows, and yet, somehow *blue* is winning. Protruding arms—or are they legs?—suggest it might be a sweater, but it's unclear whether it's meant for human use or perhaps as a species of monster yet undiscovered.

"What is *this*?" I can't help but laugh at the absurdity of the woolen disaster.

"Your next war council uniform!" Tierney declares with mock solemnity, thrusting the knitwear into my hands. "I made it just for you. I had *plenty* of time to keep busy while you were away."

I swallow the wince this time and hold out the misshapen garment at arm's length. "I'll wear it with pride," I proclaim. "I did promise after all." I let out a sigh. "And I need to keep my promises."

Tierney smiles, slipping to my bed. "Good. Now, I have some ideas about how to approach Mouric."

"Without Enna bursting in alone in the middle of the night," Mother says dryly.

"Not alone, no. But I actually believe a sneak attack is our best option," Tierney counters.

"A surprise ousting," I muse, the idea taking root. "We could do the same with Olthion." My mind spins, expanding on Tierney's proposal and considering different team members who could manage a sneak attack without being detected by Mouric's mind reading skills.

Tierney frowns. "Olthion?"

"Oh, yes. I'll need to catch you up."

"Please give us the unedited version this time," Mother chimes in with a smile. "Including more about this Callum character."

Callum

The path back to the truthteller's cottage is a tangled mess of memories, somehow taking me down the same route I walked with Enna. My heart races in my chest, each beat a reminder of what is at stake as we make our way through the dense forest. I might not have Enna anymore, but I must make sure she's safe, that Rian or Darroch (or, Gods forbid, Father) didn't capture her when I threw her from my house.

"Why *did* you agree to Mouric's demands, Eodez?" Allanagh asks, breaking the tense silence between us, her boots crunching on the fallen leaves.

"The supplies," Eodez responds, her voice tinged with amusement. "I'm basically out of the business but I am a *sucker* for good materials. The feathers and bones and yarn that man brought me! I made some of my most commercially successful work with those." She laughs lightly. "Callum actually bought one of them. The phalange piece with dried berries. Remember it, Callum?"

I swallow any response, focused more on my feet. There's no Enna to heal me if I fall this time. Only Allanagh.

"Yes, yes, how terrible," Allanagh says, but the tone in her voice tells me there's no offense. "Just Allanagh."

"It was all business though," Eodez continues, undeterred by my lacking response. "No hard feelings. Actually, now that I've met you all, I'd definitely turn him down if he asks again." She pauses. "But those feathers were awesome... Okay, I'd *almost* definitely turn him down."

I stay quiet, lost in thought about the possible outcomes of our meeting with the truthteller. As we venture deeper into the forest, a familiar enemy creeps into my vision—creeper vines.

"Wait," I say quietly, halting our trio with an outstretched arm. My gaze scrutinizes the plants and an opening to avoid them.

"This way," I announce. With deft steps, I guide Allanagh and Eodez through the labyrinth of greenery, circumventing the trap that had once almost bested me.

"Callum, you've become quite the woodlander," Allanagh says with a smirk.

"Enna's wisdom runs deep," I say, feeling a small surge of pride.

"Enna isn't here," Eodez reminds me. "That was all you."

Soon, sooner than it should, the truthteller's cottage emerges from the woods. It tells me how slowly Enna traveled for me, given it took us days to make this trip in reverse. I have little time to dwell on it as the honesty enchantment that surrounds their home glides against my skin and I close my eyes, trying to resist its beguiling pull. Eodez scoffs behind me, leaning against a tree.

"What truth do you seek?" The truthteller's voice echoes around us as they appear before us in a swirl of magic. Their black cape no longer seems so mystical in the fading light, more ominous than enchanting.

My hand trembles slightly as I draw forth another gem and offer it to them. Their eyes, twin orbs of fathomless depth, hold mine in an unyielding gaze.

"I seek the whereabouts of Enna," I say.

"Seeker of wisdom, Callum of Olthion," the truthteller muses, cradling the gem between their. "You ask for a location, but the truth you truly yearn for may be something else entirely."

Their words bring to mind their earlier warning, but confirming Enna's location, and necessarily her safety with it, is my greatest desire.

The truthteller's attention turns to the others. "And you, Allanagh of Olthion, listener?"

Allanagh waves a negligent hand. "I'll wait."

"That is the truth. But is not what you seek," the truthteller rasps.

The truthteller doesn't ask Eodez, instead lifting the gem above our heads. My heart quickens as the gem begins to spin, levitating above the truthteller's palm. Threads of light spill forth, weaving an intricate tapestry of possibilities that flicker and dance before my eyes. Beside me, Allanagh gasps at the sight. Then, with the abruptness of a thunderclap, the truthteller's declaration slices through the spectacle.

"Her validation was not the prize for you to claim either, Callum of Olthion. You know where such a prize is truly found."

A jolt of confusion strikes me like a bolt from the heavens. *Validation*? It was Enna that validated me, the first person to see my worth. The truthteller's own words pushed me away from seeking my father's validation and directed me elsewhere—towards Enna. *Did that mean she no longer values me? Have my fears been realized?*

"Callum, no," Allanagh says, sounding pained.

The truthteller begins to vanish, their form dissolving into motes of dust.

"Wait!" I plead. "Please, I must know—"

"Knock it off, Tait," Eodez says, marching up beside me.

The truthteller's—Tait's—form solidifies again, and I swear I can see annoyance flickering across those lamplight eyes. "We thought that was you, Brigantiae."

The relief I feel at their reappearance overpowers my other thoughts, and I can barely muster up the interest in why they're calling Eodez Brigantiae.

"It's Eodez now, *truthteller*," she says. "Callum asked you a question. I did *not* walk all the way here to leave with my boy all sad." She eyes me, expression softening. "Sadder, at least."

"Another gem," Tait bargains with a hiss, "and I shall reveal the location of the one you seek."

Eodez tilts her chin challengingly, the air around her crackling with a silent threat. Her ebony tresses raise with static and she appears to loom over us. I hadn't noticed it before, with her unconventional attitude and the magic she so negligently wields, but there's something unnerving about the juxtaposition of her adolescent frame, clad in a riot of colors, and the newly revealed ancient power that now seems to radiate from her core. *We're lucky she's on our side today*, I realize.

"Will you also be accepting firstborns or promises of undying fealty?" Allanagh snaps, her jest cutting through the tension like a well-aimed arrow. A smirk plays upon her lips, but her wary gaze remains fixed on Tait.

With a reluctant sigh, the truthteller concedes. "Fine. Enna arrived in Lumadh one day prior. She is unharmed, thriving even." A pause, then a hint of something unreadable briefly flashes over Tait's eyes. "And... she steadfastly refuses to part with her fox necklace."

The revelation sends a wave of relief crashing over me. I exchange a glance with Eodez. There's a smug satisfaction pooling in my stomach, knowing that Enna clung to the token I gave her. Eodez looks equally pleased that her creation has become so cherished.

"Is that all, seekers of truth?" Tait sneers, the disdain in their tone a sharp contrast to the serenity of the grove.

But before further words could be exchanged, the truthteller's form fragments into shards of light, scattering into the encroaching darkness. The air around us seems to shimmer and dance with the sudden burst of energy, leaving us all momentarily blind. And then we're back in the forest, Tait's home nowhere in sight.

"I'd forgotten how much they suck," Eodez says, crossing her arms. "What did they end up telling you, Allanagh?"

Allanagh shrugs. "I was too surprised at hearing another voice in my head, an intentional one instead of my reading others' thoughts, to make much sense of it."

"Cally!" The voice, rough and urgent, slices through the twilight hush that settled over us in the wake of Tait's disappearance. Darroch emerges from the thicket like a wild animal, searching for me with an almost desperate intensity.

"Here," I call back, my voice steadier than I feel. The hairs on the back of my neck stand up as his sharp gaze lands on me. "What is it, Darroch?"

"You're needed," he pants, barely pausing to catch his breath. His eyes are alight with purpose. "Father has called for you."

My back straightens instantly at the mention of Father seeking me out. My first thought is that perhaps something has happened with Enna and Father has found her. "I'll go immediately."

But while I am resolving to leave, Darroch suddenly realizes we're not alone. The fire of purpose in his expression changes to something much more... irritating.

"Allanagh," he says with a lecherous grin. "And who might this lovely creature be?"

Eodez regards him with an arched eyebrow, clearly not impressed by his attempt at flirtation. How fitting a primordial spellcaster is likely the first one to find him underwhelming.

"Not now," I snap at Darroch, my patience worn thin simply from his presence. "Let's go."

Chapter 19

Tierney sits beside me, arms crossed around her waist and wearing a lumpy scarf that wraps around her neck a dozen times. "Are you sure this is the best idea?"

"This was your idea, remember?" I tell her. "A sneak attack." And for me to stay in an administrative capacity this time.

Tierney bites the edge of her thumbnail. "Maybe there's a better way. We could just talk to him an—"

I interrupt her, my hand going to the fox necklace I'm still wearing. My own newly knitted eyesore slips from my shoulders with the movement, a knobby knitted cloak that I yank back around me. Tierney had just given it to me that morning. "This is a good idea, Tier. Niall and the others will be unexpected, and have the best chance for success." And just step one in my plan to make things better for all of us.

"I'm not disagreeing," says Cat from her spot on my other side, wearing her own lumpy knitted cowl. "But we are talking about deserters." She tosses her black braid and frowns at the table. "And bringing in a Netherin? We're trying to root out those who are loyal, not add to those who aren't."

I'm quick to stop this conversation before it festers. "Tier, Cat, I get it. I do. But what we've been doing hasn't been working." I sigh, staring down at the table. "What *I've* been doing hasn't been working, which we already know. We can all let go of a little control to remove the agitators and restore our country's stability. The worst that can happen is they say no."

"The worst is they join him," Tier says under her breath. Cat nods.

The beginning of a headache forms and I rub my eyes. "Just send them in, please."

Ever the loyal recruit, even when she disagrees, Catriona slips to the door. As it opens, it reveals Oisin, followed by Brendan and Cathal. Oisin's rapt gaze trips over the room, mouth ajar as his blue eyes brighten. From my review of his records before desertion, he had been a devoted soldier before a member of his training class had been killed when Mouric broke the peace at our summer summit. He'd abandoned soon after, taking Cathal with him.

"No Aoife?" I direct the question at Cat, but it's Cathal who answers.

"She remained behind, General." She bows deep, but stumbles on her leg. Cathal's file reported she took a blade to the leg, and as I suspected, it hadn't healed properly before Oisin sprung her from the medical tent.

"None of that. You're my guests today. Please, join me." I direct them towards the chairs.

Brendan sits in the chair farthest away but still facing the door. His eyes skim over my cloak monstrosity and he sneers. Cathal takes the seat beside Catriona while Oisin slams into the chair next to Tierney. Tierney only comes up to his shoulders while seated, though she's a few inches shorter than me. She cranes her neck to stare up at him, her cheeks pinking. My brows raise at her reaction.

Oisin doesn't notice, staring at me and the room. "Can't believe it. Not just my kin, but my General! I knew it from the fight with Brendan. Never met you, 'course, but I recognized that stance."

"She has a peculiar way of holding herself," Cat says, smirking.

Oisin frowns. "A good way," he says, sounding defensive. "She's a good fighter."

Cat drags a file from the center of the table. "And yet, you deserted." She slides it over to him even as Brendan scoffs.

Oisin doesn't touch the file, dragging his hand over his beard instead. "Felt right at the time." He turns to me, eyes downcast. "Sorry for what I said before I realized, about you not handling your house with that Mouric—"

I interrupt him gently, before he can work himself up more. "No, you were right. And that's why I've asked you here. Our current methods aren't working. I have plans for Mouric *and* the Netherins. You're the few with wisdom on this subject who might share with Lumadh."

Brendan scratches at his arm, exposing the small scar on his bicep where I'd stabbed him with a dagger. "What makes you think we'd want to help you?" Catriona slides a file towards him, but he slams his hand on the table, bringing it to an abrupt halt. "I know what and who I am. Tell me why the fuck I'm here."

Cat bristles beside me, but I cover her hand and squeeze it. Addressing the three of them, I explain, "Because I'm offering you citizenship papers and a spot of land for a home.

Oisin and Cathal, you're welcome to re-enlist, though I'm hoping we'll all remain off duty soon. But whether you do or don't rejoin, you'll be welcomed in Lumadh. You'll have a place here."

"If we do what?" Cathal asks quietly. Hope gleams in her eyes, confirming this was the right idea. I hold back from gloating now, but will do it later after they leave. I could use a 'win.'

"Help me get my house in order," I tell her.

Brendan glares at me. "Do we have to wear those awful yarn things if we agree?"

⊰❖⊱

Callum

Darroch, after spending an excruciatingly long time flirting with Allanagh and Eodez, finally takes me to the castle.

"Is that Eodez courting anyone?" Darroch asks as we step into the hallway closest to Father's throne room.

My head swivels to stare at him, aghast.

He shrugs, saying, "I like them small. Petite."

I'm unable to fathom the unholy union of Eodez and Darroch and I refuse to answer, instead picking up speed and barreling through the door. My father has never once called for me. That familiar knot of dread tightens in my stomach; this summons can only bring bad news.

Unlike the last time I visited him, the room is full of men I recognize as his commanders. Their faces contort into a blend of solemn disappointment and malicious anticipation. I'm accustomed to both, but never at the same time. It's obvious that Darroch didn't expect this either, as he scans the room with a frown more familiar on my face than his.

"Callum" Father says, his voice shattering the uneasy silence. "I am *delighted* that you could join us."

I stand before him, my heart racing, unsure of his intentions. "Father," I say, tipping my head respectfully.

"While you've been gallivanting off with that healer, my men have been preparing to meet Lumindar in battle."

My eyes dart to the commanders, searching for a hint of what he wants from me. "I believe you mentioned your plans when I last came before you. Did Lumindar accept your invitation?"

He grips the wood of his throne with clawed hands, his rings blinding in the light, as he glares menacingly at Darroch. "Woe, they have not. It appears both my sons are a disappointment to Olthion. However, should Darroch locate that bitch of a general, he will have the opportunity to earn my regard."

Darroch winces but I barely notice, my hands fisting at my side.

But Father isn't finished. "Callum, *you* have shown me that your ability to disappoint knows no bounds. I had mistakenly assumed that there was no lower point than not serving your country. But how lucky for Olthion that you finally exceeded our expectations."

I swallow, steeling myself for what may come. "I'm not sure what you mean, Father."

He rises from his throne with an ominous creak of leather and steel. "Private Nolan, come forward."

As the group of commanders parts, Nolan steps forward with a mottled bruise over his left eye and a cut on his lip.

The injuries look fresh, or else a healer would have taken care of them.

Elric snaps his ringed hand, likely the one that battered Nolan. "Please explain to my son what, *exactly*, he's done to earn my ire this day."

Nolan speaks in a monotone voice. "A week prior, I came upon Allanagh with a redheaded woman. She looked familiar, particularly how she handled a knife, and during training that afternoon, when we were doing archery drills, I remembered her. She was the General from—"

"The *bitch* from Lumadh," Father says, his voice filled with fury. "The very woman your brother attempted to find when he went behind my back with Rian. She was *with* you."

I lick dry lips. I could remind him I came to him when she'd appeared in my home, that I'd suggested we mine her for information. But I say nothing.

"Tell us what else you discovered, Private," Father demands.

"She was spotted over the border crossing through Morbach, by the port. Our information states she then—"

"Enough," says Father, holding up a tense hand. Nolan nods deferentially and slips back into the group while Father turns his green eyes back on me. "We lost our opportunity to leverage her against Lumindar. Do you have *anything* to say for yourself?"

"No." My voice is barely above a whisper.

Before I can react, his hand lashes out, the force of blow sending a sharp sting radiating across my face. His sharp insignia ring grazes my cheek, leaving a trail of blood. Just as he raises his hand again to strike the other cheek, something inside me snaps and I grab hold of his wrist in midair. Inhaling deeply, I feel a sense of determination wash over me, and I straighten my back.

"No," I repeat, my tone unwavering despite the familiar tendrils of fear curling around my heart, threatening to choke me. But for once, something burns them to dust. A voice rises within, telling me I'm *valued*, that I'm *good* and *clever* and *worthy*, drawing out the years of self-doubt and insecurity. It starts in Enna's smokey voice before transforming into my own.

Father's eyes widen in disbelief, his hand frozen in my grip. The room hangs suspended in silence, the only sound being the gasping breaths of his shocked commanders. I thrust his hand away from me, sending him stumbling back until he collides with his throne.

"You dare to defy me?" he thunders, his voice echoing off the walls of the chamber.

"I dare to stand up for myself," I reply, the words tumbling from my lips like a stone cast into a still pond, sending ripples of my defiance echoing through the silence of the throne room. "I *refuse* to be treated this way. All I've ever wanted was to make you proud, Father, and I tried—"

"You've never deserved my pride, you mongrel." He stalks forward, hand raised again.

Throwing back my shoulders and tilting my chin down, I loom over him. My height has never intimidated him before, but he must see something in my unyielding expression that makes him falter. I growl out, "I don't give a fuck about your opinions anymore, Father."

He glances at his commanders. "You took it, didn't you?"

I blink at him in surprise, my gaze straying from his fist towards the fear in his expression. "Took what?"

He clenches his raised fist before dropping it to his side. "Get out," he commands. "Leave and do not return."

And for the first time in my life, I leave his throne room feeling proud, a weight lifted from my shoulders, the weight of expectations I no longer need to live up to.

***

Enna

Only a day after meeting Oisin's group, a group of us leave to breach the borders of Lumindar. We make camp an hour outside the squalid town that surrounds his castle at Falias, hiding in a small copse of trees.

Lumindar's coffers, once as prosperous as ours, allowed them to provide for their people just as we did. Despite my efforts to negotiate a merger between our peoples, Mouric refused to relinquish any power. Before my stint of amnesia, I'd coordinated with a new set of advisors, hoping to ease him into a transition where he and Father would rule as regents under a combined Valenthian people, while being guided by those who know better. While the idea had potential, my demand for control was likely my downfall. It was my own arrogance that led me to accept the second meeting instead of changing tactics, instead of bringing forth force, mistakenly believing I had all the answers. Hello, trap, and hello, amnesic-Enna.

I'm not so cocky now.

As the sun sets, we approach the town, stopping in a dingy alley beside the castle gates, empty of patrolling guards. Because of my agreement with Cat and Tierney, I'm taking an administrative role and will act as commander from the rear rather than first at the front lines.

Even if I hadn't agreed to stay out of it, Mouric's limited mind reading skills would keep me from going inside before his capture. Despite my efforts to shield my thoughts, he knew my mind. But he didn't know *Oisin's* group, who could think pleasant thoughts about how they were regular citizens of Lumindar and whose minds wouldn't arouse suspicion. Niall will join them, not to oversee deserters, but because his mind is unreadable. Or, unreadable to *Mouric's* version of mind reading. If things work out and I see Allanagh again, I'll check whether he's immune to her, too.

As the moon hangs low in the sky during early dusk, we prepare for the mission ahead. My team huddles in the shadows, waiting for my final instructions.

"Remember, stay low, stay quiet. Niall, you're the key to slipping past Mouric's mental defenses."

Niall salutes me. Despite the anxiety pulsing through me and how much Niall irritates me on a normal day, his unflappable demeanor brings a sense of calm. I never enjoy sending my people into circumstances that are unknown. As good a plan as I think this is, the risk of failure looms over us. His voice rumbles pleasantly as he says, "Understood."

I heave a sigh. "The rest of you, think benign, bland things about Lumindar or, I don't know, your favorite meal. Mouric doesn't have the skills to read too deeply. Cat, you'll remain outside and only enter when you see the signal." Cat salutes too, and I turn to Oisin's group. "And the signal is?"

Cathal holds up an unlit lantern. "Three flashes in the second window of Mouric's chambers."

Oisin bobs his head in acknowledgement, smiling gleeful-ly, while Brendan remains silent.

"Won't let you down, General," Oisin says.

Oisin, Brendan, Cathal, and Niall pull up the hoods on their long cloaks to shield themselves from the cold, the fabric spelled to conceal their identities, and leave. From the alley, I watch them move in a calculated manner, blending into the shadows and avoiding the sparse patrols of Mouric's oblivious guards as they come to the gates. Niall slithers through the opening like a wraith, disappearing into the castle's dark interior. Soon, he returns and the others slip through the gate, disappearing from my view.

I let out a breath. My skin crawls with the need to run inside and join them. Better yet, attack Mouric myself.

"Brendan's attractive," Cat says, gaze on the castle, and pulling me from my unease.

Green eyes flit through my vision and I frown. "I'm not interested in fucking Brendan. He's... not my type."

Her figure shifts in the dark, and I feel her eyes on me. "I didn't think you *had* a type. Or were you lying those nights we shared a carafe of wine?"

"Don't you need to watch the windows?" I grumble.

She hums knowingly and starts down the alley. Before she turns the corner, she spins back. "By the way, I was mention-ing Brendan for *me*." And she bisects to the north to watch the set of windows attached to Mouric's chambers.

The advisors look at me until I glare at them, and they avert their gazes. We wait in silence while I wear a line in the dirt with my pacing. Soon enough, I hear the jogging feet of someone nearing me. I withdraw my daggers from their holsters, *my* daggers this time, but replace them when Cat's figure rounds the side of the building that hides the alley from sight. She salutes me again, grabs the advisors by the arms, and pulls them away.

The plan called for me to return to the campsite then and I do, moving slowly as I continue glancing back at the castle. Cat entering means Mouric should be restrained, but there's still much to be done before the sun rises and I make my entrance.

As I wait by the dying embers of the fire I started when I returned, time seems to stretch on endlessly. The cold didn't bother me. The bite of it keeps me alert as I try not to imagine all the bad things that could happen without me in that castle.

Brendan returns first, dragging a large bag behind him. The cloak he wore is torn in places.

I eye the bag. "Is that who I think it is?"

He struts to the tree trunk farthest from the fire and eases to a seat against it. "Yes."

"Is he alive?"

"Do you care?" Brendan looks up, revealing a long gash from his nose to his jaw. "We got it done. That's all that matters."

With a bitten off curse, I stalk to my supplies and start heating the dagger I lined with healing powder. "Come here," I call to him.

Unsurprisingly, he doesn't move.

I spin on my heels. "Look, I've been generous with you so far. But if you don't get your ass to the fire, I will pull rank on you and you will not like it."

He frowns, but stands quickly enough. Of course, obedience is ingrained in the Netherins, even those who try to rebel against it. When he's close, I present the blade, and he stands as still as a statue, letting me seal the wound.

"I don't have any healing paste yet, so it will scar." Yet again, I wish for the abundance of healers and healing plants found in Olthion.

He grunts. "That's fine. And yes, by the way."

I burn his congealed blood off the blade and prepare it for another possible wound, leaning back over the fire. "Yes, what?"

"Yes, Mouric is alive. Cat was pretty adamant about it."

With my back to him, he doesn't see my raised brows or the small smile I wear at how he addresses her. I've known Cat for over twenty years, fought with her for twelve, and even I didn't feel comfortable calling her 'Cat' until eight years ago, after I'd already been her commander. When my face is under control, I turn back to him. "Tell me what happened."

Brendan paints a surprisingly vivid picture. They stalked through the castle's labyrinthine passages, avoiding patrols and relying on Niall to remain ahead and confirm Mouric's absence. They arrived at Mouric's chamber, *not* the bedroom I'd remembered when I'd visited Uncle Conroy, but a second throne room, with a tall throne and a bed before it. Mouric was alone in bed, thank the Gods, and Oisin's trio drew their weapons just as Mouric sounded the alarm.

As Brendan tells it, Mouric's hubris was also his downfall. He didn't care for advisors *or* many guards, believing himself too clever to be caught out because of his, in *my* opinion, unremarkable mind reading skills and experience with a sword. Only two guards appeared, leaving them outmatched. Oisin clashed with Mouric, while Brendan and Cathal teamed up against the guards. It was Niall who seized the moment, coming behind Mouric as he and Oisin parried and thrusted. He broke off a wooden post from the bed and, with a calculated strike, smacked Mouric from behind, knocking him unconscious.

When Brendan finishes, he looks up at me from his spot under the trees, the sun rising behind him. "What's your next move?"

"Rebuilding."

He grunts. "It'll take more than a few removals to do that," he said with a hint of skepticism in his voice.

"That's what you think," I tell him, smiling. "Let's go meet *Cat*. I've got some letters to write."

Chapter 20

Callum

The sun dips low over the horizon as we set off towards Lumadh. Towards Enna.

After my father banished me from Liaf, I wasted no time in finding Allanagh and setting off on our journey. Nolan's accusation left her with no other option but to join me, as she might be considered a co-conspirator in my involvement with Enna. And Allanagh wouldn't let me go alone.

"Damn right, I wouldn't," she mutters under her breath. "Last time I left you alone, you fell in love and drove her away."

"I have no plans to do either," I tell her as we venture into the untamed landscape of Lumadh, crossing the border and far away from Father's insidious influence.

"Of course not," she says, blowing a short lock of hair from her face. "You're already in love, and I'm here to keep you from driving her away again."

We cross the border with little fuss, no contingent of barbarians attempting to murder us as we step over the line. The roads are empty of danger too, no roaming bandits or rogues trying to rob us, none of the dangers we've been told exist outside our borders.

It takes a week until we can see the sea from the coast of the Port of Bronntanas. We only survive because of my time with Enna. As a healer, Allanagh has no survival skills either. Even when she's been on duty for some of Father and Darroch's battles, the soldiers provide. We fumble through building a fire from fallen branches, stumble into finding edible vegetation and eggs to supplement what we brought, and somehow fashion a makeshift shelter beneath a canopy of trees. By the eighth night, when we stop for shelter at the edge of a dense forest, the shelter could withstand even the strongest gusts of wind whipping through the trees. If we ever locate Enna, I can't fathom how proud she'll be. I almost shudder in anticipation.

"Disgusting, that's disgusting," Allanagh says after I've finished the shelter. "Since I had to see it, you're taking the first watch."

With an eye roll, I dump our bags beside the shelter and start rummaging through them in search of our evening meal. Our forest locale means we can't create a fire, but I'll gather more berries soon. "It was my *turn* for the first watch." *And don't listen if you don't want to hear it.*

She dips to grab a handful of sodden leaves, tossing them at me. As I dance away from them, she smiles. "I like this Callum. I liked the old one, mind. But this self-assured version of you is an excellent revision."

"I like this me, too." And it isn't simply because of Enna, but she was the impetus. I found someone to value me. And if someone could value me, it meant I must be valuable. It uprooted my entire mindset. I *must* have been wrong to think I had no worth. And Father, and Darroch, and Brogan and Carrin, and everyone else in Olthion were wrong.

"You always were valuable though," says Allanagh, glancing at me as she unrolls a mat.

"But I didn't believe it. Until now."

"I'd spin some tale about how you shouldn't find your self-worth in someone else, but I don't think that's what it is, is it? It's about getting the sense knocked into you and now *you* recognize what the rest of us already saw."

The rest of us is being generous, given the list before Enna had only one name on it: Allanagh's. But still I nod. She already knows what I'll say.

"Well, so long as we agree. I'm glad I don't have to pump you up anymore." A slow smirk grows over her expression. "There are so many other things I want to pump."

"Now who is disgusting," I mutter, staring up at the first of the night's stars twinkling above us.

"I'd say you both are for that poorly phrased euphemism," a silky voice says from behind us.

We spin towards the trees, but only glimpse a gleaming sword. A man emerges from the darkness, dressed all in black and holding the blade aloft. Long black hair cascades in pin-straight locks, creating a curtain-like veil over his tanned face, only the sharp angles of his features visible. He reminds me of a raven and wraith combined. Despite the usual fear, my resolve overpowers it and I shield Allanagh behind me, my hand hovering above my sword.

"I wouldn't do that if I were you," he says. "It will not work out how you intend."

"More incoming," Allanagh whispers from behind me, her fingers clutching at my tunic.

I glance back at her. "How did you miss *him*?"

She shrugs, prompting me to turn back around towards the man I deem 'Raven.'

I raise my hands in a gesture of surrender. "We mean no harm. We're... travelers."

Emerging from the pitch black of the forest, three more jog up to Raven. Two men and a woman wear Lumadh's colors. The woman's armor looks identical to a cleaner version of Enna's. Relief washes over me, leaving behind a trail of eager anticipation.

"Is Enna here?" I ask, squinting as though I can see her hidden before me. "We're looking for her."

Allanagh leans against my back and starts to whisper.

"Quiet," Raven says. "I do not wish to kill you, but I will."

The woman steps forward, catching Allanagh's gaze before sliding her focus to me. "You're Callum."

It isn't a question, and it's impossible to stop the grin that spreads over my lips. My hands drop as the two silent men's expressions turn more curious than guarded.

"You'll come with me," the woman says, spinning and marching back into the trees, her long black braid like a whip behind her. I name her Hope, because that's what she is to me now. "Keep up if you wish to speak with her before morning."

Following a silent exchange with Allanagh, and feeling the familiar frustration of not being able to listen to *her* thoughts, I quickly set off after Hope. Raven escorts Allanagh, both trailing behind me. The two other men snatch our bags and fall in line behind Allanagh.

"Where are you taking us?" Allanagh asks, her tone defiant.

Raven lets out a rich and velvety laugh. "To *my* fearless leader, of course."

Enna

The dense canopy of the forest covers us from any spies Olthion or Naithair may have lurking about while we march to the border. My troops are spread across the south, only inspecting groups of three or more that cross the border. We may miss a few spies with that policy, but Elric's single-minded insistence on pitched battles means whatever intelligence a single spy uncovers won't help, anyway.

We left Lumindar with Mama acting as regent, the advisors supporting her. Her kinship to Uncle Conroy and former residence in the castle eased the gentle takeover, but we've a long way to go. Mouric remains with us, as a gloomy hostage-slash-bargaining chip.

"You'd think someone would have discovered travel magic," Mac says, stretching his neck.

He's part of the skeleton crew I brought with me, from my personal battalion. We were lucky with Elric and Darroch this summer, during the so-called peace summit, that my army was posted nearby and close enough that the call of the horn reached them before non-Lumadhan blood was shed. Without that, this small battalion would have been the sole line of defense against Lumadh and Elric's bloodlust.

Still clearly thinking aloud, Mac casts his gaze to the sky. "Like putting a feather in your shoes and you'd fly to your destination in one step."

Orla scoffs from his other side. "That's how you stay dry, because of the water resistance. Gods, you're an idiot."

"It's *magic,*" he says snidely. "Feathers can do more than one thing."

"That's not how magic works." Her eye roll is nearly audible.

"We don't know that. It's wondrous and powerful. Something you're not." He yanks on one of Orla's many braids and she elbows him in the stomach.

"Seems too finicky to me. Feathers and stones," Oisin says from behind them, halting the playful bickering. Mac wilts and Oisin ambles forward to walk beside him, slapping a meaty paw on Mac's broad shoulder. "Dead useful though. Brendan tried to teach me warding but couldn't pick it up. Maybe we can try together," he adds tentatively, and Mac offers him a small smile, linking their arms together. Oisin's cheeks darken.

I'll have to let Tierney down gently.

"Bren, pick him up," Cathal snaps. I look back and see Brendan dragging a seated Mouric like he's pulling a sled. Mouric isn't hurt with his long cloak over him, but it isn't likely comfortable, especially as we march over the forest's thick and knobby underbrush.

"He won't walk," Brendan says mulishly. "He's the most stubborn man I've ever had the misfortune of meeting."

Cathal and I exchange a knowing smirk. She's still no less worshipful of me, but time could cure that. *It apparently worked with Callum,* I tell myself. I push the thought aside for later. *For after, once I've created a world where he and others like him can flourish.*

"Mouric, get up," I snap. "You're better than this."

He lifts his head to direct a hateful look at me, opening his mouth to spew something no doubt insulting when the harsh sound of leaves crunching underfoot greets us from ahead. The entire unit rests their hands on their holsters, except Brendan, who grasps his bow with one hand and Mouric's hood with the other.

Loughlin appears from the dense brush before us, panting. He scratches strands of white blond hair from his mouth. "We set up the meeting spot one click away, General."

Once we've all released the tension that the potential threat created, Orla turns, offering me her back and I dig inside the pack she carries for a skein of water. After I hand it to Loughlin and he catches his breath, I say, "You did well, Loughlin, But you didn't need to race back to me to report it."

He wipes his lips with the back of his hand and gives the skein to Mac who replaces it in Orla's bag. "Bronagh saw him in the specs. She sent a small contingent to get him."

My pulse quickens as the next step comes together. But before I can react outwardly, Loughlin continues. "But, General, you should know. He's not alone."

I quicken my pace then, gesturing for the others to hurry. "Of course not."

Because that would be too easy.

⸺◆⸺

Callum

Hope—named Catriona, and I'm about to end my nick-naming habit—leads me to a clearing in the forest, after dragging me through the tree's undergrowth. My sense of direction isn't well honed, but I think we've returned south, back towards Olthion.

A figure waits in the center of clearing, her back to me and bent over a pile of notes. Five lanterns encircle her, illuminating the butter yellow of her dress, not the leathers I'm expecting to see. A nervous hand tucks a strand of brown hair behind her ear, a ring on her finger I never saw Enna wear. Even I know rings and dresses aren't the best choice for battle. A sword rests by her feet, one that looks as unused as mine.

This isn't Enna.

Catriona clears her throat, and the woman drops the parchment, spinning around to face us and grasping the sword. She bears a striking resemblance to Enna. Her eyes are the same shape as Enna's but a light blue instead of caramel. And her hair, that cascades almost to the ground, is a different, lighter, shade.

"You must be Enna's sister," I say aloud.

She slides the sword in its holster, toying with the hilt. "She told you about me." Again, it isn't a question. Her voice is unlike Enna's, softer and higher pitched. "I'm Tierney. It's nice to meet you, Callum," she says, her lips quirking upward.

My cheeks burn even as relief chases through me. "She's talked about me." Tierney's expression turns shifty and the relief fades, my heart sinking. "And it was bad, I take it."

"Not *bad*," she says with a knowing glint in her eyes.

"You'll need to do some groveling is what she means," Allanagh says from behind us. She yanks her arm away from

Raven, who stalks to Tierney's side while the two other soldiers drop our bags beside Catriona. "But we already knew that was needed."

The image of how I might grovel before me flashes before my mind before I can stop it and Allanagh grimaces. "Gross," she says, feigning vomiting, "stop thinking that while I'm around."

The entire contingent of Lumadhans turn as one to fix their attention on her.

"She didn't tell you about Allanagh's mind reading abilities?" I ask, exchanging a glance with Allanagh, who winces at her slip.

"She did not," Catriona says, her tone clipped.

Raven's lip curls, and he tosses his sheet of hair in annoyance. "Wonderful, an additional burden for me. And here I thought we removed my last one," he says dryly.

I lean close to Allanagh and speak from the side of my lips. "What's he talking about?"

"I can't read him," she hisses back. Her gaze tracks to the others. "But it seems Enna has been busy."

"Where is Enna?" I direct the question to Tierney.

She blinks guilelessly. "Right now? Trying to set up a trap for your father."

Enna

Golden sunlight breaks through the dense canopy, creating scattered patches of light on the mossy forest floor where

Darroch and another man stand. I scan the forest for any signs of unwanted listeners. This close to the border, spies are certainly likely. Despite my team already checking and confirming there are none, it's hard to let go of old habits.

I'd asked Darroch to meet me to discuss a matter of deep import for our people. Although he isn't the 'smart brother,' he should have read between the lines and realized what I wanted. At least I hope he did. Otherwise, this meeting could turn violent.

Overthrowing Mouric was easy, as I'd already had the bones of plan in place. Removing Elric is a greater challenge, and requires Darroch to literally betray his own father. While Tierney and Brendan's plan was a good one, there are no guarantees Darroch would agree.

Bronagh and the man seem to be assessing the other. Darroch's back is to me, but his armor looks scuffed and the hooks for his daggers are empty. Aidan, Darcy, and Glenn face him, their hands lightly gripping their weapons. Although I hadn't requested it, Darroch appears to be without any weapons, his raised hands a gesture of peace. The man with him seems unarmed, but an unarmed man can still be dangerous. Still, I make a show of dropping my weapons. Orla and the others behind me do the same. Oisin's crew, along with Mouric, wait outside the small glen. It's the sharp clatter of our weapons hitting the ground that catches Darroch's attention.

He spins towards me, revealing a face covered in a patchwork of bruises. "En, good to see you."

I stalk forward until I can grasp his chin and turn it into the light. "What the fuck happened to you?"

The man with him shifts closer to us, to Darroch, and Bronagh's lips curl into a snarl. *It's Nolan*, I realize, the man who flirted with me at Olthion's sorry excuse for a pub. Without being asked, Orla drops to her knees, pulling the pack from her back and rummaging through it. She hands Mac a jar—the remnants of the jar I'd kept from Allanagh that Mac had attempted to recreate. Until now, we hadn't had many occasions to assess how well his substitute worked. Mac shuffles towards Darroch, his arm trembling as he reaches forward with the jar.

"He's not going to bite," I say. "Give it here, I'll do it. And Bronagh, if you're that concerned about Nolan, pat him down. He wasn't invited, anyway." I scowl up at Darroch, his face turning a deep shade of red underneath the mottled bruises.

Bronagh smirks and inspects Nolan for concealed weapons as I dab the cream on Darroch's cheeks. In a soft tone, I ask, "Did Elric do that to you or was this one of those so-called 'friendly' brawls the soldiers engage in?"

Darroch shrugs but Nolan answers, his voice gruff. "Elric didn't appreciate that you'd left Olthion. He took it out on the lot of us."

Bronagh finishes her inspection of Nolan and looks oddly disappointed that he didn't carry any weapons. She stomps behind me to stand with Orla and Mac. My gaze shifts towards Nolan as I seal the jar. Nolan's russet face looks yellowed, evidence of recently healed bruises. But likely healed by time instead of a healer's hands.

"I'm sorry to be the cause of any pain," I offer.

Darroch snorts. "If it wasn't because of you, it would be something else."

Likely the sword, but I keep that to myself for the moment. I take in the two men, studying their messy appearances and determined expressions. Darroch's armor is ripped, but he has no defensive wounds. And Nolan is missing the four patches I remembered him having when we met. I already knew Elric hit his children, but if Elric frequently attacks his own men when he's upset and doesn't allow them to defend themselves, persuading Olthion to support me might not be as difficult as we'd thought. "Why did you come, Nolan?"

"I'm here to make sure this isn't a trap," he says, his brown eyes fiery.

"That's what your people do," Mac says under his breath. Nolan rolls his eyes and Bronagh looks ready to pounce on him. Loughlin's pale hand rests on her shoulder, causing her to slouch and cross her arms in defeat.

"Thank you for the healing paste," Darroch says, cutting through the rising tension. His cheeks look better, and I make a mental note to talk to Mac about producing more of the cream. "But... I'm surprised you sent me a letter and not Callum."

That's next. Just as I'm about to come up with an excuse, Nolan lets out a dismissive snort. I shoot him a glare, my eyes narrowed. "What's that supposed to mean?"

The tension rises again, and my battalion assumes a battle-ready stance. Nolan raises his hands, his palms facing upwards, a sign of surrender. "Nothing meant. Only that Callum is gone, so the letter wouldn't have reached him."

My own shoulders slump and my battalion eases back into their at rest formation. I knew the meeting would be intense, but I never expected the emotional storm to start with me. *Damn Callum for distracting me.* But even though I know it isn't the point, I can't resist asking, "Where *is* Callum?"

"He went to find you," Darroch says. A surge of relief floods through my veins, washing away the doubts and fears that grew after Callum had dismissed me from his cabin. *He's looking for me. He probably regrets the fight, too.* I won't let him slip away from my grasp. Not this time.

Darroch's voice cuts through my thoughts. "But you mentioned you had a proposition for us. I'm listening."

I take a deep breath, forcing down thoughts of Callum and instead steeling myself for the task ahead. I can seek out Callum once we've fixed the country. "Elric has done nothing but bring chaos and suffering. But we have a plan." I look over Darroch's shoulders at Nolan. "Our strategy involves enlisting all the dissatisfied soldiers from Elric's court and outmaneuvering him. He likes games and betrayal, but he'd never expect someone to try his own tactics against him. Lumindar will agree to a pitched battle on Valenthian soil in one week. But we'll take him hostage and let his second-in-command negotiate a ceasefire. As a symbol of our united aims, we'll leave the former Lumindar leader with you, while Elric remains in Lumadh."

I inch forward and clasp Darroch's arms. "I know I'm asking for a lot, that I'm asking you to betray your own father and put your country into brief turmoil. But Olthion won't be the only one grappling with the new normal. Lumindar and Lumadh will face these challenges alongside you, with you. And I truly believe we can ally together and stop the bleeding."

"And Rian?" Darroch asks, his gaze on my hands.

My nose wrinkles dismissively. "The united triumvirate of Lumadh, Lumindar, and Olthion can certainly handle *Rian.*"

The glade is quiet, as Darroch and Nolan exchange a heavy glance. Finally, Darroch says, "I thought about what you asked. When you left Callum's cabin. And I am tired. Nolan too."

"Several of us are," Nolan agrees. "You'll have your contingent of the dissatisfied ready to depose Elric. We can have them ready in a week's time. But war is in our blood. The troops won't want everlasting peace. Especially without the hybrid lily tea, thing's won't be easy."

I raise my brows, wondering what happened to the tea, as footsteps muffled by the thick carpet of pine needles sound behind us. We turn to see Brendan, dragging Mouric behind him. "Then we'll give them something else to do," Brendan says.

Darroch's brow furrows. "Do I know you?"

"Fuck me. *Brendan?*" Nolan shouts, rushing forward to clasp hands with Brendan. "I thought you died."

"I thought I had too," Brendan admits. "But I've found something else to keep going for. And I know the soldiers will, too."

Darroch's expression softens, a flicker of hope igniting in his bright blue eyes. "Alright, En. We're listening."

Play the game, beat the player, I remind myself. I clasp Darroch's shoulder. "First, and this might sound unbelievable. But... have you ever heard anything about your father's sword?"

Chapter 21

Callum

We follow Tierney to the spot where the fake battle is expected to unfold. Although *follow* might be too generous. She adamantly refused to abandon us in the wilds of Lumadhan, but the others seemed anxious, suspecting us of being clumsy spies. We correct that assumption quickly, or I do. They even let me keep my sword and help with the night watches.

But there is still a lingering hesitation whenever they encounter Allanagh. Mouric must have put them off mind readers. To win them over, she offers her touch healing, but only Tierney accepts. While Allanagh works on soothing Tierney's sore leg muscles, the cantankerous Niall never lets her out of his sight, his glare piercing the back of her head.

Throughout the trip, Niall positions himself behind Allanagh like a sentry, his scowl a constant presence. We retrace our path, reaching the border where Lumadh, Olthion, and Naithair converge. Although the battle acceptance apparently came from Lumindar, the rugged mountains at the border make Lumadh territory the most practical location. Father would likely interpret it as a sign that Mouric has taken control of Lumadh, given Enna's supposed absence. Catriona said she hadn't revealed herself publicly yet.

On the seventh day of our journey, we arrive at the battle-ground: a hazy, fog-filled valley that stretches from Lumadh to Olthion. Catriona begins barking orders. The other two men position scopes, aligning them towards the sprawling valley ahead. From this distance, I can see someone has arrived, but not which side. Tierney drops herself gracefully on an overturned stump, fussing with her skirts. Niall dips beside her to brush off the dirt on her hem with a frown.

I fix my eyes on the valley, eager to use the scopes. Catriona informed us about the plan, which involves staging a fake battle to capture Father. But Father is wily, there's no telling he won't expect a trick. And it requires Darroch to deceive him, who is as thick as—

"Callum, find something to do other than distract Phelan and Kael," Catriona snaps at me.

I swallow down my immediate reaction, that I'm not doing anything but waiting, rather than upset Catriona more. She looks nervous, and I recognize the worry churning in her gaze.

Instead, I sit next to Allanagh, who is leaning against a tree at the edge of the grove. From there, we have an unobstructed view of the valley below. "You finally lost your shadow," I tell her.

Allanagh sighs, staring at Niall who is casting some kind of spell on a bone. I absently wonder who he planning on cursing. "He was babysitting me," she says, her voice filled with disappointment. "He's the only mind I can't read, and they were using him as a buffer."

"Did it work?"

"Sort of," she says, crossing her arms and sliding to sit beside me. "I still hear them, but there was a blank spot for the first time in forever."

"And you *miss* him?" He reminded me of a hawk-like badger, grumpy and ferocious.

She elbows me hard in the stomach. "It was... nice. Having that momentary silence. And I got used to the scowling. And the nose. You know what they say about men with big noses?" The frown falls off her expression and she waggles her eyebrows playfully.

"No." A shiver escapes me as my cheeks flush with embarrassment. "I refuse."

"Niall and Kael," Cat shouts, calling the men back to her. "You're with me. Phelan, you'll stay with Tierney and our guests."

Niall stalks forward to whisper in Cat's ear, causing Allanagh to frown.

"Never mind. In Cat's opinion, he's apparently unavailable," she says with a sigh.

"I need you at the front. You know this. Tier will be fine with Phelan," says Cat. With a flick of her wrist, she gestures them forward. "Move out."

As soon as they trip down into the valley, I leap for an open scope, knocking into Tierney who had the same idea. She takes over the other, a blush on her cheeks from our momentary midair struggle.

Despite the morning fog, I can make out Enna near the middle of the valley, surrounded by a group of soldiers. She greets Catriona with a hug, Kael with a pat on the shoulder, while Niall only receives a head nod. Oddly, he pulls a bird from an inner pocket of his cloak, tossing the bird into the sky, which swoops over Enna's small battalion until its circles widen to take in the entire left half of the field. I blink rapidly as my eyes start to adjust to the bird's movement. It is dropping something, bird seed or specks of sand, I can't tell, but suddenly it appears as though Enna's tiny army expands to one that would rival Father's.

He's a spellcaster, I realize. He hadn't used any spells that I could tell on this trip with him, or else I was too distracted by the idea of seeing Enna again. But this must be the spellcaster that left her wary of other practitioners. And, now knowing him, I can't blame her. With his spell engaged, Niall quickly drapes something over his head and vanishes from sight.

Even with the glamour over the field, Enna's sword remains holstered, and my heart starts to pound with the growing realization that this might fail. Tierney devised the plan and, like me, had little exposure to battles and rarely witnessed them firsthand. I observed battles through the scopes, at least. *What if Father sees through it?*

The ground rumbles as blood red dots emerge from over the valley and cascade towards the center where Enna waits. Darroch leads the charge, his black armor a dark void amongst the soldiers clad in red behind him. I spin the scope, searching for Father atop his horse. He is known for being at the front with Darroch, before swiftly galloping towards the tents, where he finds safety behind strong barricades far from any actual battle. I keep searching until—there. He isn't on horseback but hiding behind the men, his face twisted with malice. He takes off in the opposite direction of the battle.

He has something planned, he must. A banal pitched battle against Lumindar wouldn't sate him, not while on Lumadh land. There's something—*what is that on the other side of Enna's contingent?*

Before I realize I'm doing it, I'm running down to the field, my feet thudding against the ground in time with my frantic heartbeat.

<hr>

Enna

The sound of my pounding head is all I can hear while we await Elric's appearance. My small battalion stands beside me, united and ready for whatever lies ahead.

This plan called for so many moving parts. It's like a delicate puzzle, where removing just one piece could cause the entire structure to collapse. If Darroch changes his mind, I've taken my people to a bloodbath. If Elric figures out the trick, I've as good as killed them. *We could have tried something different. We* could *have snuck me back into Olthion*—Cat shifts beside me and I swallow down my unease. *Trust in the plan.* At bottom, it's playing Elric's game by tricking him into coming for a battle that will never happen. Instead, his men will revolt and we'll take him into custody.

As the king's army advances, Darroch stands at the forefront of the wall of soldiers. I quickly count them. Two hundred men follow behind him. The entire army is closer to five hundred, and Elric never brings more than half to a battle, meaning there's nothing out of the norm here. I release a relieved breath. *This could work.*

Nolan walks beside Darroch as they confidently march forward. Once they reach the center of the field, their soldiers stand at ease. Darroch flicks his eyes to the side. During a typical battle, the leaders first salute one another, followed by the soldiers beginning combat. *But where is Elric?* Niall's bird will run out of dust soon and the small size of our battalion will be exposed.

"Enna!" a voice shouts.

My sword—normal, not magical *or* unbeatable—slides smoothly out of its holster as I twist my body, pointing it at the unexpected visitor. Bronagh and Aidan quickly step in front of me, ready to protect me from what they think is a threat. But it's Callum, with his long black hair flowing behind him, sprinting towards me.

"He's coming from the other way," Callum pants, his breath coming in short, desperate gasps.

I blink up at him, my mind slow like syrup. I know he was looking for me, but he's supposed to be deep in the Lumadhan wilderness. I expected to need Niall to scry and find him once we'd taken care of Elric. "What are you—what are you doing here?" I glance at Cat, who smirks at me.

But Callum doesn't explain, clutching my shoulders. "There's no time for that, Enna. Elric's coming. Did Darroch betray you?"

I search for Darroch, finding him stomping towards us. I sprint towards the center of the field, Callum following quickly behind, where we encounter Darroch. Callum's presence causes murmurs among Darroch's soldiers, but Callum straightens his back, ignoring them. Nolan follows behind Darroch, wrinkling his nose at Callum but staying silent.

Callum stands nearly nose-to-nose with Darroch. They look even more similar now, long wild hair in different shades, tall figures, determination etched into their faces. "What did you do?" Callum snarls.

Darroch exchanges glances with Nolan. "What Enna said to do. What are you talking about? Where is Father?"

"He's changed something," I tell Darroch, cutting off the growing tension between the brothers.

Darroch's blue eyes widen as he scans the battlefield, no doubt searching for Elric. "What is his plan, then?"

"It's likely a pitched battle still," Callum says, grimly. "But another army approaches from the opposite ridge, half the size of Darroch's. If he *doesn't* know this is a trap, he... he must plan to box Lumadh in."

As if speaking it aloud was the signal they needed, a contingent of soldiers materializes out of the fog from the opposite direction, like Callum predicted.

"They're flanking you," Nolan says, frowning.

"Us," Darroch says with a curse.

"Are they in on the plan?" I ask, hoping the answer I assume is wrong.

Darroch inspects the advancing red blur, furrowing his brow. "We brought every soldier who privately expressed dissection. The numbers exploded once they realized we had no more tea. But we swore them to silence. I don't know how Father did this. He knew nothing of the plan."

"It looks like the reserve unit," Callum says. "See the cross over their hearts? He simply needed to call them up, and they'd arrive. They've no requirement to report to you first, but to the reserve leader."

Darroch blinks in surprise, as if the possibility had never crossed his mind, and my eyes involuntarily shut in frustration. *Damn Olthion, damn Elric, and damn me for not realizing this was a possibility.*

"Why would he do this?" Nolan asks, shaking his head. "We were careful. This is the *exact* size for a battle against a Lumindar detachment."

"Likely punishment," Callum says quietly. "For Lumindar refusing to accept the earlier offers. A Valenthian spy would notice a larger army coming with you. But the reserve unit is scattered, only coming together when called."

"Or fear," Darroch adds, reminding us all he isn't only brawn. "They live lives outside battle. They don't need the tea to wake up each morning. He might have feared the normal regiment wouldn't be as motivated."

"Idiot," Nolan says. "The tea dulls the pain, it doesn't stop the press for bloodshed. They have nothing else but war. The tea just keeps them from acknowledging it."

When I reopen my eyes, I squeeze Darroch's armored arms. Callum flinches at the touch, but there's no time to worry about what Callum thinks. "We didn't bring a full force, Darroch. We can have one here in an hour. But until then, are your men willing to fight their own?"

"War is war," he says, frowning.

Nolan nods and offers a forced smile. "I told you they enjoyed fighting. They'll probably be even happier they got armored up for an actual battle. It makes the march towards death's inevitability more meaningful."

"What about the sword?" Darroch asks, looking at the blade I'm still pointing at the grass.

My expression is strained, chastened. "This wasn't to be a real battle, remember?"

Darroch nods, offering me one last salute before turning away. Callum shakes his head as Darroch and Nolan return to their men and begin barking orders, leaving Callum and I alone in the middle of the battlefield.

"You need to—" I start.

"I'm sorry," Callum blurts out. "I wanted to tell you, in case something happens. It wasn't about you, but my own—"

I yank him down by the collar of his tunic, cutting off his apology, to better stare into his eyes. "After, tell me after."

He bites his lip before nodding. His green eyes trace down my face, landing on my lips. One hand trails over my cheek down to the bottom of my chin and he tilts my head up. Then he kisses me.

This isn't the soft kiss I expect from him. It feels like he's pouring his unsaid apology into it. He sucks on my lip and tastes every inch of my mouth. I grip his tunic to press him even closer, as though we can become one on this fucking battlefield.

There are catcalls all around us, and I hear Brendan (or maybe Glenn) pretending to retch.

"Save that for after too," Cat says, gently pulling us apart. "Ready, General?"

I lick my lips and secure my grasp on my sword. It's lucky I didn't accidentally stab him with how he's distracting me. Godsdamnit, he isn't even wearing armor. "Ready. Callum, go back behind the lines."

His expression shifts and I don't have time to hear him agree before it's too late to focus on anything but keeping alive and resurrecting our plan. From behind us, Elric gives a formal salute and then runs through the soldiers towards safety. Just in time, as Niall's bird caws sharply and vanishes into the trees, exposing our meager size.

And then the battle is on.

With a thunderous roar, the king's reserve unit surges forward. Darroch shouts his call too, and the red tides of death and destruction charges towards each other. There's a moment of shock on the King's side, when Darroch's contingent surprises them by pointing their weapons at them instead of my small battalion in blue. But the surprise attack does little to give us an advantage, as the Oltion's battle hardened soldiers effortlessly respond. The battlefield echoes with the clash of steel as swords collide with shields and arrows rain down from the sky like violent lightning.

My vision narrows to the spot where Elric has disappeared, using his men as human shields and cowering behind them like a coward, as usual. Why I expected better of him when he doesn't have an unbeatable sword with him, I'll blame on a busy few weeks. I carve my way through the enemy ranks, my sword singing as it cleaves through flesh and bone, each swing of my blade taking me closer to my goal.

Darroch catches up to me, and with each step, we draw nearer to Elric's elusive hiding spot. His blade flashes in the hazy light as he strikes down enemy after enemy—his own men—with deadly precision. But the soldiers are relentless, their numbers seemingly endless. For every enemy that falls, two more appear to take their place, their bloodlust driving them forward with no thought for their own lives.

"They won't stop," Darroch shouts as he butchers a man who could have been his comrade. "But neither will we. And we outnumber them."

With another war cry, Darroch's men push forward beside us, joined by my small battalion. My resolve is unshakable as I cut a path through the chaos, searching for the end of this sea of soldiers and where I will find Elric. If I can capture him, I can end this.

Elric's voice echoes towards us, spewing insults and accusations at us as he remains hidden. "You dare to challenge me, do you? You are nothing but traitors and cowards!"

Darroch flinches, but his grip on the sword remains steady.

My jaw tightens as I switch out my sword for my two daggers. "Come out and say that to my face, Elric." But I don't wait for his response, spinning in place, shouting, "Niall! To me!"

Two of Darroch's soldiers leap between us and tackle the few reserve members blocking our path to where Elric must be. My battalion fans out and together we cross the reserve army until there are no more soldiers before us, only open grass and sky. Cat signals and my battalion swiftly adjusts its formation to surround Elric's remaining loyalists, flanking them as they'd hoped to do to us.

An unseen force grasps my shoulder, undoubtedly Niall's hand, and I forcibly stop myself from attacking. Through clenched teeth, I hiss, "Can you uncover him?"

Niall's silky voice whispers in my ear, saying, "Do not doubt me."

And just like that, Elric's invisibility is stripped away as a sudden downpour materializes above him, drenching him in water and revealing his true form. He stands before us enraged, his fists clenched at his sides. "You think you can open your legs for my son, and he'll betray me? Darroch, stop this nonsense now and I may yet let you live."

"Enna has promised to treat you well in Lumadh," Darroch says, his eyes pleading. "Surrender peacefully, and we will grant you mercy."

Elric's scowling face twists into a nasty smirk. "You know," he says almost conversationally as he slowly inches towards us. "This is how I overthrew my father. I found the sword and cut him down."

The air thickens with tension as we brace ourselves for whatever he might do. His mouth curls into a snarl, spittle spraying out as he sneers, "I'd be proud if it weren't all due to some *bitch*."

Elric's words hang in the air like a foul curse, the tension palpable as we wait for his next move. Darroch's grip tightens on his sword, his knuckles turning white with the strain of keeping his composure.

I step forward to meet Elric's gaze head-on. I think about Callum's self-confidence and the emotional scars that won't heal, Darroch's bruised face, my brother's corpse in the ground. "This bitch holds your fate in her hands. How does that feel?" My voice drips with venom and my body trembles with rage, ready to strike at any moment.

Elric launches himself forward. I'm expecting it, so is Darroch, and the two of us prepare to block whatever attack he intends. But before he reaches us, there's a sudden blur of movement as a soldier knocks into him, sending him sprawling to the ground.

Elric's head hits the earth with a hard crack. Before he can recover, the soldier quickly stands and plants his booted foot on Elric's chest. Elric's eyes narrow with contempt as the soldier swiftly unsheathes his sword and presses the tip against the vulnerable dip in Elric's throat.

"You will not touch her," the man growls.

I blink. I know that voice, and I know that sword. The soldier turns, his long black hair swaying to reveal Callum, decked in torn red armor.

Callum

Looking down at my father, I can see the fear reflected in his gaze and the vulnerability etched on his face, mirroring the same expressions I've worn countless times. His green eyes—my green eyes—stare up at me in disbelief. I think of all I'd like to say to him, every swallowed curse and suppressed demand for respect. But I didn't need his approval anymore, I don't need anyone's.

It should be an exciting moment, like I'd felt when he'd thrown me from his throne room. This is the end of the reign of the man whose actions have caused me and others so much harm. But all I can feel is an overwhelming sense of exhaustion.

"It's done, Father," I say. "You will drive this kingdom into dust before considering there could be another way. So, we've taken the choice from you." I look back over at Enna, who nods encouragingly. She looks like the warrior princess I knew her to be, her armor covered in blood, her chest heaving with exertion.

With a heavy sigh, I withdraw the sword from his throat and motion for Darroch to come and take him. Darroch and an unfamiliar woman, one of Enna's soldiers, start lifting him up and securing his hands with tightly bound ropes.

"What happened?" Enna asks, rushing towards me.

My fingers sink into her hair, finding the lingering stickiness of blood that her fierce fighting left there. "Borrowed a set of armor from one of the fallen. I couldn't let you do it alone."

She smiles. "You are full of surprises. Clever, clever Callum." Her hands grasp the armor I borrowed, and a sharp pain shoots through my body as she accidentally hits a tender bruise. She frowns apologetically, her hands gently resting on my hips as she looks up at me. "You were in the middle of apologizing to me, I believe. And then it will be *my* turn."

I lean down, planning to kiss her again, when a sharp crunch echoes through my ribs, and I stumble backward. "I think I... I think I hurt myself," I stammer, peering down at my armor. It was already stained with blood when I'd put it on. But I... there are new tears. I catalog them absently as my head starts to pound in time with my heartbeat.

The pounding slows and slows, like a fading drum.

"When do we get to get rid of our hostage?" one of her soldiers says, a thin man in blue wearing double bows. My eyes widen in surprise as the man looks identical to Brendan. Oisin's double stands behind him and waves.

"I think... I think I need Allanagh," I say. Enna clings tightly to me, her beautiful brown eyes filled with fear, but she can't keep me upright. Losing my balance, I crash down onto the unforgiving, solid ground. Red tendrils spread out from my legs, like a fiery halo. It reminds me of finding Enna and cleaning her of dye. I meet her gaze and furrow my brows. "I just hallucinated that Grasshopper was here."

"He's really here," Enna says, her voice rising in pitch. "Niall, find Mac."

"The touch healer came with him," a voice that *sounds* like Niall says. But there's no person attached to the voice. He must be invisible.

I lean to the side until my body falls to lie down. *Being invisible sounds nice*, I think. *Father's men would stop attacking me if they couldn't find me.* I'll have to suggest that... to

Father's spellcasters... the next time they try to change me... One of these days, the spells will work... and I'll make him... proud...

"What's wrong with him?" That sounds like Darroch. "Cally? Don't lie down. Callum, you hear me? Sit up. You can't sleep."

It can't be Darroch. Darroch would never worry about me.

"Get fucking Allanagh!"

Chapter 22

Callum

The air is heavy with the scent of healing paste and whispered conversations. I'm no stranger to waking up with a sticky layer of healing paste on my skin, a result of my former comrades from the Oige launching unexpected attacks. But this time, something feels off, and I can't quite pinpoint what it is. I open my eyes, struggling against the weight of pain and confusion. It's nearly dark, the sun's rays barely visible through the window of a room I don't recognize. The last thing I remember was—I frown.

"Do you know who you are?" Allanagh sits by my bedside, idly tossing a jar of healing paste from hand to hand.

"Yes," I say, my brows furrowing. Callum, son of Elric, of Olthion.

Her eyes are pinched at the corners. "And do you remember *when* you are, and what's happened over the past few months?"

The memories of the battle flood back, sending a shiver down my spine, before they're quickly replaced with Enna's smiling face, and I nod slowly.

"Good, there was some concern," she says, standing. "I'll let the others know you're awake."

"The others?" I sit up, feeling a dull ache pulsing throughout my body. I stare down at myself. My chest is bare, but no bruises dot my skin.

Allanagh frowns. "Sorry. There's still limited healing potions here. I healed the internal injuries, but I must have accidentally left some of the soreness because there were too many others that needed help." She leans forward and places a hand on my uncovered stomach.

I jolt at the cool touch of her hand. "Don't waste your energy," I tell her, shifting away from her. "What others?"

"Cat, Niall, Tierney, Phelan, Kael, Bronagh..." She rattles off a dozen more names, each one unfamiliar to me. "And Darroch and Enna, of course."

"Enna's here?"

Allanagh smirks. "Where do you think you are?"

Without waiting for my reply, she quickly makes her way to the window and flings open the airy linen curtains. Lying in bed, my view is limited, but I can still make out the ominous sight of several pitch black spires reaching towards the sky in the distance. Spires that block out the sunny day outside. Spires I've never seen in Olthion.

Allanagh heads towards the door to leave. "Welcome to Euthia. I'll let Enna explain."

My eyes stay fixed on the view from the window, wondering what it means that Enna brought me here. That Darroch is here. Elric was captured, I remember that. I'd momentarily forgotten when I was bleeding out. *But what does it mean for Olthion?*

Allanagh pauses at the door, gripping the frame tightly as she glances back at me. "I'm really glad you're okay."

I give a pained smile.

Her expression shifts from genuine to mocking and I brace myself for whatever vulgar thoughts she might spew. "Seriously, because Enna's thoughts about you are repulsive, and I'd like you to bang them out of her."

I toss a pillow at her, but it narrowly misses as she ducks. The pillow lands in the hallway with a thud. Her laughter grows fainter and fainter as she walks further away.

"That was very brave of you," a voice says from the hall. *Tierney*, I think. I lean in, straining to catch her words.

"It was nothing," Darroch says, his voice oddly subdued.

"I thought Allanagh was the only eavesdropper we had to worry about." Enna leans against the doorframe, back in her leathers, no longer blue but a rusty brown, and holding the pillow I'd tossed into the hall. She looks tired, her eyes bruised, and there's a tremble to her frame.

"Are you alright?" I ask.

She comes into the room and stands beside my bed, tucking the pillow under my head. "I should ask *you* that question."

"I will be," I tell her.

"Me too," she says. She gestures to the bed. "May I sit?" After I nod, she perches lightly on the bedframe. "That was very idiotic of you. You've never been in battle."

I swallow the reflexive flinch that wants to arise. "I stand behind it."

She makes a soft humming sound. "From my vantage point, you're not standing yet."

I place my hand, palm facing up, on my knee and feel a burst of relief that she intertwines our fingers. Staring down at her hand, so small in mine but so strong, I ask, "Can you tell me what I've missed?"

Enna gives me an overview of the current situation. Two weeks have passed since the battle. The open trade route with Lumadh is helping some, but there remains significant strife in Olthion. *Brendan* has an idea and some of Enna's advisors are helping him keep the soldiers occupied to avoid a second revolt.

"Darroch has proposed a council, with two people from each province. One elected, one chosen by the remains of the government," she finishes.

"*Darroch* did?"

"Tierney actually, but they think I don't know," she says, a sly smile playing at the corner of her lips. I wonder what I'm missing as I try to decipher the mischievous glint in her eyes.

"There will remain a limited monarchy," she continues. "More like a regent over the council, who will hold significant power. They're still working out who the regent might be. We need someone who is completely different in demeanor from Elric, but still able to command respect. And someone who will work with my parents, but not feel cowed by them."

I purse my lips. I'd wanted to be second-in-command one day, only because Father would never release his grip on the crown. In my wildest dreams, I'd wanted to be king, to wield the power I spent a lifetime chasing.

But things had changed. I found power elsewhere.

"You can work it out with Darroch, or... You can be the ambassador to Lumadh," Enna says hesitantly. "Only if you want to though. It is your choice."

My gaze shifts towards her, noticing the slight twitch in her frame and the hesitation in her request. There's no demand this time. Things must have changed for the both of us.

"Perhaps," I say. "I'd like to get back on my feet first. And once I have, we can finish the discussion we started on the battlefield?"

As she wets her lips, her amber eyes grow darker. Trailing her gaze over my face and down my torso, she says, "Is that a discussion you need to be standing for?"

My stomach clenches. "I suppose not. What did you have in mind?"

Lust pools inside me as her voice takes on a husky tone. "I think that's a conversation best had on your knees. What do you think, Callum? Are you willing to kneel for me again?"

And there's only one answer I can give her as I slip from the bed onto the floor.

Author's Note

Thank you for reading *A Kingdom to Remember*, a stand-alone in a new fantasy romance series, *Kneeling Kingdoms*, with interconnected stories. Watch for *A Kingdom to Protect*, which will follow a new couple as Lochmorae deals with the aftermath of Elric's removal and learning more about the sword and other gifts given to the world.

If you're interested in more of my writing, check out my website (**kmalady.com**). You can find other fun information there about my other projects, like *The Ascend Trials* (a romantic YA portal fantasy all about subverting tropes), *Threads of Fate* (an NA romantic fantasy series adapted from Greek myths), and more!

www.ingramcontent.com/pod-product-compliance
Lightning Source LLC
Chambersburg PA
CBHW061658190726
48289CB00006B/1923